SHADOW RIVER

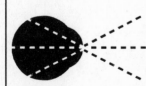

This Large Print Book carries the
Seal of Approval of N.A.V.H.

SHADOW RIVER

RALPH COTTON

THORNDIKE PRESS
A part of Gale, Cengage Learning

GALE
CENGAGE Learning·

Farmington Hills, Mich • San Francisco • New York • Waterville, Maine
Meriden, Conn • Mason, Ohio • Chicago

GALE
CENGAGE Learning®

LIBRARY OF CONGRESS CATALOGING-IN-PUBLICATION DATA

Cotton, Ralph W.
    Shadow river / by Ralph Cotton. — Large print edition.
        pages ; cm. — (Thorndike Press large print western)
    ISBN 978-1-4104-6967-0 (hardcover) — ISBN 1-4104-6967-0 (hardcover)
    1. Arizona Rangers—Fiction. 2. Burrack, Sam (Fictitious character)—Fiction.
3. Outlaws—Fiction. 4. Undercover operations—Fiction. 5. Large type books.
I. Title.
PS3553.O766S534 2014
813'.54—dc23   2014009507

Published in 2014 by arrangement with NAL Signet, a member of Penguin Group (USA) LLC, a Penguin Random House Company

For Mary Lynn, of course . . .

■ ■ ■ ■ ■

PART 1

■ ■ ■ ■

CHAPTER 1

Blood Mountain Range, Old Mexico

Above a stone-lined water hole seated in the foot of the Twisted Hills, Arizona Territory Ranger Sam Burrack lay on his belly in the arid dirt hidden between two brittle stands of mesquite. On the sand flats a hundred yards below him, he saw four men on horseback riding toward the water hole at a gallop. Their duster trails flapped on the hot Mexican wind like tongues waggling from the mouths of lunatics.

With a dusty telescope to his eye, he moved from face to face, studying the men in the circular lens. The only face he recognized was that of Clyde Burke, a gunman he had left at this same watering hole a month earlier. The other men were just three hard-set faces darkened out beneath wide hat brims. Sam lay in wait like some predator of the desert floor, his duster and trail clothes long faded to the color of desert and stone.

At midmorning the scalding sun had already cast and drawn a wavering curtain of heat between a clear blue sky and rolling desert floor. Behind him at the edge of the water hole, Sam had left his dun and a spare horse, a mottled white barb, to draw their fill, having tied their reins around a rock spur standing up from the gravelly sand.

And now to wait, he told himself.

He lowered the telescope and let his mind pore over the events leading up to now.

It had been a month — over a month, he decided — since he'd left Crazy Raymond Segert lying dead on a hotel balcony in Agua Fría. He had no regrets about killing Raymond Segert. It had been his job to bring down the outlaw leader. Yet, recalling that day, he still saw the body of a peddler girl named Lilith Tettovia lying dead in the street below the hotel balcony. Segert had thrown her over the balcony rail, but it wasn't the fall from the balcony that had killed Lilith Tettovia. Her death had come from a bullet through her head as Sam had held her weakened body in an embrace.

Four inches to the right, the bullet would have struck him in the back of his head. But as it turned out, the bullet came in just over his shoulder and hit her squarely in her forehead. He still hadn't decided if the long-range rifle shot had been meant for the woman or for him. But he had a strong feeling it was for him. Whomever it was meant for, the shot was made by one of Segert's men, a Chinese-Mexican named Jon Ho. Sam had every intention of killing Jon Ho, he reminded himself.

He was still working undercover; he was still careful to keep his identity a secret.

His objective a month ago had been to infiltrate the gangs operating back and forth across the border out of Agua Fría and the Blood Mountain Range. He hadn't been successful in joining either group of outlaws, but he had found out that the two gangs were in reality only one gang run by one man — Bell Madson. It was useful knowing the head of which snake he needed to cut off. Now that Segert was dead, Madson was, without question, the head of the snake.

Sam had also established himself as a hard case, a gunman who was out to do anything that had a dollar attached to it. While Madson might not trust him yet, there was no one on Madson's payroll who suspected him of being an Arizona Ranger working on the sly. Even better, he reminded himself, after he'd killed Madson's right-hand man,

11

Crazy Raymond Segert, in a straight-up gun battle, there would be few in the gang who would be quick to lock horns with him mano a mano. Strange as it sounded to him, he had established himself as an outlaw a lot faster than it had taken him to establish himself as a lawman. And he had managed to do it well enough that most hard cases prowling the desert knew him — or thought they did.

Good enough. . . .

Now he was back on the job.

Sam remained in the mesquite cover the next twenty minutes, watching the four riders draw closer, riding abreast, to a path leading up to the water hole ahead of a wide, roiling stream of trail dust their horses raised. Sam shook his head. *Nobody rides abreast this time of day,* at least nobody who wanted to keep the hair atop his head. When he raised the lens back to his eye, Sam looked out past the four riders all the way across the sand flats to a stretch of sloping hills standing beneath the Twisted Hills. At this time of morning, he could still see the hills well enough to distinguish any signs of life and what that life-form might be. Another hour or so and the wavering heat would obscure these foothills from view for the rest of the day.

Good Apache weather, Sam told himself.

The Apache knew this; they used the time of day or night to their advantage. Their knowledge of earth and weather was as instinctive to them as the scent of blood to a wolf, the sense of sight to a hawk. Sam knew that not seeing the Apache in the foothills this time of day did not mean they weren't there. It meant they knew the desert wouldn't yet hide them from watchful eyes. When the wavering heat overtook the flatlands, the Apache would venture down. They would cross toward the place where they had first spotted the wide trail dust.

So, here we go . . . , Sam told himself. It appeared his first job of the day would be to save the hides of some of the men he was sent here to kill. That struck him as darkly ironic, he thought, rising onto his knees, his rifle pressed to his shoulder, levered and cocked at Clyde Burke from ten feet away.

"Whoa, now!" Burke shouted, all four riders and horses startled at the sight of something rising from the sand that way, sand pouring down from Sam's shoulders. The riders struggled to keep their spooked horses from bolting away beneath them.

"Everybody, freeze up!" Sam shouted, hoping that he wouldn't have to fire his rifle.

13

On the slimmest outside chance that the Apache in the foothills hadn't seen the trail dust, he didn't want to send a rifle shot resounding in a five-mile radius.

The three other men tightened on their reins but kept their hands chest high. So did Burke.

"Jesus, Jones!" he said. "What the blazing hell are you doing here?"

"I felt bad leaving you, so I came back," Sam said, thinking quick. He stood up, the rifle still pointed and cocked.

"After a *month*?" Burke said. The other three men watched and listened.

"I got sidetracked," Sam said. "But I'm here now. I even brought you a horse."

"As you can see, I already acquired a horse. A gun too," said Burke. He gave a mirthless grin. "Like you said, there seemed to be plenty of guns and horses drifting around out here."

"Glad it worked out for you," Sam said, not sounding as though he cared one way or the other.

"And I heard how you were *sidetracked* too," said Burke. "I heard how you killed Segert and a couple of his men in Agua Fría. Stuff like that always gets around."

"I was ambushed by them," Sam said. "I did what any clear-thinking man would do.

I killed the ones I should. I chased away the one that had no stake in the game."

Burke nodded. He stared at Sam as he spoke to the other three gunmen.

"Pards," he said sidelong, "this is Jones, the man I told you about. Be advised that every damn thing he just said is most likely a blackguarding lie."

"So, this is Jones," said a tough-looking gunman wearing a high Montana-crowned Stetson. As he spoke, his hands lowered a little. He and the other two men began to inch their horses away from Burke and form a half circle around Sam.

"Clyde," Sam said calmly, his rifle still leveled at Burke's chest, "you might explain to your pals how the closer they try to get around me, the tighter my finger gets on this trigger."

Burke knew enough to realize that this man Jones had no hesitancy about killing. Yet he only sat staring at Sam.

"I meant to tell you fellows," he said to the other three, "Jones here is one of them suspicious kind of folks, always thinks everybody is out to get him."

"Adios, Clyde," Sam said with finality. He braced the rifle in his hands, ready to fire.

"Hold it, Jones!" said Burke. He quickly recommitted to raising his hands chest high.

15

He gave the other three men a jerk of his head, calling them back in. "There's no need in you breaking ugly the first smallest thing we might disagree on."

As the three inched their horses back beside Burke, Sam kept his rifle tensed, ready.

"We disagree on a lot, Clyde," Sam said. "The last thing you told me was that I'd better hope I never see you again."

"It was?" said Burke, looking surprised. Sam saw that he wanted to ease the tension, get the rifle bead off his chest.

"It was," said Sam.

"All right," said Burke. "I admit I was piqued at you, leaving me out here with no horse, no gun, Apache crawling all around —"

"The question is," Sam said, cutting him off, "are you and your pals here going to do something to cause me to drop this hammer?" He gestured his eyes toward the distant hill line. "The minute this rifle barks, the Apache are going to come to see what's left to pick over."

Burke looked off toward the Twisted Hills. "You figure they're still here?" he said.

"They've been here a hundred years or so," Sam said. "I've seen no sign of them leaving."

16

"I meant, right here, right now," Burke said.

"They locked on to the four of you the minute they saw you stirring up dust," Sam said. "Only fools ride abreast that way. It makes too wide a rise of dust."

"Hey, watch the name-calling, Jones," the man with the Montana-crowned Stetson warned. "Killing Dirty Tommy Mullins and the Argentinean doesn't cut you a wide swath, far as I'm concerned."

Sam didn't answer. He looked back at Burke.

"Want to sit here and see if I'm right about the Apache?" he asked Burke.

Burke scratched his beard stubble as if in consideration.

"You brought me a horse, huh?" he asked.

The other men gave him a curious look. They couldn't believe he was falling for it.

Sam nodded.

"He's over there watering," he said.

"What about a gun?" Burke asked.

"No gun," Sam said. "I didn't trust you that much." He gestured at Burke's mount. "Now that I see you've already got yourself a horse, I'm keeping the one I brought as a spare."

"This man thinks we're idiots, Burke," the man with the Montana-crowned Stetson cut

17

in. "He didn't come here thinking you were still here after all this time."

"Hush up, Montana. I know why he come here," said Burke without taking his eyes off Sam. "He come here headed the same place we're headed. Am I right, Jones?"

Sam only nodded.

Burke took a deep breath. "Jones, this is Jarvis Finland, the Montana Kid," he said. "If you think Montana won't kill you, you'll be wrong starting off."

"*The* Montana Kid," Sam said, eyeing Finland up and down.

"One and the same," Finland said proudly.

"And this is Stanley Black," said Burke, gesturing toward the next gunman, a rat-faced young man with pinched cheeks and a crooked nose.

Sam only nodded.

"And this is —" Burke said, gesturing toward the third man.

"We met already," said the third man. He pushed his hat brim up and Sam recognized him as the gunman he had chased out of town the day he'd shot it out with Segert and his men. "I'm Boyd Childers," the third man said.

"Oh, that's right," said Burke. "I nearly forgot, you two have met." His sly grin told Sam that he hadn't forgotten a thing. "Boyd

18

here told us how you and him stood each other to a truce after the gunfight. Said you watched him mount up and ride out of Agua Fría. Is that how you recall it, Jones?"

Sam recalled telling this man to leave town, not slow down and not look back. The man had raced away on foot, and had not even stopped long enough to mount his horse — left it standing at a hitch rail. He stared at Boyd Childers, letting the nervous-looking gunman wonder what he would reply. Childers looked embarrassed with Sam's eyes searching his.

"Yeah, that sounds about right," Sam said finally, letting Boyd Childers off the hook. He saw relief flood through the gunman.

Sam turned to Burke. "I figured, when I saw you coming, you're headed out to find the three bags of gold I hid from Segert."

"You'd be right in thinking that," said Burke. "Would I be right, figuring you're headed the same place?"

Sam only stared at him. "Wherever I'm going, you'd also be right figuring I don't want any partners," he said bluntly. "How were you going to find the gold anyway? Turn over every rock on the hillside?"

"Might have had to," said Burke. "But now that we're all here, let's talk about partnering up."

"Didn't you hear me, Clyde?" Sam said. "No partners." Yet even as he objected, he began working the idea around in his head. He still needed to find Madson and his men. Burke was part of the gang. "I figure with you riding for Madson, you'd be prone to letting him know about the gold, maybe even giving it up to him," he said.

Burke started to answer, but before he could, something sliced past his face. "What the . . . ?"

He looked around just as Childers let out a yelp and grasped an arrow shaft sticking from his shoulder. Another arrow thumped into Montana's saddlebags. His horse reared. As it touched down, he drew his Colt and fired wildly into the rocks above the water hole.

Stanley Black also let out a sharp yelp and stiffened as an arrow sliced across his hat and left the front brim hanging down below his eyes.

"Injuns!" shouted Burke, gigging his horse forward, making for cover. Upon hearing Finland's gunfire, he jerked his own Colt from its holster on his hip.

"Don't shoot!" Sam yelled, but it did no good.

Montana fired wildly in three different directions. So did Burke. Stanley Black did the same as arrows streaked in, broke and bounced off rocks, sliced through mesquite and low cactus.

Sam ducked down, rifle in hand, and ran in a crouch toward his two watering horses. He got there just in time. A small bent figure had taken the reins to the two horses and turned to lead them off into the rocky hillside. But this was no warrior, Sam realized at once. It was an ancient relic of a woman in a ragged checked dress and a straw skimmer hat. Upon seeing Sam rise with his rifle, she stumbled and fell and let go of the horses' reins. With guns roaring behind him, Sam saw that the silence on the desert floor was broken.

Sam had brought his rifle to his shoulder. Yet upon seeing that it was an elderly woman instead of a warrior, he held his shot. He watched as her terrified face looked at him from thirty yards away. She stumbled to her feet, her toothless mouth agape, and scurried off out of sight.

An arrow slid across the ground at Sam's feet. He ducked and swung his rifle in the arrow's direction. Again, he held his shot, seeing a half dozen children racing away like young jackrabbits across stone and brush in the same direction as the old woman. They carried bows and arrows in hand.

Babies . . . , Sam told himself. But babies whose arrows could kill a man.

He released a tense breath and hurried to the two horses as they stood milling about where the old woman had turned them loose. Leading the two horses hurriedly back to the crest of rocks surrounding the water hole, Sam kept himself and the animals covered by a large boulder as he called down to Burke and the others.

"Hold your fire," he shouted. "It's only kids and old folks. They're gone." He stood in the ringing silence after the final shot was fired. Had there been any question of the Apache across the sand flats knowing they were here, the gunfire had answered it.

CHAPTER 2

Sam and the four gunmen led their horses into the safety of rock higher up the sloping hillside above the water hole. Burke walked alongside Sam, his Colt out of its holster, his eyes searching every rock, every slice of blackened shade in the midmorning sun.

"Old women and little kids, huh?" he said to Sam.

"That's who hit us," Sam said. "But now every warrior around knows somebody's here. Unless they have something better to do, they will be coming to feel us out."

"Damn Injuns," said Burke. He spat in disgust. "They act like they own both sides of the border."

Sam just looked at him.

"You know what I mean," Burke said. "It's got to where a white man can't go nowhere or do anything without stepping on some Injun's tail."

"This is how it's going to be all the way to

where I hid the gold," Sam commented, walking on.

"Aha," said Burke. "So I'm right, you are headed there?"

"I never denied it," Sam said, knowing it would make no sense, him being an outlaw and not greedily going after gold he'd hidden a month ago. "Segert set me up, made it look like I sold rifles to a band of Mexican rebels. Hiding his gold is all that kept me from a *federale* firing squad. I figure the gold's rightfully mine."

"With what just happened back there," said Burke, jerking his head toward the surprise attack, "we're doing you a favor offering to ride with you."

"Like I told you, Clyde," said Sam, "you ride for Madson —"

"Forget Madson," Burke said. "We get the gold and split it up, I'd be a fool to ever let Madson know we got it."

"What about those three?" Sam asked, appearing to consider it. He wanted to get into Madson's gang, and Burke was his best means of doing so. But he wanted to be talked into it.

"They're not fools either," Burke said. "But if you don't trust them, we can always kill them soon as we get our hands on the gold." He shrugged.

24

"That's true," Sam said, seeming to consider it some more.

"Crazy Raymond Segert did a lot of dealing on his own," Burke continued. "It wouldn't surprise me if Madson didn't even know about the rifle deal. We could take this gold and go ride for Madson and he'd be none the wiser." He grinned.

There it is . . . , Sam told himself. That was exactly what he wanted, a way into Madson's gang. Once he was in, all he had to do was get close enough to Bell Madson to kill him.

They stopped at a turn in the hill path to let the others catch up to them. Boyd Childers grimaced, holding a hand pressed around the arrow sticking from the side of his shoulder above his upper arm.

"What do you say, Jones?" Burke asked, keeping his voice lowered. "You and me, even split? I take care of these three when the time comes?"

"The more I think of it, the better it sounds," Sam said, letting go of some of his reluctance.

They stopped talking when the three other gunmen gathered up closer to them.

"How's the arm holding up, Childers?" Burke asked.

"Hurts like hell," Childers said sullenly.

25

"Why the hell was we palavering in clear view back there, knowing Injuns are swarming like flies?"

Burke stared at him.

"We all learn from our mistakes, don't we?" he replied sarcastically.

Childers looked away, muttering under his breath.

The Montana Kid spat in contempt and wiped his gun hand across his lips, his Colt gripped in his fist.

"If that's their best they just hurled at us, we've got nothing to worry about, if you ask me," he said. "I can shoot at young'uns and old folks all day long, means nothing to me." He slickly spun his Colt into his holster.

Sam eyed him.

"Even if they're facing you, shooting back?" he asked flatly.

"Are you being funny, Jones?" he asked. His hand rested on the butt on his holstered Colt.

Sam didn't answer. Instead he turned to Burke.

"We've got a deal, Clyde," he said, "if you can keep this one from firing his gun every time the wind changes."

"We were fired upon, Jones," said Finland. "When fired upon, I generally find it help-

26

ful to fire right back. Especially when it's a band of border-jumping Apache out to lift my hair."

"Yeah, look at my arm," Childers put in. "I say kill them all, to hell with them. Where did all the old women and the kids come from anyway?"

"My guess is they're a different tribe than the ones over in the Twisted Hills," Sam said. "What we've got are a lot of remaining White Mountain Apache, Tontos and Chiricahuas. They're moving into the Mexican hill country, taking anything with them they find along the way. The old woman, the children? I'm thinking they're what's left of Pinaleños or Mescaleros, after what the U.S. Cavalry has done to them."

"Well, well, fellows," Montana said with a dark grin. "It looks like we've got ourselves a 'pache *expert* on our hands."

Sam bristled a little, for show — just one hotheaded outlaw that took no guff or goading from anybody.

"I'm no expert on Apache, Montana," he said. "But I know when to start shooting or when to ride wide of them. About the only thing that draws these tribes together is the chance to kill some white men and spike their scalps and testicles on a lodge pole. Most times they go out of their way to avoid each other. We need to leave them that way."

"I will," said Montana, "unless they come calling on me." He patted his holstered Colt. "When that happens, I'll burn them down, same as I would a coyote."

Sam turned his stare from Montana to Burke. Burke shrugged and offered a grin.

"What can I say, Jones?" he said. "The Montana Kid likes to settle things with a gun — don't we all?"

"Yeah, I suppose so," said Sam, looking back at Montana, "but we're going to try to shake any warriors off our trail that we might have picked up today. We're going to slip as quiet as we can up to where the gold is buried, get it and get out." He looked all around at the gunmen's hard faces. "Anybody who's not all right doing that needs to turn his horse around and get his knees in the wind."

"We hear you, Jones," said Burke. "Now let's yank that arrow out of Childers and go get ourselves some gold."

Sam looked from face to face, seeing the front of Stanley Black's sliced hat brim drooping down to the tip of his nose, the outlaw's eyes staring out above it.

"Fix your hat brim, Black," Sam said. "We don't want to be mistaken for a traveling circus."

Burke and the Montana Kid chuckled under their breaths. Black grumbled, red-faced.

Sam turned to Childers and looked at his wounded upper arm, the arrow sticking from the side of his shoulder.

"Sit down over there, make yourself comfortable," he said to Childers, gesturing him toward a low rock. "I'll slice that thing out of your shoulder."

"I'm thinking *wait up on it,*" Childers said, gripping his shoulder around the sunken arrow shaft. "See if it loosens up some. It's awful sore right now." He'd taken out a bag of tobacco and papers from his shirt pocket to roll himself a smoke.

Awful sore right now . . . ?

Sam just looked at him.

"I can slice your arm and take it out with a knife, or I can chop your arm off later with an ax." He shrugged. "It's your arm. Let me know if you decide to keep it."

"No cause for you getting a mad-on over it," Childers said, his cigarette paper in one hand. He shook a stream of tobacco across the paper and pulled the drawstring on the bag shut with his teeth. "I just want to wait until the soreness eases up some. It ain't every day a man lets folks go digging down into his arm." He offered a nervous laugh

29

and looked around at the others for support. The gunmen only looked back at him with caged eyes.

"Sounds good to me," Sam said to Childers. "While you're waiting, practice rolling your smokes one-handed."

"Damn it to hell, Jones," Childers said. He wadded the half-constructed cigarette and threw it away. "All right, next stop we make, you cut it right out of here."

"Wise decision," Sam said over his shoulder.

Seeing Sam mount his dun and take up the lead rope to his spare horse, the gunmen gathered their horses as well. As Sam put his dun forward at a walk, the four mounted their dusty animals and rode on, Boyd Childers at the rear of a single line up the steep switchback trail.

When they had moved farther up onto the rocky hillside, Sam, Burke and the other gunmen made a fireless camp in the early afternoon. After leaning Boyd Childers back against a rock, Sam fed him shot after shot of whiskey from a canteen Burke had handed him. Sam watched for a moment as Childers' head began to bob toward his chest. Finally Sam drew a long knife from his boot well and mopped the blade with a touch of whiskey on a bandana. Then he studied Childers' face closely.

"Are you ready, Childers?" he asked stoically.

"Ready as I'll ever be," Childers said with a whiskey thickness to his voice. He sat shirtless, having pulled off his shirt and maneuvered it over the embedded arrow shaft.

Sam spread his hand around the shoulder wound and reached in with the knife to go to work. As the others had drawn back to watch from a few yards away, Childers took a piece of wood from his mouth that he'd been given to bite down on and spoke to Sam in a slurred, lowered voice.

"You don't think much of me, do you, Jones?" he asked.

Sam just looked at him, knife in hand.

"I don't think of you one way or the other," he said. "You best bite down on that." He gestured toward the short piece of dried ironwood.

"I mean me running out of town that day, not even taking my horse," Childers said.

"I figured it to be a wise move under the circumstances," Sam said quietly. "Am I taking this arrow out, or not?"

"I just don't want you thinking me a coward," Childers said. "I'm not."

31

"Bite down, here we go," Sam said. He laid the point of the knife alongside the arrow shaft.

Childers barely got the piece of wood between his teeth before Sam stuck the blade down into his shoulder flesh. With a widened wound opening, Sam gave a slight twist of the knife blade and yanked the arrow free, fast and slick. The pain was sharp, deep and searing, but it ended as quickly as it had started. Childers grunted and bit hard on the wood. Then he relaxed and slumped back.

Sam inspected the blood-smeared arrow shaft. He found the metal head intact.

"You're lucky, Childers," he said. "If this was a flint head, pieces of it could have broken off deep. I'd have been digging it out a little at a time, the next hour."

"Lucky me," Childers said halfheartedly. He looked at the iron arrowhead himself.

"Usually the warriors only give their kids stone heads, for hunting. They keep the iron heads for themselves, for killing us white devils."

Burke had walked up as soon as he saw the arrow was out of Childers' shoulder. He stood bent, palms on his knees, looking at the arrowhead.

"What do you suppose it means?" he asked.

"I don't know," Sam said. "It could mean the warriors have enough rifles and pistols, they can afford to give the war heads to their sons for hunting."

"Rifles, huh?" said the Montana Kid, he and Black venturing in closer. "How far are we from this buried gold?" As he spoke, he looked all around, back across the desert floor below. The wavering afternoon heat had cut the vision across sand flats by half. Anything moving over a mile away was lost in the rising, swirling heat.

"Two days," Sam said, "three at the most, depending on what pushes us forward or holds us back." He pitched the arrow across Childers' lap. "Here's you a souvenir," he said.

Childers picked up the arrow and flung it away.

"I won't need reminding of it," he said.

Sam placed a folded bandana on the bleeding wound and pressed Childers' hand on it. He twisted another bandana and tied it around the wound as Childers removed his hand from it. Black stood watching, his hat brim tied flat against his hat crown with a strip of rawhide.

Sam looked off and up at a higher switch-

33

back trail circling in the distance above them.

"We need to get up there before dark," he said. "Whoever's coming this way across the sand should be getting here about dark. They can't make any more time than we can on these hillsides."

"You mean we'll get on up there and camp the night real quietlike?" Burke asked.

"No," Sam said. "We get up there and rest our horses for a while and move on. We ride all night. Tomorrow we'll cross more desert, put some miles between us and them, maybe shake them off our trail. Right now they're curious about us. But the curiosity will wear thin when they see how hard it is to catch up to us."

"I've heard 'pache can track a ghost across running water," Black said.

"So you want to give up, throw ourselves on their mercy. Maybe we could ask them where we can and can't go?" Montana said critically.

"I'm just saying, is all," said Black. "The 'pache ain't people to be fooling with."

"Don't make them bigger than they are," Sam said.

"Yeah, we're gunmen ourselves," said Burke. "We don't bow and scrape to no-body. Am I right, Jones?"

"Yeah, why not . . . ?" Sam looked all around, taking stock of the hills, the winding trails. "Besides, we're so deep in the Mexican Desert hills now, we're going to be ducking and fighting them whether we go forward or turn back."

The Montana Kid chuckled, seeing the look of trepidation on Stanley Black's face.

"Hell," he said, "if this gold was too easy to take out of here, I expect I wouldn't think it worth my time."

"You're talking crazy, Montana," Black said.

Sam wiped his knife blade back and forth in the dirt and shoved it down into his boot well. He walked toward his dun and the spare horse.

"Let's get moving," he said over his shoulder. "Tomorrow we'll all try to keep our guns quiet."

"Be advised, Jones, if I'm fired upon, I'll fire back," the Montana Kid called out, taking Sam's words to be aimed deliberately at him.

"So I've seen," Sam said without looking back.

As he walked on, he heard Black speaking to Burke in a lowered tone.

"Who put him in charge?" Black asked.

"Keep your mouth shut, Stanley," Burke

35

growled in reply, "before I stick a rock lizard in it and sew it shut."

Sam stared straight ahead at his dun and the spare horse. Yes, he could see he was taking the lead with these men, but so be it, he told himself, walking on toward the horses. Somebody had to take charge. This harsh land had no respect of person or his objective. It didn't matter that he was a lawman working under cover. In this deadly terrain, staying alive dwarfed all other purpose and intent.

CHAPTER 3

At dark, the five had reached a high summit and stepped down from their saddles. They led the tired horses under a limestone shelf overhang and dropped the saddles from their sweaty backs. They poured tepid water from their canteens into their upturned hats and held the sparse offering up to the horses' muzzles. Sam took a dried goat shank from the supplies carried by his spare horse. Walking over to where the men had fallen to the ground and leaned against their damp saddles, Sam pitched the meat down to Burke.

"Here, take some and pass it around," he said.

Burke caught the shank and gazed at it hungrily as he pulled a knife from a sheath at the back of his trouser waist and carved a thin slice.

"Obliged," he said up to Sam. "No matter where I've gone in life, there's always goat meat waiting for me." He chuckled and passed the shank to the Montana Kid.

Montana cut himself a thin slice and handed the shank on to Stanley Black, whose severed hat brim dropped again, in spite of the rawhide strip holding it. Instead of dealing with tightening and retying the rawhide, Black jerked the hat from his head and slapped it to the ground. He quickly took a slice of goat and passed the shank on to Childers.

Childers turned down the meat, looking as if even the sight of it sickened him.

"How's the shoulder coming?" Sam asked, noting the wounded gunman's lack of appetite.

"It's pounding like a drum straight up from hell," Childers replied. "It's pounding inside my head as well as in my shoulder." He leaned his head to the side and spat in the dirt. "I'd like to catch the kid who arrow-spiked me and beat him senseless with a stove poker. That would teach him."

Teach him what?

Sam considered it and only nodded, knowing it was Childers' pain talking.

"If you can make yourself eat some, you should," he said matter-of-factly. "You're going to need all your strength if we're riding all night."

Boyd Childers didn't answer. The other men gave one another a guarded look. Burke finished chewing a mouthful of goat and swallowed it dry.

"Speaking of riding all night, Jones," he said, "do you suppose that's the best idea?"

"I wouldn't have proposed it otherwise," Sam replied. He stared flatly at Burke, anticipating more to come. The others sat chewing, watching intently. This was something the four had talked about among themselves along the trail, Sam decided. "Why do you ask?" he said.

Burke coughed and cleared his throat. He winced a little before speaking.

"The thing is, we was wondering why we can't lay up here for the night. Get ourselves and our horses rested —"

"We talked about this already, Clyde," Sam said, cutting him off. He took the goat shank from Childers and wrapped its canvas cover back around it.

"I know we did. We're just wondering, is all," Burke said. "But we're all worn out here. Our horses are worn out. Childers is hurting like hell —"

Sam turned and walked away, goat shank in hand.

"Hold on, Jones," Burke called out. "Where you going?"

39

"On," Sam said, "by myself."

"Wait, damn it," Burke said, scrambling to his feet. The others followed suit, still chewing their goat meat. "Can't we just talk about it?"

"We did, *twice,*" Sam said without looking back. "I'm not talking about it again." He stopped at the dun and the spare horse. He scooped his saddle off the ground, slung it over the dun and cinched it.

Burke and the others looked at one another.

"Damn it to hell!" said Burke.

Sam swung atop his saddle, the spare horse's lead rope coiled in his hand. He turned the dun and gave a pull on the spare horse's rope, guiding both animals toward the trail.

"If I start looking smaller, it's because I'm riding away," he said, touching his hat brim toward the staring gunmen.

"Jones —" Burke started to call out, but a distant sound of gunfire resounded from far down the hillside, causing him to stop and stand in silence. The others did the same.

Sam stopped the dun, but only for a second. As the gunfire increased, erupting into a full-fledged gun battle, he touched his boots to the dun's side and rode on, leading the spare horse close alongside him.

"Jesus!" said Burke. He let out an exasperated breath and snatched his saddle from the ground. "I've never seen a man so damn intolerant of others." He hurried toward his horse, the remainder of the group right behind him.

Sam rode on, keeping the dun at a steady but easy pace, knowing the others would be hurrying to join him. Before he'd gone two hundred yards, he heard their horses' hooves thundering up behind him.

"Damn it, Jones!" said Burke, riding up beside him, well ahead of the others. "You can't just ride off and leave us. We've still got a deal."

"I've got no deal with dead men," Sam said, playing it hard as stone. "If you fool around in the country, you'll be decorating some warrior's lodge pole."

"All right," said Burke. "We were all worn out, but here we are now, ready to ride. Giving it all we've got."

"Yep, here you are," Sam said. "But let me make sure you understand, I'm not going to waste my time keeping you alive if dying is all you're good for. Either give it all you've got to begin with or go lie on a rock and blow your heads off — save yourself the trouble." He booted the dun up a little. Burke rode alongside him.

41

"You've got it, Jones," he said. "What do you suppose all that shooting is about down there?"

"I've got no idea," Sam said. "But it's coming from the trail we're on. When they're finished fighting, if they haven't all killed each other, they'll be coming up this trail." He slowed the dun a little as the other men came galloping up in a hurry, still stretched out single file.

Seeing the men slow their horses, Burke looked down at the sound of the battle raging below them. He looked back up at the men as Sam booted the dun forward.

"What the hell are you all waiting for?" Burke said to the other three. "Let's get the hell out of here."

On the lower trail the battle raged full bore for over an hour. For the next three hours sporadic gunfire continued. From the upper ledges just short of the hillside's crest, Sam and the four gunmen heard the straggling battle spread out, diminishing farther down along the trail and out across the sand flats. After midnight a lasting silence had set in. From the crest of the trail, the five sat their horses in the purple light of a three-quarter moon and gazed down across black shadowy darkness.

"Well, I'm glad they worked everything out between them," Burke joked. The three other gunmen laughed until Sam raised a hand, hushing them.

"Did you feel that?" Sam asked almost in a whisper. He listened in every direction. The men sat in a tense silence.

"Hear what?" Burke whispered.

No sooner had he spoken than a small powerful tremor bored through the stony hillside beneath them, the rumble akin to that of an oncoming train.

"Jesus, what's that?" Black asked.

"Get off your horses, quick," Sam said.

The men didn't question his order. They slid down from their saddles just in time to feel another rumbling quake down deep under the hillside. The horses spooked and whinnied, but they didn't attempt to bolt away, their legs feeling too wobbly and unsteady to support such an effort. They stood their ground, trembling along with the hillside, and struggled to remain upright.

Sam grabbed the dun's saddle horn and stood with his feet spread shoulder width apart. Burke collapsed against the side of his horse and held on as the trembling earth jarred through him. Childers jumped farther away from the wall on the inside of the trail as small stones and gravel sprayed down like heavy rain. Stanley Black and the Montana Kid pawed and grabbed at each other, and fell to the ground like impassioned lovers no longer able to resist.

"Da-da-da-damn!" Burke stuttered. He fell the rest of the way down his horse's side, caught on to its stirrup and hung there.

The sound of loosened rock and dirt shuffled and rattled and slid. Brush and sparse timber rustled. Sam tried to look all around in the darkness, but his eyes would not focus just right. The night, the sky and the hill itself seemed to try to rise as if suddenly intent on relocating themselves. Sam felt his hat tremble loosely atop his head.

Then, as if having changed its mind, the earth fell into place with a bone-shattering thump, the feeling of some gigantic underground ledge slipping and falling and settling onto some lower level.

The calmness set in so fast Sam turned loose of his saddle horn and steadied himself in place, his arms out on either side as if to test his balance.

"That was . . . an earthquake," Burke said unsteadily.

"I noticed," said the Montana Kid, turning loose of Black and jumping to his feet. He brushed him off and straightened his clothes and gun belt. He drew his Colt and checked it nervously.

Sam didn't waste any time. He pulled the dun forward by its reins with one hand and pulled the spare horse along by its lead rope. The two horses needed little coaxing.

"Get up over this hilltop, find us a wide spot," Sam said, dirt and rock still raining in spite of the earth having settled back into place.

Managing to stay single file, the men and horses moved upward the short distance to the top of the hill. Once on wider, flatter ground, with no rocks to fall from above them, they stopped and looked back in relief.

"That was close," Burke remarked.

Almost before he'd finished his words, the four turned their heads toward what sounded like angry waves breaking on a rocky shoreline.

"What the hell?" Childers said, his hand clasped to his wounded shoulder.

A roiling brown-black cloud rose on the darkness and spread down along the sky and trail side as far as the men could see. The sound of ocean waves revealed itself to be a shifting, sliding bed of loose scree, unseated stone and boulder. The men watched as if transfixed. In slices of purple moonlight, they witnessed and felt a new rumbling beneath them as the top layer of hillside tumbled and bounced and flung its stone and sparse flora mantling downward toward the distant desert floor.

"Landslide . . . ," Burke whispered, staring as if in awe. "Damnedest place I've ever seen."

"I want out of here," Black said, with no pretense of courage. He started to jerk his horse's reins, but Sam stopped him.

"Stand still," he said to the frightened gunman. "This hilltop is the best we've got until everything settles down."

"Hell, I guess I *know* that," Black replied, his voice turning deeper, affecting a braver tone. He stopped and stood quietly.

The sliding stone and scree waned on the hillside. Louder rumblings resounded farther back along the hill line behind them. In front of them miles ahead, peaks of the Blood Mountain Range stood jagged and endless against the purple sky.

"One thing," Burke said, turning and looking back through the roiling dust of the dislocated hillside. "Nobody's coming up behind us now."

"That's a fact," Sam said, staring back at the roiling brown cloud of dust.

"How much gold are we talking about

here?" Childers asked, trying to sound casual.

"Talk to Clyde about it," Sam said to Childers. He turned and led his two horses over to a rock. He took a canteen down from his saddle horn and sat down. Clamping the rope and reins to the ground with his boot, he sipped water and sat listening to the men talk back and forth among themselves. The dun stuck its muzzle in close and stretched its lip out, probing toward the open canteen. The spare horse stuck its muzzle in right beside it. Sam rubbed their muzzles and pushed them away gently.

"I'm saving you boys a drink," he said to the two horses.

In moments the men walked over and stood in front of him.

The Montana Kid stood closer than the others.

"What now?" he asked Sam bluntly on all their behalf. "Like Burke said, there's nobody behind us now."

Sam looked up at him in the pale moonlight as he capped the half-full canteen and held it on his lap.

"I've learned there's *somebody* behind *everybody*, Montana," he replied. He wiped a hand across his mouth.

47

"Come on, Jones," said Montana. "You know what I mean. What's to keep us from resting the night right here? Take up toward the ruins come morning?"

"Who said we're going through the ruins?" Sam asked.

"We all know there's water around those ruins," said Montana. He glanced around at the others, then back to Sam. "We'd be foolish not to go through there."

Sam only stared at him.

"Water is all the more reason to push on tonight," he said firmly. "We don't know what shape the quake left this trail in ahead of us. It'll be easier on thirsty horses traveling tonight while it's cooled down."

"He's got a point, Montana," Childers cut in, holding his wounded shoulder. "There might not be any more trail before us than there is behind us."

Montana looked at the men's faces in the moonlight. Then he looked back down at Sam and let out a breath.

"Have you been in any of these quakes before?" he asked.

"A few," Sam said. "It seemed like there was one every time we turned around a month back." He kept his voice as civil as Montana's. "Have you been in any?"

"Last month, like you said," Montana

replied. "I was on flatland every time, though. What about you?"

Sam gestured a nod toward the hill line, the looming brown-black dust. "My first time seeing it this bad," he said. "So I can't say what to expect between here and the ruins."

The Montana Kid nodded, appreciating the truth.

"All right, then," he said. "We're both on the same spot. None of us here knows any more than the other."

Sam stood and stretched and hung his canteen back on his saddle horn.

"That about the size of it," he said. "I'm still pushing on. Make up your minds if you're still riding with me."

Montana looked at the others, then back at Sam.

"I'm not speaking for anybody but myself," he said. "I expect if you're still riding on, I'm still riding with you." He gave a thin devil-may-care grin. "If this is turning into an adventure, I can't wait to see what's next."

CHAPTER 4

In the gray-silver hour of dawn, the five men stood beside their horses overlooking a trail below them that they could plainly see had been knocked out and overcoated with a layer of rock and broken pine twenty feet deep. The long slope of broken and unseated rock lay spread and reseated down the steep hillside beneath a silvery morning mist. The long slide looked as if a sound no larger than a whisper or a cough could loosen the whole hillside and send it plunging downward again.

"There we have it," Burke said in disgust. "Who'd ever guessed I'd someday be on a mountain and the damn thing fell out from under me?"

"Call it the luck of the game," said Montana, leading his horse beside Burke. He gazed down as if in deep reflection.

Sam had noted that Montana had taken on a better attitude since the quake and the subsequent landslide.

"I remember once when I was a young boy," Montana said quietly. "For no reason at all, a little boat I was standing on just sank . . . no reason. . . ." He shook his head wistfully. "I mean, for no reason at all."

Sam just looked at him.

On Sam's other side, Childers stood holding a hand to his wounded shoulder.

"It sort of makes you wonder, don't it?" he commented quietly to Montana.

Burke and Stanley Black sat listening until Burke could take it no more.

"Jesus . . . ," he said, sounding irritated with the two gunmen's conversation. "Wonder about *what*?"

Childers shrugged with his good shoulder.

"Just, you know . . . everything, I reckon," he said.

Sam shook his head and backed the dun and the spare horse away on the thin trail.

"Where are you going, Jones?" Burke asked, backing his horse up as well.

"I'm going to find a game path or something," Sam said. He gestured at the hillside that had risen beside them as they'd traveled down from the higher summit.

"What if there's none?" Burke asked.

Sam just looked at him.

"I'm just asking," Burke said.

51

As the others turned and led horses in behind him, Sam spoke to them over his shoulder.

"Spread out along this back trail, look for any kind of path not too steep to lead these horses up," he said. "Anybody finds one that leads up and around the slide, call out . . . only not too loud," he added. "This whole hillside looks a little like it could take off sliding again any—"

His words stopped short beneath the long, loud bellow of a monstrous grizzly that suddenly stood up on its hind legs only twenty yards up the rocky hillside.

"Holy Joseph, shut up, you big son of a bitch!" Burke called up to the bear, trying to keep his voice as quiet as possible.

But the bear would have none of it. It continued to bawl out long and loud, the sound echoing like cannon fire along the shaky hill line. The horses spooked and whinnied and stamped in place as the men held them firm.

"You won't shut it up," Sam said. "Look at it. It's beaten something fierce."

"Whoa, it is," Burke said. He raised his rifle in his hands and stood with it loosely pressed against his shoulder.

Sam gave him a warning look.

"Just in case it comes charging at us,"

Burke said, regarding the rifle. "I don't want to be caught short by a wounded griz."

The men stood staring at the big bawling brute, noting streaks of blood glistening down its sides, its big head, its raised paws.

"Oh yeah, this one is hurt bad," Montana said quietly. "I'd say it got caught up in the slide and rode it down until it could get out of it."

As the bear bellowed and postured and threatened, its claws spread and its big mouth open wide, showing long bloody teeth, the men backed away. Leading their terrified horses, they eased away along the trail, mindful of small streams of gravel and loose rocks starting to stream down among the freshly formed slide bed. Burke kept his rifle ready, as did Black and Montana. But in a moment the bear wore itself out and dropped onto all fours. They watched as the big animal turned and waddled away up into the rocky hills.

"Which way are you going, Burke?" Sam asked.

"Huh?" said Burke.

"To search for a path up around the slide," Sam reminded the shaken gunman. "Which way are you going?"

"I'm going whichever way the bear *ain't,*" Burke said.

The men spread out along the trail as they had started to do before the bear announced itself. It took the men four unsuccessful starts before they found a path that didn't stop short, but rather led all the way up the bald and scathed hill and around the upper edge where the rock slide had started.

Once having found the path, the men spread out with ten yards between them and led their horses single file, silently and carefully upward. Halfway around the upper edge, Sam stopped and looked back past his two at Burke, who moved toward him almost on tiptoes. Burke kept a wary eye on the hillside still above them, much of its scree and loose stony surface held back only by a large boulder sunken to midgirth.

Looking away from the precarious boulder and forward along the path, seeing Sam had stopped and stood looking back at him, Burke grumbled under his breath. He moved forward, and when he caught up to Sam and had to stop for him, he wasted no time trying to hurry him forward.

"Why the hell are you stopped, Jones?" he asked, keeping his voice lowered.

Sam looked at him.

"Just want to tell you, I can see a trail up ahead that looks like it runs down back onto the switchbacks," he replied.

"That's great. Real good," said Burke. "Can we keep moving? Do we have to stop right here?" He eyed the boulder and the large buildup of loose rock and broken pine behind it.

Sam turned and walked forward, leading his two horses.

"It's going to be a steep downhill climb to it," he said. "But once we make it, I believe it will take us on down to the desert floor by evening — on to the ruins by tonight."

"Sounds good to me," Burke said hurriedly. "Keep moving."

"I will now that I've told you which way I'm headed," Sam said, looking past Burke, back at the others. "But you've got to stick here until Childers catches up to you. Then you tell him, and he'll wait here for the next one."

"Jesus . . . ," said Burke, not liking the idea of waiting for the next man. But looking ahead at the path and how it dropped out of sight, he realized how easy it would be to get separated up ahead. "All right, just go," he said, forcing himself to calm down.

"You need to settle yourself down, Clyde," Sam said quietly.

"Man! I do *not* want to die on this miserable godforsaken Mexican hillside," Burke said.

Sam stared at him.

"Neither do I," he said, seriously. Then he turned and led the horses away along the narrow rocky path.

For the rest of the morning and into the afternoon, the four riders followed Sam down one steep path after another. Finally they reached a switchback where they were able to collapse for a short rest in the heat of the day. The horses milled and blew and raised their muzzles in the direction of a water hole that lay in a wide clearing along the trail on the next level down. Sam looked down and saw nothing blocking the trail between them and the water. Then he divided the contents of his canteen and served each horse from his upturned hat.

The mottled white barb took its water first. The dun poked its nose back and forth impatiently and stamped a hoof.

"I told you I'd save you both a drink," he murmured to the horses, pushing the spare horse back and pouring the rest of the water for the dun.

As the dun sucked up the water in a fast gulp, Sam patted the horse's lowered head. The dun nipped the inside of Sam's hat, wanting more.

"Mind your manners, now," Sam said. The dun slung his wet hat and bit down with its teeth until Sam managed to take the hat and shove the dun's nose away. "We've got water coming. Take it easy," he said to the parched animals.

The men stepped up into the saddles and followed Sam down the trail. They were scuffed and bruised and cut and covered with thick dust, but grateful to at last be on horseback. When they reached the small water hole on the inside of the trail, they sank their canteens into the water while their horses stood knee deep at the edge and drew their fill. The water hole stretched fifteen feet out from the trail and backed up against the stony brush-covered hillside.

Even as the thirsty animals drank, Sam noted a skittishness about them that caused him to take a step back and look all around at the boulders and stones strewn about on the hillside. He held his palm on the butt of his holstered Colt, his rifle already in hand.

"Something's got them spooked, sure enough," Burke said quietly to Sam, moving up close beside him, seeing how the horses were acting. He also held his rifle in hand.

Instead of answering, Sam stepped sidelong around the water's edge and stooped down and looked at fresh elk hooves and bear paws in the softer wet dirt. He gestured Burke over to him and pointed at the tracks as he gestured his eyes toward the rocky hillside. The other men stood watching quietly as the horses filled their bellies.

Burke nodded and whispered, "Same bear, you think?"

"I don't know," Sam whispered. "These quakes have everything stirred up. Either way, it's on this hillside, probably watching us right now." He drew the other men's attention to the hillside and ran his hand back and forth in the air, signaling them to watch the rocks. "We need to finish up here and slip away as quick as we can —"

Before he finished his words, the big grizzly stood up from behind a land-stuck rock straight across the water hole. The bear let out another loud bawl. This time its big paws were not spread wide but rather hanging almost limply at its sides. The bear's presence was not as threatening as earlier — only a weak warning, nothing more.

"Stand still, he's not going to charge," Sam called out to the four gunmen, who had to grab their horses by their reins as the animals pulled back from the water to turn and race away.

No sooner had Sam gotten his words out of his mouth than Montana's rifle barked and bucked in his hands. The bullet hit the bear high in its shoulder, half turning the animal on its hind legs.

"Don't shoot!" Sam shouted, although he knew the shot couldn't be taken back. Across the water, the big bear staggered a step forward, appearing to stare straight across at Montana. Without hesitation, Montana fired again, then a third time as the bear bolted forward two steps, splashed into the water and fell forward on its face.

Sam and the others stood in silence as the sound of the rifle fire echoed and bounced away along the high hilltops.

"He's cooked us," Burke said with a deep sigh. He stepped over to where Black stood holding the reins to his and Burke's horses. Burke took his horse's reins and glared at Montana.

"What?" Montana said. "The bear was coming at me! I shot him. I did it without even thinking."

"I can believe that," Burke said, still glaring. The other men settled their horses and watched the two stare each other down.

To keep down any trouble, Sam took a coil of rope from his saddle horn, stepped over between the two and looked all along the high cliff edges and hilltops.

"All right, let's finish up and go," he said. As he spoke, he dropped coil after coil of rope.

"What's this you're doing?" Burke asked, eyeing Sam's rope.

"We've got to pull the bear from the water hole, keep it from ruining the water," Sam replied. "Like as not, there's no one around near enough who cares about us after that quake."

"Then what's our hurry?" Childers called out.

"It's just in case I'm wrong," Sam said, stooping, grabbing his full canteen from the water and screwing the cap down on it. He threw his hat off his head so that it hung on his back from its string and splashed water on his dusty face. Then he trudged into the water and made his way out to the bear, his rope trailing out behind him.

"Son of a bitch," Burke growled. He grabbed a rope from his saddle horn and splashed out into the water behind Sam. "I'd never live in a place where you can't shoot a gun without every pig-licking bastard coming to see why."

"I didn't do anything wrong," Montana called out, taking down his rope as well. "The bear was coming at us. I shot him!

Who can blame me?" He walked through the water toward Sam and Burke. The three began tying the rope to the bear.

"Nobody blames you, Montana," Sam said. "Any one of us might have done the same." He swung up atop the dun and turned both horses toward the trail with Burke.

"Well, now, that's damn big of you, Jones," Montana said with sarcasm. "I'll be damn sure to get your approval anytime I go to shoot something —"

"Shut up, Montana," Burke snapped at him, jerking his horse around toward him, his hand on his Colt. "We're all worn plumb to the bone and still got a long ride ahead of us."

Montana settled himself, staring at Sam.

"Jones, I wish I hadn't fired those shots, but I did. There's nothing I can do that'll change it," he said, his voice taking on a calmer tone.

"Forget it, Montana," Sam said. "Like Clyde says, we're all worn out." He turned and walked the rope back to the water's edge and tied it off to his saddle horn.

Montana shook his head and walked back and tied the rope off to his saddle horn as well. So did Burke. Black and Childers stood guard, looking back and forth along the wavering desert floor, rifles in hand.

In minutes the three had pulled the dead bear out of the water and onto a bed of gravel and small rock. They gathered their wet ropes and recoiled them. As Burke and Sam mounted their horses and rode away, their trousers dripping water, Montana let out a breath and hung his coiled rope back on his saddle horn.

"If there was one place on me that's not sore, I'd stab myself there just to make everything match," he said. "How much gold *are* we talking about?" he asked Childers, having heard Childers ask Sam that same question the night before. Beside them Stanley Black mounted his watered horse and rode away behind Burke.

"Talk to Clyde about it," Childers replied to Montana, swinging up into his saddle, giving Montana the same answer he'd gotten from Sam.

The two mounted and rode off behind the others, each man keeping a ten-yard interval between himself and the man in front of him.

Fifty yards farther down the winding trail, they bunched up again at the edge of an overgrown cliff ledge. Sam and Burke sat their horses, looking through a sheltering stand of young pine at a wide desert stretched below.

"What do you think?" Black asked, pulling his horse up on Sam's left.

Sam studied the empty desert floor, his wrists crossed on his saddle horn. Below them, long evening shadows encroached out onto beds of gravel and farther out through embedded stones the size of steers. Sand the color of copper and pearls lay windbanked among the stones. Pale dry sage clung to the desert floor as if in a last stand before tumbling off to parts unknown.

"Make a dark camp until midnight," Sam replied to both Burke and Black. He spoke sparingly, knowing he'd have to repeat himself when the other two arrived.

Black let out a tired sigh.

"That's sort of what I figured," he said. "I hope folks are still drinking hot coffee by the time we get out of this wilderness."

They waited as Childers rode and stopped, followed a moment later by the Montana Kid.

Sam looked around at them, then back out across the low rolling sand flats.

"We'll stick up here and rest a few hours," he said. "After midnight, we go down and lead our horses along the rocks, stay this side of the gravel beds."

The men gave a low collective groan.

"The longer we lead these horses, the longer it'll take us to get to the ruins," Childers pointed out.

"I know," Sam said. "But anybody wants to find our trail, at least they'll have to work for it."

The tired, battered men nodded in agreement.

"Each of us stands an hour of guard," Sam said, having their attention, knowing he was in charge. "When the last man has stood guard, we move down from here and get under way."

"You got it, Jones," Burke said. "I'll take guard first, unless anybody objects." He looked at each exhausted dust-caked face in turn, then gave a thin, tired chuckle and said, "I didn't think so."

CHAPTER 5

They slept the short night four men at a time, while the fifth man sat awake, wrapped in a blanket and backed against a rock. Sam had pulled his hour of guard third in line. At three in the morning, he arose from his spot among the rocks where the other sleepers lay sprawled like dead men awaiting burial and walked quietly to where the Montana Kid sat blanket-wrapped, his rifle hugged against himself like some talisman meant to ward away evil in the wide desert night.

"I'm awake," Montana said in a lowered tone, as if denying an accusation before it was made.

"I figured you were," Sam whispered in reply. "It's time we shake them out."

Montana reached beneath his blanket, took out a pocket watch, opened it and cocked it against the pale moonlight.

"I make it five more minutes," he said, a

man suddenly dedicated to the precision and distribution of time.

Sam leaned against the rock beside Montana and gazed out through the purple-black-striped desert floor below them. Overhead, stars lay spread on a wide silken trail leading off into the endless depths of the heavens. A three-quarter moon dozed, its cleaved edge leaning against the western sky. On the ground below them, Sam watched as a shadowy black line of coyotes rose and fell in their silent stride, their red eyes darting upward toward the scent of man infringing on their domain.

"They make a ten-minute circle," Montana said quietly. "Seeing if our smell is changing any — figuring us for fresh kill." He paused, then said, "Might be catching some of Childers' dried shoulder blood on the air."

"Their scenting don't miss a thing," Sam offered, watching the coyotes file out of sight into the greater blackness of rock shadow.

"Sons a' bitches hunt with their nose better than we can with our eyes," Montana said. He paused, then added, "All we've got is brains, and they don't work right half the time."

"You'd choose to be a coyote instead of a

man?" Sam asked.

"I never choose either one," said Montana. He stood up and gestured a nod in the coyotes' direction. "Neither did they." He cocked the watch against the pale moonlight again, then snapped it shut soundlessly and put it away under his blanket. "Now it's time to shake them out," he said.

Sam nodded and walked away. From one sleeper to the next he walked, kicking each man's feet as he passed.

"S'wrong?" Burke mumbled when Sam gave him a wake-up kick. He jerked upright in his blanket, but kept his voice lowered.

"Nothing. Time to go," Sam whispered.

"Damn it. I feel like I just lay down," Burke grumbled as Sam walked away.

At the horses, Sam drew the cinch on his saddle and laid the stirrup down the dun's side. He took out the remainder of the goat meat and shared it with the others. The men twisted off a small portion and passed it along. They wolfed the meat down or held it between their teeth as they readied their horses for the trail.

Clyde Burke took his bite of meat and swallowed dry and shook his head. "I always said a big breakfast can ruin a man's whole day."

The men gave a sleepy half laugh. The

67

worn horses grumbled and blew and scraped their hooves.

Sam took his bite of meat, downed it and stood waiting with the lead rope to the white barb in hand. When the men had shaken off their sleep and bridled and saddled their animals, he led his horse around and stood waiting. A moment later, Burke stepped up into his saddle, saw his mistake and swung back to the ground. He cursed under his breath and led his horse over behind Sam's.

One by one the others stumbled over, leading their horses, and fell into line like lost souls searching for the other side. Finally, without a word, Sam walked away from the dark, cold camp onto the thin path leading to the last stretch of the downhill trail.

As dark as it was on the upper hillside, it turned darker yet over the next hour as they moved down with the moon standing on the other side of the hill line. What moonlight lingered lay sliced and darkened out by black shadows of boulder and cliff shelves lining the winding trail. Another half hour and the darkness waned around them as the larger boulders grew sparse as if having abandoned their rugged domicile one and two at a time, taken over by the long

68

beds of scree sloping on either side of the trail.

Where those loose talus beds banked against the rounded steer-sized rock the men had become acquainted with, a wide bed of gravel and sand lined the lower slopes and spilled and spread out into stands of brush and low cactus garnishing the wide desert floor. When the men reached the long gravelly boulevard near the bottom of the hill, in the east the first thin wreath of silver-gold began to glow below the black edge of the earth.

"I make it we'll all have one leg shorter than the other by the time we're off this hillside," Burke whispered to Sam, walking a few feet behind him. "I'm thinking I'll walk backward a ways just to make up."

They trod the gravel bed two miles to its end, their boots and the horses' hooves leaving a low crunching sound in the silent darkness. When the crunching gravel turned quiet and the land turned stiff and rocky beneath them, Sam led his horses a few feet to the side and waited until the last man and horse filed past him.

Kneeling in their tracks, Sam eyed back through the grainy predawn light, seeing the efforts of their travel recorded in the gravel like words embedded in the printed page.

Yet it would still be less clear to the searching eye than a line of tracks made out in the open across the sand.

It's the best you get, he told himself. He knew it wouldn't trick Apache; it wasn't meant to. He only hoped it showed them this trek was not led by a fool.

He stood and looked all around, seeing not fifty feet from him the red glow of eyes and the black silhouettes of the coyote band. He saw three sets of eyes blink and glow closer to the ground. *Pups* . . . He stooped and picked up a round quarter-sized piece of gravel and threw it back along the path of boot and hoof. The red eyes all shot in the direction of the slight sound of the rock skittering away. Then the eyes turned back to him, blinked curiously and vanished. Sam turned, rifle and lead rope in hand.

And he walked on.

As first boiling sunlight spilled up over the horizon, the riders rode back up onto the rocky hillside. At midmorning they fell among rock shade like men shot dead from afar.

"Don't wake me 'less a fish bites," Burke said, collapsing.

They rested in silence, corpselike, until the heat and glare of sunlight rolled and spread and began to waver like spirits dancing in the middle of the desert floor. While the others lay spent, Sam found a large boulder farther up the slope and positioned himself in a way that gave him a clear look in every direction. As he rested, he held the battered telescope to his eye and gauged the obscurity of the view across the low rolling desert. For the next hour he probed the wavering heat every few minutes with the circled lens until he decided he and his band could not be seen any better than they themselves could see anyone on the other side. He rose and walked back to the worn-out men and horses.

"Fish biting," he said, kicking the sole of one of Burke's boots. The outlaw's boot soles stood toe-up from the ground, leaning away from each other like a pair of weathered grave markers of some lesser cretins with issues unresolved.

"I'm up, *I'm up,*" Burke mumbled, jerking upright, then stumbling to his feet. He picked at the seat of his dusty trousers as he pushed his hat down atop his head. "Jesus! Do you ever sleep?" he said to Sam.

"You'd have to be awake to know it," Sam replied, kicking Montana's boot, stepping away, kicking Black's, then Childers'.

Sam watched the men drag themselves to

71

the horses and take up their reins. The horses yanked against their reins, getting sharp-tempered, hard to handle.

Testy with thirst . . . , Sam noted. Even though the horses hadn't been ridden all day, the heat throughout their travels was starting to take its toll. He took a deep breath, walking to the dun and the white barb. He had checked the desert floor as best he could. With the Apache making war on the Mexicans and anyone else they came upon, all he could do was keep the men moving — stay out of sight.

He felt his senses slip a notch beneath the heat and his own thirst. But he shook his head free of a white blankness and looked around to make sure the others hadn't noticed.

"Let's lead them out of here," he said quietly. "There's water waiting up ahead."

The men gathered and stretched and settled their thirsty horses and walked on in the scorching afternoon heat.

It was early dark when the riders came to the water hole that lay no more than two hours from the hillside ruins. Two miles before reaching the water, Sam and the men led their horses down off the rocky hillsides onto the sand and stepped up into the saddles. When the horses had caught scent of the water, they had become cross and unruly. It was easier to ride them and let them lead the way than it was to try to keep them in check.

Once at the water hole, Sam and the men stepped down at the water's edge and lay prone beside their watering horses, reins and empty canteens in hand. They sank their canteens into the water to fill them and rinsed their mouths of the day's sand and dust, squirting the water out. Then they drank their fill, their hot scorched faces and chests submerged in the water, finding the tepid water to feel as cold as a winter stream after their torturous day in the desert sun.

When they finished drinking, the men lay on the wet ground at the water's edge until the horses had drunk their fill. Stanley Black sat on a rock keeping an eye on the trail they'd ridden on while the others took their horses up onto the hillside above the water. There they rope-hobbled their forelegs and left them to graze on pale clumps of wild grass standing among rocks the size of melons.

"I got to hand it to you, Jones," Burke said. "You've kept us a clean trail in both directions."

"We're not there yet," Sam cautioned,

looking around the darkness as he spoke.

"But we will be soon enough," Burke said. "What say, after we get this gold and split it up, you ride on with me?"

Sam just looked at him, the two of them sitting with water running down from their wet hair.

"I mean it," Burke said. "I'll put in a good word to Bell Madson for you. He's got lots of moneymaking gun work coming up."

"What about me killing Segert?" Sam asked, not wanting to sound too eager. In fact, this was exactly what he'd been hoping for.

"A fair fight is a fair fight." Burke shrugged. "Anyway, I figure there might have been a bone between the two of them. Why else would Madson be pulling so much away from Crazy Raymond?"

"I didn't realize he was," Sam said.

"Well, he was," Burke said. "I saw it. So did some others. Anyway, it's all about business to Madson. With Segert dead, who better to have riding for him than the hombre who killed him?"

"Makes sense to me," Sam said. "Far as I'm concerned, set me up with him, so long as everybody keeps their mouth shut about this gold."

"They will, you can bank on it," said Burke.

The two stood up as the other men gathered at the water's edge, capping their full canteens. On the hillside, the sound of the horses grazing resounded quietly.

"How long you figure?" the Montana Kid asked Sam, gesturing a nod toward the dark silhouettes of the horses, their heads lowered to the ground.

"We'll give them an hour," Sam said, taking on the authority the men were giving to him. "It's the only graze we'll find between here and the ruins."

The men nodded in agreement, Sam noted. That was good.

"Think we've shook free from any more Apache?" Childers asked, holding a wet bandana to his healing shoulder wound.

"No," said Sam. "We'll have them down our shirts as long as we're here." He looked around the darkness again. "The Apache size everybody up, see how they act, how strong they are. The first thing they look at is gun strength. We've got that. The next thing they look at is how smart you are. They see you traveling wise, leaving little sign of yourself, they know you're strong, not foolish. The Apache don't abide fools. They only respect strength and wisdom.

Show them weakness, show them you don't know your way around on the desert, they'll take everything you've got and chop you down fast."

"So what we're saying is that stupidity won't cut it, fellows," Burke cut in, wanting to show himself sided with Sam.

The men nodded again.

Childers gave Black his tobacco fixings and Black rolled each of them a smoke.

"How's the shoulder, Boyd?" Sam asked Childers.

"Better," said Childers, sitting on a low rock. "I'm damn glad you made me go ahead and have you tend it when you did," he said. "I don't know what I was waiting for. I think the sun might have had me thrown off some." He took the rolled cigarette from Black and lit it with a flaming match Black held out to him.

Sam looked around, making sure the larger stones around the water hole kept the flare of the match from being seen down on the desert floor.

"Is this all right?" Childers asked, holding the cupped cigarette down close to the ground.

Sam only nodded.

An hour later, the five wet, thirst-slaked men had walked up onto the hillside and gathered their horses, mounted and ridden away.

With the horses grazed, watered and rested, they rode forward along the desert floor at a gallop, cool air moving down around them from the higher Blood Mountain Range. Above them the moon stood full and bright in a cloudless purple sky.

In the middle of the night, the five fell into a single file and rode up off the sand flats onto a path Sam had traveled before. Within an hour they turned off the moonlit trail onto a thin path that brought them to an ancient grown-over stone ruins that stood pressed against the mountainside where it had been since time unrecorded.

"And here we are, hombres," Burke chuckled quietly to the other men. He tapped his horse forward at a walk, then jerked it to a halt as the long squall of a panther resounded from somewhere far inside the ruins' vine-clad walls.

"Easy, now," Sam whispered to his horses, feeling the dun tense up beneath him, the white barb draw back on its lead rope. The men sat tense and silent.

"There's a panther living in here," Sam said.

"Yeah, she's the one I told you et up Mick Galla," Burke put in.

"We'll just keep watch for her," Sam said, nudging the dun forward, pulling the white alongside him.

The men eased their wary horses forward as another squall resounded out and down from the hillside. The sound was far enough away to not cause alarm, yet, having seen firsthand what the big she-cat could do, Sam decided to steer clear of it.

The men followed Sam as they wound around inside the ruins and reached a wide area surrounded by a ten-foot stone wall. As they stopped their horses and stepped down from their saddles for the night, the panther let out another cry.

"That ol' pussy sounds hurt to me," Burke said. "Whatever's got her so cross, I hope she don't come blaming us for it."

Sam listened as he led his horses over to a young ironwood growing flat and misshapen against the stone wall and hitched them to it.

"I'm going to see what's ailing her," he said.

"You're going to *what*?" said Burke incredulously.

"You heard me," Sam said. "Do you want to sleep with an injured cat prowling around all night?" He dropped the saddle from the dun, stepped over and pulled the pack off

78

the white barb.

"Well, hell, you're right," Burke said with a deep sigh. He paused, then said, "If you're loco enough to go looking for a hurt panther in the dark of night, I expect I'm loco enough to go with you."

"Stay here and get yourself some rest," Sam said. "I shouldn't need any help."

"Huh-uh, I'm going," said Burke. "You're the only one knows where that gold is buried. I ain't going through all this and have you et by a cat the way Mick Galla was — leastwise, not until we've got our hands on that gold."

Sam shook his head, but he waited until Burke dropped his saddle and slid his rifle from its boot. Turning to Black, Sam said quietly, "We're going to see about the panther, find out if she's dangerous to us. We can't have her spooking the horses all night."

"She sounds hurt," Black replied. "I'll build us a fire down out of sight. You'll have coffee waiting when you get back."

"Obliged," Sam said. "We won't be long."

79

CHAPTER 6

Sam and Burke climbed up over a vine-draped stone wall and struck out uphill in the direction from which they'd heard the panther's pained wailing. Scaling the stony hillside like two dark insurgents reconnoitering some greater plane, they pulled themselves up and over boulder, stone terrace, wall and earthed embankment. A half hour later they stood on what had likely been an ancient marketplace, complete with an overgrown stone-tiled floor and a long stone bench that had served as a public privy above a deep brush-covered ditch.

"This is where we left Mick Galla, after the cat et him up," Burke said in a lowered tone, looking all around, recognizing the vine-draped wall and the remainders of weathered-out stone columns.

"Yes, it is," Sam said. He gestured upward along an earth- and vine-covered stone wall. "Her lair is right over that wall."

"At least we know she's not there tonight," said Burke, moving forward, searching as he went for the body of the ill-fated gunman, Mickey Galla, in the pale moonlight.

Before going three yards farther, Burke stopped short and stared down at the ground beside what was once a stone bench.

"Good God, there he is," he said. "Or what's left of him," he threw in as Sam walked over and stood beside him.

On the ground in the moonlight lay scraps of trousers, a brass belt buckle and a human skull lying on its cheekbone. Ragged patches of hair still clung to blackened skin atop the head. Beetles crawled freely in and out of the open eye sockets.

Burke shook his head.

"You figure she et him the rest of the way up?" he said, unable to take his eyes off Galla's skull. Sam saw other bones scattered here and there, including part of a rib cage a few feet away.

"She probably had her turn with him," Sam said.

"Damn it, I wish we'd buried him," Burke said, also looking around now at Galla's other bones and remnants. "Although, I'll be the first to say, we had no shovel with us." He shrugged down at the skull as if explaining himself. "It don't seem right, feeding ol' Mick to the very cat who killed him. She probably brought her cubs down, just had themselves a big ol' time —"

Sam cut him off.

"Put it out of your mind, Clyde," Sam said, seeing Burke going further and further with the matter. "The panther and her cubs are not the only thing that dined on the dearly departed." He boot-toed a black-gray feather lying on the ground. "There's been buzzards, rodents, rollbacks and now rock beetles — ants next, if not already."

Burke winced at the picture Sam painted while beetles roamed the skull on the ground.

"I know it's true," he said. "But I don't like seeing it, close up."

"Neither do I," Sam said, already stepping away. "But it's a hungry world. Everything takes its turn at the table."

"Jesus," said Burke. "Mick was strong and tough as a Canadian grizzly. Look at him now." He blew out a breath and tore himself away from staring at the bones and skull of the strong, tough man he'd watched fist-fight the she-panther there a month earlier. "It just goes to show you . . . ," he added, moving along with Sam.

"Goes to show you what?" Sam asked.

"Hell, I don't know," said Burke. "A lot of

things, I guess."

They walked through the lower ruins and back onto another stone-laden hillside. After climbing another fifteen minutes, they stood up in the full moonlight onto a walled and leveled spot that was strewn with jagged stone that appeared to have been spat from the sky over time. Upon appraisal of the level area, its character suggested that it might once have been a parade field or some ancient sports arena.

"Um-hum, just what I thought," Burke said, staring across the stony echelon toward the far wall and beyond it to the more up-slope hillside. "We'll be climbing rock all night. And I'll tell you something else," he added. "I've already gone farther than I wanted to. If that ol' cat's on the move, she could drag us along for miles —"

"Shhh," Sam said, holding up a hand to quiet him as he listened toward something beyond the far wall. They listened as the panther cried out, her voice sounding closer, but weaker in the moonlit night.

"She's no threat to us anymore," Burke whispered. "Let's go on back."

"Wait," Sam said. "There's something else. Hear it?" He listened more intently. Burke attempted to close in on the sound beside him. From the same direction as the cat's cry came the low indistinguishable mutter of voices and laughter.

"Oh, hell," Burke whispered, the two crouching instinctively, their rifles coming up ready in their hands. They listened even more intently for a moment. Finally Burke whispered, "I can't make it out. Is that 'pache or English?"

"I don't know," Sam whispered, easing forward. "But we'd better slip in closer and find out."

"Wait!" said Burke. He grabbed Sam's arm, stopping him. "If that's 'pache camping the other side of that wall, I'm nearer than I want to be already. Slipping closer does not sound all that rewarding."

Sam gestured a nod back in the direction of the other three men camped unsuspectingly inside the ruins.

"Any least sound from back there and we're going to have a fight on our hands," Sam said. "We need to know how many we're looking at before we go back and tell the others."

"Bad as this sounds," said Burke, "I'd sooner we slip off into these ruins and wait till everybody's smoke settles. We can get out of here then with a full head of hair and go on and get the gold for ourselves."

"I don't leave anybody behind to die if I

can keep from it," Sam said, shaking his forearm free from Burke's hand.

"Damn it, Jones," Burke whispered. "When did you become such a do-gooder? There's not a son of a bitch back there thinks he's going to live forever. Let's find a cave and go deep — save our own skins and pick through what's left come morning."

"Do what suits you, Clyde," Sam whispered, gesturing toward the deeper ruins. "But get out of here as quiet as you can. I'm going on like I said."

Burke hesitated and watched as Sam moved forward toward the far wall.

"Damn it, Jones," he cursed under his breath, finally hurrying forward and moving along beside Sam. "I'm nothing but a damn fool when it comes to gold. If I have to keep you alive, I expect I will. You had no right heaping guilt on me that way. I'd hate to die saving somebody just as ornery as I am."

"I'm not planning on dying," Sam said sidelong to him. "And I didn't heap anything on you." He stared straight ahead at the dark far wall. "We're going in and out of there as quiet as ghosts." He paused, then added, "You're going to be glad you did it, once it's done."

"Ha. That's real funny, Jones," Burke said in a critical tone, moving along quietly beside him.

They crept across the rocky field until they hugged against a pile of collapsed stone at the bottom of the overgrown wall and listened to the sounds from the other side. In the last few yards, they had seen the slightest glow of a firelight wavering from the other side. The quiet voices they heard in the night were not Apache; they were Spanish. Through the voices they heard the constant low whine and growl of the cat. The sound was that of an animal that had spent itself threatening and resisting, and was now exhausted from its efforts.

"Mexicans. We can go back now," said Burke in a whisper, sounding relieved by their discovery. He shoved his hat up and looked at Sam in the moonlight as the she-cat groaned in pain. "They've most likely wounded that ol' gal and are just watching her die for the hell of it. Mexicans are good for that sort of thing."

"It might be *federale*s," Sam whispered in reply.

"So?" Burke whispered. "*Federales* are still Mexicans." He stared at Sam. "They still love to torture a cat."

"They'll be no different than Apache if they catch us here," Sam said.

"Then let's get out of here, like I said,"

Burke said.

"We will," said Sam. "As soon as I see how many there are over there."

"How are you going to find out without tipping our hand?" Burke whispered, getting a little put out.

Sam gestured up at the top edge of the wall as he handed Burke his rifle.

"Here, hold this, I'm going up," he said.

Burke took the rifle Sam thrust to him and looked through a stand of brush and dry tangled vines hanging from the wall.

"No, wait! That's crazy," he said. But it was too late. Sam had already darted up a rock pile and huddled back down out of sight.

"Lord God, he's got us both killed," Burke whispered to himself. He lay silently, rifle ready, watching as Sam slipped forward again and cloaked himself in the hanging vines.

Sam grabbed two thick vines and tested his weight on them. Finding the vines strong enough, he wasted no time climbing hand over hand until he pulled himself atop the crumbling wall. Like some silent reptilian creature, he burrowed in beneath a thick bed of dried vines lining the wall's upper edge. There he lay perfectly still looking down into the circling firelight below.

On the ground in the outer glow of fire-light, he saw a two-wheel mule-killer cart loaded heavily with supplies and ammunition, covered with a ragged trail canvas. Behind the cart stood two brush-scarred mules tied for the night alongside six horses to a drawn rope along the stone wall.

Too much ammo and supplies for only this many men, he told himself, looking at the six *federales* lounging closely around the campfire. The six men, their dusty tunics opened down the front, passed around a bottle of mescal and made gestures and laughed at the she-panther, who had been stretched out Christ-like between two thick low branches of a twisted hackberry tree. The panther hung there panting, hopelessly bound by ropes, her head lolling on her outstretched shoulder. Sam saw fresh red blood on her exposed chest. Her milk teats hung loose on her belly. Against the tree stood a long crudely whittled lance made from a pine sapling. The sharp tip of the lance was red with blood.

Uh-oh . . . Not necessarily panther blood, Sam told himself, seeing six young Apache warriors seated across the campsite, a guard standing over them with a rifle at port arms. Moving his eyes along the warriors from face to face, Sam saw dried-over untreated bullet and saber wounds on their chests, heads, arms and bellies. He reminded himself of the fierce battle he and the outlaws had heard on their way up the hill trails. This was the outcome.

Looking closely, he recognized one of the warriors as the prisoner of the three scalp hunters he'd encountered over a month ago on his way to Agua Fría. He'd given the warrior a drink of canteen water; later the warrior had managed to untie himself and get away from his captors. Looking at the bloody, familiar face, Sam saw the warrior turn his eyes ever slightly up and appear to be looking back at him.

Sam started to duck down, but he caught himself and froze in place. The warrior could not have seen him, he told himself. If he had, Sam doubted he would say anything to his Mexican guard. Still, he decided, he'd seen what he'd climbed up here to see. He started inching back out over the edge of the wall. Before dropping down, he saw one of the soldiers walk over drunkenly and pick up the lance from the tree. He poked the point of the makeshift lance into the she-panther's already wounded side. The panther jerked and squalled out weakly, but she could do little else.

"Por favor. Baile para nosotros algún más, la anciana!" the soldier said to the half-conscious panther. The Apache prisoners looked on stone-faced.

"Por favor, por favor, anciana." He poked her again, this time not as hard, but it didn't matter. The *old woman* was not going to dance for him as he'd requested at the end of the sharp lance. The cat was exhausted, maybe dying, Sam told himself. He thought for a second about the she-panther's cubs — cubs he'd never seen, cubs he didn't even know for sure existed, he reminded himself. Then he dropped over the wall into the hanging vines and started to climb down as quietly as he'd ascended them. But he stopped when he heard a short burst of the soldiers' laughter, a weak growl from the tortured cat.

All right, that's enough!

He climbed back up and slipped beneath the tangle of vines. Looking all around from his loose cover, he saw a break in the vines a few yards ahead of him. Below the break, the gourd around the wall lay in blackness outside of the circle of firelight. Silently he inched forward on his belly like a stealthy snake, causing only a slight rise and fall atop the dry layer of vines as he passed beneath them. At the break, he crawled out onto the wall and dropped down onto a sloping pile of broken rock.

He crawled around in the blackness at the bottom edge of the wall until he stopped and watched the soldier lean the lance back against the tree. The soldier shrugged at his friends, walked back over and joined them at the campfire. Sam saw the bottle of mescal make its rounds from man to man.

Wait a minute. This is crazy, his own voice inside his head told him. *Why are you doing this?* He stopped suddenly in the black darkness and lay as still as stone against the bottom of the wall. He thought about it. This had nothing to do with his job, with why he was here, with what was expected of him. This panther had killed at least one man that he knew of — he'd seen her do it. She would kill him too, if she got a chance. Anyway, she was probably too far gone. Nobody would risk their life doing this!

I know all that, he replied to himself, dismissing all the questions running back and forth through his mind. *But this will only take a minute. . . .* He cocked his leg at the knee and brought his boot close enough for him to reach back and pull out a big knife in his boot well. As he inched forward again, he froze at one point when he could have sworn the young warrior he'd recognized looked around toward him as he crawled down into a shallow water-cut ditch that ran along the wall behind the hackberry tree.

Keeping an eye on the soldiers, Sam rose behind the tied panther, his knife in hand. The panther had been hanging there motionless. Yet, when her drooping eyes opened and she saw Sam's face not more than a foot from hers, she showed her fangs in a low hiss and tensed her claws in her rope bindings.

Sam ducked away quickly, knowing the soldiers had heard her. But as he peeped around the tree, he saw them only look her way, then fall back into talking and drinking. Sam waited for a moment before attempting to cut the panther loose. This had not been one of the best ideas he'd ever had. But he was here now, and had already gone this far. *All right, here we go,* he told himself. As he started creeping back up a fork in the tree's trunk, he heard gunfire break out in the distance, in the direction of the other three outlaws.

The soldiers, hearing the gunfire, scrambled to their feet and began buttoning their tunics as if that was them doing their part. Sam watched them all hurry to an open gap in the wall and stand looking in the direction of the battle. Even the rifle-man guarding the Apache left his position and ran to the others. The Apache prisoners sat stone-faced, staring straight ahead, as if none of this mattered to them.

Hurriedly, Sam rose with the knife and cut through the rope circling the tree, holding the panther's right front and rear paws stretched out. As soon as the rope went slack, the cat swung her freed paws back and forth as if searching for Sam, her big claws bared, ready to slice open anything that got close. As the wounded bleeding cat sensed her freedom at hand, she found a new burst of energy and swung about wildly on her left paws.

Sam quickly sliced the rope drawn around the tree holding the cat's left fore and rear paws. As soon as he cut the rope, he dived backward into the ditch. But he saw the cat hit the ground and catch herself and look all around, crouched on all fours. Blood dripped from her wounded side. But she was free, and wasting no time. Each of her four paws had a two-foot length of cut rope hanging from them.

Given her new resurgence of strength, Sam knew her next move would be to leap up onto the wall and bound along it and disappear off onto the hillside into the night, ropes and all. Yet, in the flicker of a second, it dawned on him how crazy this cat had acted from the very start.

"Oh no," he said, seeing the big cat had spun and stood staring at him huddled there in the shallow ditch. At the gap in the wall, the soldiers had heard the cat squall out. They turned, guns in hand, just in time to see her spring forward onto Sam and roll and wallow atop him down in the ditch.

Sam had just enough time to draw his Colt as she hit him. But in spite of her wounds, her rage was so sudden and intense, his knife flew from his hand in one direction and his Colt in the other. The cat was weakened enough by its ordeal that Sam managed to get his hands around its throat and hold it back, but it did him little good. The long, sharp fangs didn't reach his face, his neck, his jugular vein, but the claws slashed at his chest, at his shoulders.

Across the campsite three soldiers raised their rifles as one and fired. The shots missed the cat, but the roar of explosions and the impact of bullets knocking chunks of stone from the wall caused the cat to leap away and up atop the wall. By the time the soldiers fired again, Sam heard the cat breaking through the vine bed and vanishing into the darkness.

The Apache prisoners still sat watching stone-faced as Sam struggled to his feet, his hands raised high, four red slashes of the cat's claws stretched across his bare chest. Blood ran down from the claw marks. Rifles turned and trained onto him, their barrels already smoking. He froze in place, seeing the other soldiers also raise and aim their rifles.

"Tenga su fuego!" a soldier shouted, ordering them to hold their fire. But one rifle shot exploded anyway just as he finished his words. *"Tenga su fuego, embecile!"* he repeated, staring hard at the bungling soldier. He started forward cautiously toward Sam, a long saber in hand. Beyond the walls in the distance, Sam heard the battle raging in the ruins farther downhill. He only hoped Burke had lain low as he told him to do. He glanced all around as the soldier drew closer, the saber rising slowly, pointing at him, glistening in the firelight.

"Who are you, hombre?" he asked in stiff English, "and why do you come to disturb our entertainment?"

CHAPTER 7

Clyde Burke lay hidden among the rocks on the stretch of terrace where Burke told Sam he would wait. He'd heard the gunfire coming from the direction of the other gunmen camped inside the walls of the lower ruins. He also heard the commotion and gunfire from the other side of the wall in front of him. He knew nothing else to do for the time being but lie low, hoping Sam would get back so they could get out of here. The longer he waited, the less likely he thought that was going to happen.

Damn it, Jones!

He stayed buried down in the rocks as the gunfire waned from the lower ruins. When the sound of hoofbeats rumbled up a trail and stopped inside the wall in front of him, he poked his head up for a second for a look-see, then ducked back down quickly when he saw horsemen come out from behind the wall and ride almost straight toward him.

There was no way he was going to get up in the light of a full moon and make a run for it. *Huh-uh. Not now,* he warned himself. He'd waited too long. All running would do now is get him a back full of Mexican bullets. He lay frozen, almost as if pretending the hoofbeats closing in around him had nothing to do with him. He hugged his and Sam's rifle against his chest and lay with his eyes squeezed shut. But he winced and snapped his eyes open when the closing hooves stopped and a voice called out to him.

"You in there, come out," a *federale*'s voice demanded in clear but broken English.

Burke waited, tense, silent.

"So, you are not in there, eh, hombre?" the voice called out with almost a dark laugh. "In that case, I will have my men start shooting until we decide you are dead." A pause; then the voice said to the circled riflemen, "Ready, aim —"

"No hablo español," Burke called out in a shaky voice. But the *federale* leader was having none of it.

"— fire," he shouted.

"Wait!" said Burke. "Here I am, see?" He stood up with his hands high and empty.

"Step out, keep your hands high," a *fede-*

97

rale captain demanded.

Looking Burke up and down, a sergeant sitting his horse beside the captain gestured for two men to step down and take Burke prisoner. As the men dismounted, the sergeant leaned a little in his saddle.

"You see, *Capitán,* I said there would be more out here. These gringo pistoleros are everywhere — like flies."

"What were you and your amigo doing out here?" the captain demanded as the soldiers lowered Burke's hand behind his back and quickly bound them together with a strip of rawhide tethering.

"Believe it or not, *Señor Capitán,*" Burke said, getting his nerve back, "I was just out taking a stroll, the night being such as it is." He rolled his eyes toward the purple starlit sky.

"Alone, eh?" said the stocky sergeant, swinging down from his saddle. He stood with his face only inches from Burke's.

"Sergeant, he has two rifles down here," said one of the two riflemen who'd bound Burke's hands. He held up the two rifles from among the rocks.

"Ah," said the sergeant. "The other one belongs to the man they captured inside." He gazed back at Burke as he spoke over his shoulder to the captain. "These men are all a part of the rebel forces. They support our enemies."

"These men . . . ?" said Burke, as if in surprise. "It's just my pal and me here. Like I told you, we were out taking a stroll —"

"Shut up your lies, idiot!" the sergeant bellowed, cutting Burke off with a hard fist to his belly. Burke's knees buckled from the blow. He almost sank to the rocky ground, but the two soldiers caught him, held him up until he collected himself and stood swaying in place.

"We know there are more than the two of you," the captain called down to Burke from his saddle. "We found the rest of your band of pistoleros camped farther down. My patrol brings the survivor up to us even as I sit here speaking."

"Survivor?" said Burke. This time he really was surprised. "You mean there's only one man left alive?" His voice was weak and strained from the hard blow to his gut.

"You do not ask us the questions, gringo. We ask you," said the sergeant.

"Sergeant Bolado," said one of the soldiers still mounted, "here comes the patrol now." He pointed out toward a shadowy line of riders topping into sight on a narrow trail up from the lower ruins.

"Good," the sergeant said, staring into

Burke's eyes. "Soon we will know the truth." He turned to the two soldiers. "Rope this one and walk him up to the camp. Let him and his amigo see each other, so they will both know that all is lost."

All is lost?

In spite of the pain throbbing in Burke's stomach, he stifled a chuckle and shook his head. "Sergeant, if you don't mind me saying so, you're making a whole lot more of this —"

His words stopped short as the sergeant launched another hard blow to his stomach.

"Every time this one opens his mouth, hit him again for me," he ordered the soldiers. He gestured a hand. "Now get him out of my sight."

The soldiers shoved Burke roughly over to their horses. One took down a lariat, uncoiled it and looped one end of it around Burke's waist. Burke made it a point to keep his mouth shut as the soldiers stepped atop their horses and turned them toward the approaching patrol as both parties of riders spotted each other.

When the two parties joined at the top of a rocky rise, Burke saw a body draped over a horse in the moonlight; he recognized his horse and the others led by one of the soldiers. He caught a glimpse of someone riding slumped in the saddle, his hands tied behind him, two soldiers flanking him. But Burke couldn't make out the face in the pale grainy light. He lowered his head and stood waiting, wondering what sort of plan his pard Jones would have for getting them out of here.

Sam stood across the campsite from the stony-eyed Apache warriors, his chest bleeding from the panther's claw marks, a short welt on the side of his head from one of the soldiers' rifle barrels. A soldier stood in front of him, a rifle in his hands at port arms, ready to crack Sam in the head or shoot him if need be. Luckily, when the soldiers had tied Sam's hands, they tied them in front of him rather than behind his back. He wasn't sure how long that would last, noting that the six Apache prisoners' hands were all tied behind them. A long rope ran behind their backs, through each man's tied wrists, keeping them roped together.

Sam and the warriors stared at each other. The young warrior Sam had given water to a month earlier leaned near the older warrior seated beside him. Sam saw the young warrior gesture first toward the tree where the cat had been hanging, then toward the wall where the cat had escaped. The two warriors sat almost expressionless, yet Sam could see they had just shared a joke at his expense. He glared at them.

When the captain's patrol rode into the camp, both Sam and the Indians turned and watched them intently. Sam saw Burke stumbling along in front of them at the end of the rope. He saw Boyd Childers' body draped over a horse's back. On horseback he saw Stanley Black, his severed hat brim once again drooping down below his eyes. As the soldiers at the campsite looked at Black, they laughed among themselves. The front brim of Black's hat lay sagging just under his nose. It rose and fell slightly with each breath he took.

An angry look from Black caused one of the soldiers to shove him from his saddle and goad and probe him toward Sam with his rifle barrel. Another soldier shoved Burke over beside Sam. Burke cursed at them over his shoulder as he staggered forward across the campsite, his wrists tied behind his back. Seeing Sam standing there, his wrists bound in front of him, he stopped and eyed Sam up and down.

"All right, Jones, how come you're getting such favored treatment?" he asked Sam as he stopped and stood close beside him.

"Just special, I guess," Sam said quietly. "Where's Montana?"

"He must've got away," said Black, his sagging hat brim drooped below his eyes. "Leastwise I haven't seen his body."

"Good for him," Sam said.

"No talk," the young soldier said.

Burke and Black ignored him. Both of them scrutinized the claw marks on Sam's chest and shoulders.

"I see you found the cat," Burke whispered. "Was she happy to see you?"

"It's a long story," said Sam. "But no, not real happy."

"No talk," the guard repeated. He took a threatening step forward.

Burke gave the guard a hard, cold stare.

"Don't go getting your drawers in a knot," he said calmly. "It would be a bad mistake, you thinking we can't take that rifle of yours and shove it —"

The seasoned gunman stopped and rocked back a step as the soldier's rifle butt gave him a quick short stab to his chest. Burke staggered but managed to stay upright. He continued giving the young soldier his hard, cold stare.

"Take it easy, Clyde," Sam whispered, even as he stared at the soldier. "We're going to need all our strength here."

103

Burke settled down and let out a tight breath.

"Lucky for you I'm in a good mood tonight," he said to the soldier.

As he talked, other soldiers strung a rope along behind their backs the way they'd done with their Apache prisoners. Yet in Sam's case the rope ran around the front of him and between his tied wrists. In a moment the captain walked up and stood in front of Sam. Sergeant Bolado stood at the captain's side. Two riflemen flanked them. Sam noted that his own bone-handled Colt stood in the sergeant's waist sash. He'd have to keep watch on the Colt and whose hand it wandered into, having learned that guns had a way of traveling full circle here in this desert badlands.

"So," said the captain to the sergeant, "this is you, the man who decided to fight the loco panther who lives here?" He stared curiously at Sam and grinned, noting the claw marks and blood.

"*Sí*, Capitán Flores, he is the one," said Sergeant Bolado.

With a gloved hand, the captain flipped up the loose shredded shirt cloth hanging down Sam's bloody chest.

"How did that go for you, gringo?" the captain asked Sam, stifling a cruel smirk.

"I didn't come here to get into a fight with the panther," Sam said calmly. "I came here to see if you were Apache warriors camped up here."

"Oh?" the captain said. "Then why is it that you slip into our camp?" He gestured toward the hackberry tree where the tortured cat had been hanging. "Why do you set the panther free, so that she can inflict more injuries on my men?"

Set the panther free?

Even Burke and Black leaned forward a little and gave Sam a curious look when they heard the captain's question.

"I didn't come here to set her free," Sam said. "I came here to see what was wrong with her. I was concerned. We heard her squalling all the way down the hillside."

The captain and the sergeant stared at each other. The captain laughed and looked all around at his gathered men.

"This one goes looking for panthers in the night. He is concerned!" He grinned openly and spread his gloved hands in an understanding gesture.

The men chuffed and laughed.

After a moment, when the captain stopped laughing, the sergeant settled the men with a raised hand as three more mounted soldiers rode into the camp and stepped down

105

from their horses.

"*Capitán,* I sent for Corporal Valiente from the ranks," he said to the captain. "He has arrived."

"Ah, good," said the captain. "Now we will find out if these men are wandering around in our desert like mindless ones do, or if they are rebel supporters and arms dealers." He gave Sam a dark piercing stare.

The three newly arrived soldiers walked over to the captain and stood beside him. One of them wore a corporal's uniform and had his left arm in a sling. He stared at Sam for a moment.

"These two I do not know, *mi Capitán,*" he said to the captain, gesturing at Burke and Stanley Black. He gave Black's drooping hat brim a curious glance. Then he looked back at Sam and said with certainty, "But this one was with the wagon that carried the guns to the rebels."

"Are you certain of this, Corporal Valiente?" the sergeant asked.

"*Sí,* I am certain, Sergeant," said the corporal. "I stood this close to him before the Apache attacked and killed all of our soldiers. He delivered the guns and ammunition to our enemies and took the gold for the rifles."

"That will be all, Corporal," said the

captain. He turned to Sam as the corporal walked away.

"Too bad for you," the captain said to Sam, shaking his head slowly. To Burke and Black he said, "And it is too bad for the two of you as well, for being with this one."

Burke swallowed a dry knot in his throat and looked at Sam, then back at the captain.

"I would not go so far as to say we're *with him, Capitán,*" he said somberly. "It's more like we come across him out here on the sand flats and just sort of happened to be going the same —"

"Shut up," the sergeant snapped at Burke. "You do yourself no good to lie. You will still hang."

"He's telling the truth, Sergeant," Sam put in. "They had no part in the rifle deal. Neither did I, the truth be known."

"The *truth be known?*" the captain repeated. "Then you deny what Corporal Valiente tells me — what he has seen with his own two eyes? Perhaps you will say you have never seen him before?"

"I've seen him before," Sam admitted, recalling the corporal from over a month ago when he was arrested for gunrunning. "He rode with a captain named Silvero."

"Yes, a very good amigo to me, Capitán Silvero," said Captain Flores. "May his im-

107

mortal soul rest in peace. He was killed by these murdering Apache." He slid a dark glance to the stone-faced Indian prisoners who sat staring at them. "For which they will hang." He looked back pointedly at Sam. "It is Capitán Silvero's death, and that of his men, and the selling of firearms to the rebels that brings me out here, *investigating,* in this blasted devil's inferno."

What can you say . . . ? Sam told himself. He wasn't about to give up his identity. Even if he did, what good would it do? Who would believe him? He couldn't tell this very good friend of Captain Silvero that his amigo Silvero was taking money from Crazy Raymond Segert. For all Sam knew, so was Flores. All he could do was play this thing on out, hope to get himself, and yes, even these two outlaws standing beside him, out of this situation alive.

"Capitán," said Sergeant Bolado, "now that Corporal Valiente has identified this one, do you want me to form a firing squad for him and these two gringos?"

Sam stood tense, ready, watching the captain consider the matter. He was not going to stand here and be shot down without trying to save himself. He glanced at an ornate-handled saber hanging at the captain's side. He poised, on the verge of leaping out, grabbing it up with his tied hands and slashing his way to the horses. But he had to stop and settle himself when the captain spoke.

"No, Sergeant," Captain Flores said. "We will not shoot them here. We will march them to Fuerte Valor, along with this stinking Apache rabble." He wrinkled his nose in association with the warriors' offending smell.

"If you will permit me to say so, *Capitán,*" said the sergeant, "these gringos do not deserve to be taken to Fuerte Valor. These men are no better than dogs."

The captain gave him a dark glare. Sam, Clyde Burke and Stanley Black stood listening intently.

"I do not permit you to say so, Sergeant," the captain said bluntly. He folded his gloved hands behind his back in rigid military style. "The Apache will hang as a public display of our military might. These gringos will be further questioned about the death of Capitán Silvero and his men. They will then be shot as supporters of a rebel force that threatens the sovereignty of Mexico."

The sergeant turned from the captain back to Sam. "Perhaps, *Capitán,* you will allow me to shoot this one myself, when the

109

time comes." He patted Sam's bone-handled Colt standing behind the sash around his waist. "With his own *pistole,* perhaps?" He grinned evilly at Sam.

"We will see, Sergeant," the captain said. He turned a cruel smirk to Sam and said, "You'd better watch your step, pistolero. My sergeant does not like you so much."

"I caught that right off, Captain," Sam replied drily.

Relieved, he let out a breath, glad to hear that he and the other two were headed for Fuerte Valor — Fort Courage, he translated to himself. Once there, when the time came, he would reveal his true identity and his reason for being here.

■ ■ ■ ■

PART 2

■ ■ ■ ■

CHAPTER 8

In the night, Sam, Clyde Burke and Stanley Black sat in a row opposite the Apache warriors. Both lines of prisoners stared at each other from ten feet apart. A rifle guard walked slowly down between the two rows of prisoners. At the end of each walk, he warmed his hands at the fire ten feet away, turned around and walked back, fulfilling his monotonous routine between caged and watchful eyes.

"Good thing my hands are tied behind me," Burke whispered as the guard held his hands out over the fire. "I know I'd choke this fool to death, take his rifle from him and fight my way out of here." He paused for a second, staring at the Apache. "Maybe put a bullet in a couple of these Injuns while I'm at it."

"Take it easy, Clyde," Sam said. "Now's not the time."

"Then when is the time?" Burke asked.

Sam didn't answer.

After a pause, Burke asked Sam quietly, "Any chance of you doing that for us, Jones?" He wiggled his hand behind his back. "It appears you're the only one with hands that can do any choking."

"Not a chance," Sam whispered with no hesitation. Without taking his eyes off the warriors staring back at him, he said, "There'll be better chances of us making a break while we're on the trail. It's a long march to Fuerte Valor."

"Fort Courage, my ass," Burke translated in a whisper. He spat in the dirt in contempt. "I've left more courage running down a privy wall." He leaned his head and wiped his lips on his shoulder.

"Jones is right, Clyde," Stanley Black whispered on Burke's other side. "There'll be better chances on the trail."

"Jesus!" said Burke, jerking his head around toward Black. "Let a man know when you're sneaking up that way."

"I wasn't sneaking, I'm sitting right here," said Black.

Burke drew away from Black, seeing his face, his eyes peering at him from the narrow gap between his hat's sagging brim and its crown.

"You sure as hell are," said Burke with

114

sarcasm. He shook his head, staring at Black. "Stanley, do you have even the slightest idea how stupid you look wearing that Gaw-damnable hat?" His voice grew a little louder as he spoke.

"No talk," said the guard, turning toward them from warming his hands at the fire.

Sam saw by the look on Burke's face that he was losing control.

"Oh yeah?" Burke shouted out at the guard. "Why don't you go *fummmmph* —" he said, his words muffling suddenly behind Sam's cuffed hands clamping over his mouth. Burke thrashed back and forth. But Sam held on until Burke finally settled. Across from them, the Apache looked on blankly, firelight glittering in their black eyes.

The guard adjusted his rifle in his hands and walked straight toward them.

"Get yourself in hand, Clyde," Sam whispered, letting go of Burke as the guard drew closer. "It'll do us no good to make a move, you with your face bashed in by a rifle butt."

The guard stopped and looked down at the three pistoleros. Sam spoke up before Burke got a chance to say anything.

"He was asleep," he said, gesturing toward Burke. *"Habla en su sueño, éste."*

"Ah," said the guard. "This one talks in

115

his sleep?"

"*Sí,* he does, he wakes himself shouting out," Sam said. "I'll watch over him — see to it he doesn't do it again."

"You do that, gringo," the guard said, leaning in close to Sam and Burke. "If he talks in his sleep, he can die in his sleep."

"We understand," Sam said quietly. As the guard turned to walk away, he looked down at Black, cocked his head curiously, seeing the eyes look up at him from above the sagging brim. Chuckling under his breath, he walked away, shaking his head. When he was out of whisper range, Burke leaned close to Black.

"See? Even these fools think you look like some damn circus clown," he whispered harshly. "Get rid of that hat. I mean it."

"Go to hell," said Black.

"Both of you shut," said Sam. "Try to rest for a few minutes. We'll be heading out of here before long."

The two fell silent, Burke grumbling something under his breath before doing so.

Sam took a deep breath and sat staring at the Apache in the shadowy firelight. He wished he knew what they were thinking — what plans they had to get free. But they weren't going to give up any plans any more than he was.

And that's how it is. . . .

There was nothing he could do about it, he reminded himself, staring at their dark formidable eyes. He fought sleep, yet after a moment he felt his head lower to his chest and his eyelids droop and finally close altogether. It felt like only moments later when he opened his eyes quickly and saw that first light had mantled the far upper peaks of the Blood Mountain Range. The guard and three other soldiers began to roust both sets of prisoners to their feet and then formed them into two lines. While the rest of the camp gathered, saddled and readied their horses for the trail, three soldiers walked from prisoner to prisoner. While the guard looked on, one soldier untied the ones whose hands were tied behind them and retied them in front. The second soldier carried a large pot of cold red beans from the night before, along with a wooden dipping spoon. The other soldier carried a canvas sack half-full of cold, hard bread.

"Hold out one hand," the soldier with the beans ordered. As the prisoner's hand came out, the soldier slopped a spoonful of beans into it.

"Your other hand," the soldier carrying the bread sack ordered. As empty palms

117

turned up, he plucked up a torn chunk of bread from the sack and dropped it onto each empty hand.

"How about a plate or bowl or something?" Burke called out to the soldiers.

The one carrying the bean pot looked back and grinned.

"Yo no hablo ingles," he said.

"Don't speak English, my ass!" said Burke. "Your sister does," he called out, but not loud enough for them to hear him clearly.

The soldiers both looked back at him curiously.

"I say *yum-yum,*" Burke said mockingly, giving them a wide, superficial smile. As the soldiers walked away, he stared down at the beans dripping from his hands. "What's the gospel truth is this is how they all eat at home." He raised his voice toward the two soldiers. "They never heard of washing their hands. They lick at them all day like a damn cat —"

Sam gave him a push with his elbow to shut him up.

"Leave it alone, Clyde," he said in a low voice. "Eat your breakfast. Your hands are out from behind your back. Let's see if they keep them there."

"Be thankful they fed us at all," Black

said, through a mouthful of beans and bread.

"Right you are, both of you," Burke said, taking on a better attitude. He laughed. "I'm grateful for everything every son of a bitch ever done for me." He raised his beans and bread to his lips and managed to take a bite of each, leaving crumbs and a red smear in his beard stubble. "Speaking of cats, how's your claw wounds this morning?"

"Better," Sam said. "They'll be even better still if we stop at a water hole long enough for me wash up."

"What was the captain talking about, you cutting the panther loose?" Burke asked.

"I don't know," said Sam, giving a slight shrug.

"Was you?" Burke asked.

"Was I what?" Sam said.

Burke just looked at him.

"Was you trying to set her loose?" Burke asked.

"What do you think?" Sam said.

"I don't know," Burke said. "That's why I'm asking."

"I wasn't," Sam said. "So forget about it." He turned and looked off toward the soldiers. "That's the craziest thing I've ever heard of."

Burke shrugged, his beans and bread in

his cuffed hand. "I was just thinking about it, is all."

"You want something to think about?" Sam said. "Think about us walking all the way to Fort Courage."

"I already am," Burke said grimly.

The mounted Mexican army patrol led the two lines of prisoners down from the hillside ruins onto the desert floor. They traveled forward through rock, gravel, low cactus and sand, in the direction of Fuerte Valor. Fortunately Sam's and all of the other prisoners' hands were left tied in front of them. Unfortunately the two rope lines of prisoners were traveling afoot among horseback riders whose object appeared to be keeping them too hungry, thirsty and weak to think about making a getaway.

It was noon before the soldiers directed the exhausted gunmen and Apache off the desert floor and back onto the hillside. They headed into the rock and cactus shade of the water hole where the Montana Kid had shot the wounded gizzly bear. Buzzards stood feasting on the bear's large carcass on a bed of gravel and small stone. Newcoming scavengers circled overhead, and stood randomly on rock and cactus watching, as if awaiting their turn at the feast.

Upon arriving at the edge of the water, rifle guards held the prisoners back until the soldiers drank their fill. They continued holding them back while the soldiers let their horses and the team of mules slake their thirst.

While Sam was standing in line waiting, a soldier led Sam's dun and his white barb past him. The dun was bareback; the barb had been stripped of its pack frame and supplies. The dun pulled against its reins and tried to nose over to Sam, but a soldier jerked the horse away and slapped the dun with a leather quirt hanging from his wrist. The dun resisted, half reared against the sting of the quirt. Sam jumped sidelong toward the soldier, but Burke and Stanley Black grabbed him and held him back.

Sergeant Bolado stepped in and gave the young soldier a sound slap across his shoulder.

"What good is a soldier who cannot control and water horses?" he said harshly. He grabbed the dun and the barb's reins, settled them expertly and handed the reins back to the humiliated young man.

"Now go," he said with a dismissing gesture. As the soldier led the horse on to the water, Bolado turned to Sam.

"Those two are your horses, *sí*?" he said.

"Yes, they are," Sam replied, swaying a little from thirst and the relentless heat.

"Where were you going that caused you to need a packhorse and so many supplies?" he asked. "Most of you gringo pistoleros travel with only your guns — your guns and your whiskey." He gave a faint smug grin.

Sam stared without reply.

The sergeant leaned in close as if speaking in secret. "Perhaps you were going somewhere important, eh? Somewhere that would require such provisions?"

"It was for all of us, Sergeant," Sam said.

Bolado looked back and forth as if making sure they weren't being watched or heard.

"I don't think so, pistolero," he said secretively, even as Burke and Black looked on, trying to listen. "I think you were going somewhere by yourself until you joined with these others." He studied Sam's eyes intently, searching for answers there. After a moment he gestured toward Corporal Valiente, who stood a few feet back behind him. "He thinks so too," he said.

"Like he said, Sergeant," Burke cut in, "it was supplies enough for all of us. Leave him alone. You want to pick at somebody, pick at me." He gave a defiant grin. "You hit like a woman, Sergeant. I sort of like it."

The sergeant started to turn on Burke, but then he saw that was exactly what Burke was trying for. He raised a finger and shook it at Burke.

"Don't worry, *embecile*," he said to Burke. "I will hit you some more, only later." He turned back to Sam, but as he started to speak, he caught sight of the captain riding forward. Tugging his tunic down into place, he said to Sam, "I will talk to you later. We have much to talk about." He stepped a few feet away from Sam to meet the captain.

"Why are we not watered yet and ready to go, Sergeant Bolado?" the captain asked, swinging his horse around quarterwise to the sergeant and the corporal.

"It is the heat, *Capitán*," Bolado said, he and Corporal Valiente almost snapping to attention. "The men and the animals are moving slower becau—"

"Do not explain to me the heat!" Captain Flores shouted, cutting him off. "Get these prisoners watered and ready to travel."

"Yes, *Capitán*, right away," said Bolado. He and Valiente snapped a salute to the captain, turned briskly and walked toward the soldiers and horses at the water hole. "Why are these horses and prisoners not watered and ready to go?" he called out, almost mimicking the captain's words.

As the soldiers hurriedly led the animals away from the water's edge, guards led Sam and the others forward. Both gunmen and Apache dropped onto their chests in the water and drank their fill, their tied hands folded out in front of them as if paying homage to some greater being farther up the rocky hillside.

When the prisoners were watered, they stood back from the hole in line, dripping wet. Sam's blood-crusted chest had washed clean, and a thin trickle of fresh blood had begun to run down his belly and beneath his shredded shirt. As the soldiers gathered the spare horses and the team of mules, Corporal Valiente weaved his nervous horse around on a thin path leading through a strip of larger stone standing between the men and the bear's carcass.

Sam watched him ride in close to the dead bear for a look, then back his horse when the buzzards screamed and batted their greasy wings at him. Cursing the big birds, he turned his horse and had started back along the path when a monstrous bear stood up atop a rock in front of him.

"Good Lord God Almighty!" said Burke. "It's the bear's big brother!"

The large brute stood high on its hind legs and bawled out loudly.

Valiente's horse whinnied and reared so high it almost fell backward. The corporal, his arm healing in a sling, tried to get the horse in check and grab his rifle from its boot. But before he could do anything, the big bear rumbled forward from the rock and knocked both horse and rider to the ground with a long powerful swing of its wide paw. Valiente hit the ground as the horse crawled and whinnied and scrambled up, finally racing away limping, its saddle hanging under its belly.

"Shoot it! *Shoot it!*" the corporal shouted, almost hysterically, his hand fumbling at his empty holster, his pistol having been knocked away by his fall. He stumbled to his feet.

The soldiers swung their rifles up to their shoulders, but before they could fire, the bear knocked the corporal down, grabbed him under his shoulder with its powerful jaws and stood erect, the corporal dangling and screaming in the air.

"No, don't shoot!" Captain Flores shouted, seeing that any shot made would more likely kill the corporal.

"He's got him," Burke said, the gunmen and the Apache gazing on with interest.

The bear stood shaking the corporal back and forth in its jaws like a bundle of rags.

The soldiers hurriedly ran along the path through the rocks to get position. Seeing them coming, the bear clamped a big arm around the helpless soldier and squeezed him tight against its chest. The corporal screamed, the bear's teeth gripping him and stabbing deep into the flesh up under his arm. Valiente's arm swung limply, broken and bleeding.

Before the soldiers got through the rocks, the bear dropped onto three legs and loped away across a large stone, climbing upward onto the hillside. The prisoners stood watching as if spellbound as the bear and the screaming, sobbing corporal disappeared from sight.

"That's one bear ain't foraging for berries tonight," Burke said quietly to Sam, keeping three guards standing nearby from hearing him.

"Sergeant, keep your men after it!" the captain called out, staring along with everyone else, watching Bolado and a half dozen men scrambling upward over the rocks in pursuit of the bear. A barrage of rifle fire resounded from the first few men who had gotten up the hillside ahead of the others. Sam watched gray gun smoke rise and drift from among the rocks. They heard the corporal's screams grow louder in spite of being farther away.

"Might as well get comfortable," Burke said. "This could take a while." He plopped onto the dirt, pulling the rope taut between Sam and Black. They sat down with him, still staring up the hillside. Across from them, the Apache did the same.

"There they go firing guns out here," Black commented. "Wonder who that'll bring calling on us."

Burke looked around at him and his drooping hat brim and shook his head.

"It's anybody's guess," Burke said. He looked at Black sourly. "Please get rid of that hat, Stanley," he said. "I swear to God it's killing me looking at it."

"Tough knuckles, Clyde," said Black. "It keeps my head from burning up."

Watching the hillside, speculating on the gunfire, Sam said, "If there're Apache out there, they'll be coming for their own."

"Yep," said Burke. "I figure in a few minutes when the bear gets shed of these soldiers, we'll be hearing some bones popping and cracking up there." He shook his head. "It ain't going to be no pretty sight, a bear eating a Mexican."

"I bet it's not," Sam said, running his fingers back through his wet dripping hair.

CHAPTER 9

Shortly after the soldiers went in pursuit of the big yellow-brown Mexican grizzly, a series of terrible gut-wrenching screams resounded down from the upper hillside, followed by a deathlike silence.

"*Bon appétit,* as the French say," Burke chuckled under his breath. "He's got himself a big mouthful of heart and liver right now, sucking and munching." He let out a deep breath and continued. "They say a Mexican griz will go in through the softest spot, root around and eat the innards first off," he said quietly, lest the already rattled guards hear him. The young soldiers stared transfixed upward in the direction of the dying corporal's screams.

"Most any grizzly does that," Black cut in. "Not just these Mexican browns."

"I'm just saying." Burke shrugged. He looked away as he spoke, owing to the displeasure he found in Black's sagging hat brim.

Sam sat quietly gazing up the hillside. And for the next hour, the two rows of prisoners sat in the dirt facing each other from ten feet apart. Four riflemen guarded the grim dirty lot of them. Two more riflemen stood in front of a pitched tent where the captain rested behind the tent's flapping thin gauze-like sides, out of the scorching sun.

Three more soldiers guarded the horses and the mule-killer cart while most of their comrades scoured the rocky upper hillsides chasing the big yellowish brown Mexican grizzly.

Suddenly, after an hour of quiet, the stillness of the afternoon was shattered by a large volley of rifle fire far up the hillside.

"If that didn't kill the big brute, they best all run for their lives," Burke commented.

Both soldiers and prisoners fell silent again, the soldiers appearing gripped by apprehension.

After another ten minutes of silence, the hillside shuddered and rumbled as a powerful quake rippled through the earth deep beneath its rocky surface. As the earth rumbled and churned, the guards staggered in place and managed to keep their footing, their rifles ever ready. The Apache were the first to turn their eyes upward in time to see a heavy rock slide tumble down less than a quarter of a mile away on the trail behind them.

As the three American gunmen stopped swaying in the dirt, Stanley Black turned to Sam and Burke.

"The day's been anything but uneventful, you have to admit," he said under his breath. He gestured toward the large dust looming above the settling rock slide, and added, "There goes any thought of turning back."

Surprisingly, one of the young guards standing over the three looked down at Black.

"The Mexican army does not go back, only forward," he said in broken English.

"Ha. Now you're habloing Eng-lace, all of a sudden," said Burke, recognizing the soldier who had served them beans at breakfast.

Sam leaned and whispered in Burke's ear, "Stop it, Clyde. Keep him talking." Burke sat back and let Black and Sam handle the conversation. Black picked right up on the change in the guard's attitude.

"How long before you figure we move out of here?" he asked, keeping his English slow and clearly spoken.

"I don't know," the young soldier said, shaking his head as he searched back and forth, making sure he wasn't heard by the other guards. "The captain only gives his orders to the sergeant at the last minute. The sergeant tells us when he thinks we need to know."

"What's your name?" Black asked in a whisper.

"I am Private Roberto Deluna," the soldier whispered, standing straight and rigid above them for the sake of appearance. "But do not think that because I am talking I will reveal anything I should not, because I will not."

"I'm hurt that you'd think it," Burke put in.

"I know how men like you are. I have a brother who was a pistolero and a bandito."

Burke shook his head.

"Jeez," he said. "Pistolero, yeah maybe . . . but a bandito? That's getting a little rough, don't you think?"

"Yes, it is a harsh thing that I say about you," he said with a slight shrug, not seeing that Burke was playing him along. "But it is true," he added. "True about you and also about my poor brother, Roberto, may God show him mercy." He crossed himself quickly.

Burke looked confused.

"I thought your name was Roberto?" he said.

"It is," said the private.

Burke looked even more confused.

Sam leaned in.

"Don't try to figure it out. Keep him talking," he said. "We need someone who'll tell us what's going on."

"When my brother, Roberto, was hanged for rustling goats and shooting a wealthy patron," Roberto said, "I took his name as a form of pittance to redeem my family name for the bad he did. I must go for years in shame with his name on my shoulders."

Burke sat staring curiously.

Sam leaned in again.

"See what I mean?" he whispered to Burke.

"This sure as hell ain't Missouri," Burke said.

"I should not even be telling anyone, especially prisoners," said Private Roberto. "Only, in your case, I know it is all right that I do so."

"Oh? And why's it all right telling us?" Burke asked.

"Because when I tell you, I know that I am talking to dead men, and it will never be revealed what I say," he replied casually.

"Why, you little —" Burke started to stand, but Sam jerked on the rope between the two of them and pulled him back down.

"Any idea what we'll have for supper?" Sam asked in an effort to keep a conversation going.

"No idea," said the young soldier. He stood silently for a moment, then said, "Beans, I think. Beans and salt pork."

"Frijoles y puerco salado?" Burke said in poor Spanish, keeping the sour look from taking over his face.

"Yes, *Frijoles y puerco salado,*" the young soldier repeated. "Beans and pork."

"Good," Sam said as if delighted. "That's what we were all three hoping for."

"Yum-yum," Burke said. "I say a man can't live on a handful of cold beans and salt pork, he don't much deserve to live at all."

The conversation stopped as a volley of rifle fire resounded from up the hillside, followed by a long pain-filled bawl of the bear that ended abruptly.

"Maybe beans and bear," the young soldier said, with the trace of a grin.

"Eating a bear that just et a Mexican does not pilot my appetite in the proper direction —" Burke said, interrupted once again, this time by Sam's elbow in his side.

"We can hardly wait," Sam said, taking over from Burke. "Any chance of us getting some tin plates under it?" he asked.

The soldier stood in silence for a moment, then said quietly to Sam, "I will see what I can do."

"*Gracias,* Private Roberto," Sam said, sitting back in the dirt, feeling they had made some headway with the young private.

It was later in the afternoon when the signs of trail dust came down the hillside. Foot soldiers and soldiers on horseback followed. The soldiers on foot who had scrambled and bounded up over rock and boulder going after the bear now trudged down into the camp, worn out and filthy. Behind them on the trail, Sergeant Bolado supervised from his saddle, leading two other horsemen into camp dragging the dead bear. Across Bolado's horse behind his saddle lay a short rolled-up bloody canvas. At the water hole, Bolado stopped. Two soldiers trotted over and hefted the canvas down and lowered it respectfully to the ground.

"There's the good corporal now," Burke said quietly, the three of them staring at the half-eaten body wrapped in bloody canvas.

"Uh-huh," Black agreed, his mouth slightly agape, his neck craned for a better look out over the sagging edge of his sliced hat brim. Across from them, the Apache also stood up and stared. Both groups watched as soldiers back from the hunt fell facedown into the water and swished their heads to and fro as they drank. While they slaked their thirst, they slung their wet hair and milled about. A soldier walked up to them with a three-foot-long wooden crate that he set on the ground and opened.

"Tome su escoge," the soldier called out, telling the soldiers to take their choice from inside the crate. Stepping back, he watched the soldiers gather over the crates and pick out butchering tools. They fell upon the bear carcass with knives, both long and short, and saws and bone-chopping cleavers. As the prisoners and the captain and sergeant looked on, the soldiers dismantled the big bear onto a canvas laid out for storage wrapping. With the bear's head still attached to its thick, furry hide, four soldiers carried the bodiless bear to a side and draped the hide over a large rock.

Standing nearby, the two mules and the spare horses nickered nervously and shied away on the rope line they stood reined to.

Young soldiers showed up and relieved the guards while Sam and the others were engrossed watching the bear butchering.

135

Close to where the bear was being quartered, boned, separated and wrapped in canvas, a large fire began to flicker skyward in a pile of brush and deadfall timber.

"Think they've got a big enough fire?" Burke said with sarcasm as the flames licked high upward against the evening sky.

"Yep, plenty," Sam replied. "If they leave it burning after dark, we'll have lots of company coming."

"No talk," said one of the relief guards.

"Well, well, look who's here. *No Talk* is back," Burke said, his voice lowered but still defiantly loud enough to be heard. "Bet he missed us." He grinned at the soldier.

"Let it go, Clyde," Sam whispered. "We need to let them forget we're even here."

Burke nodded. He corrected himself and took a deep breath.

"Somehow I don't look for that to happen," he whispered sidelong to Sam.

"No *talk,*" the soldier insisted adamantly.

Burke chuckled but only shook his head.

While they stood watching, Roberto and the relieved guards had walked off behind some rocks. When they returned to the water, they stooped and watered themselves with cupped hands, their rifles leaning across their knees. When they stood up slinging their hands dry, they walked with three other soldiers for a moment, then walked back to the relief guards and sent them away.

After a moment, the relief guards had walked away, back to where chunks of the bear were being spiked and laid on the licking flames. Looking all around, first Sam ventured talking to the young private some more.

"You were right about it being beans and bear meat for tonight's grub, Roberto," he said quietly.

"Yes," Roberto said with a half smile. "I am known as one who listens closely but says little." He beamed proudly.

"I bet you are," Sam said. He paused for a moment, then said in the same quiet voice, "After a big meal like this, we'll be lucky to get ten more miles in."

"I'm told we will be spending the night here," Roberto said. "I do not mind saying I was glad to hear it."

Here, after all the gunfire, and now a big fire . . . ?

Sam looked out across the desert floor below, then over at the stone-faced Apache warriors. The Indians looked back at him with an almost bemused look in their dark eyes, as if having figured out what he was thinking — agreeing with him, despite their

137

own sinister intent.

Turning away from the Indians, Sam saw Sergeant Bolado walking toward him. As the sergeant drew closer, he took Sam's bone-handled Colt from his waist and twirled it on his finger. When he stopped in front of Sam, he brought the spinning Colt to a halt with the tip of the gun barrel only an inch from Sam's belly.

"Do not think I have forgotten about you, gringo," he said, standing menacingly close, his words lowered privately between him and Sam. "Corporal Valiente is dead, but earlier today he told me of how you and the gringo Raymond Segert argued over you hiding his gold from him."

Sam just stared.

"Any gold Segert had coming was from selling rifles to your enemies, Sergeant," Sam said.

"Don't take me for a fool," the sergeant said. "I don't care where his gold came from. You have it, and I want it." He poked Sam's own Colt into his ribs. "Corporal Valiente said you hid Segert's gold up on the hillside where the Apache attacked Capitán Silvero and his men. When the time comes, you will lead me to that gold. Make no mistake about it," he said in conclusion.

"You're out of your mind, Sergeant," Sam said.

"We will see who is out of his mind," said Bolado. He turned away quickly when he heard his name called, and looked around, seeing the captain wave him over to where the bear lay broiling in chunks on long iron spits. "I will talk more with you later, gringo," he said to Sam.

"Seems like a real likable fellow, that one," Burke said, watching Bolado walk away. "I think we're going to have to find a way to drive a stake through his heart, else he's going to be after that gold at every turn."

"You listened to everything?" Sam asked.

"It'd be hard not to," Burke said. "Our living conditions being such as they are." He looked all around, then said, "Do you figure he could get us out of here if we took him on for a share? We're down two men. We can afford it."

"Maybe," Sam said, considering it. "He's got to have me figured for taking him to the gold. He's not going to take my word for where it is."

"No, he won't," Burke agreed. "But it's going to be hard getting him to take Black and me along too. Most likely once you take him to the gold, he's going to drop you dead as soon as he gets his hands on it."

139

"Sounds like you have the man figured out real good, Clyde," Sam said, staring over to where Bolado stood talking to the captain beside the large raging fire.

"He ain't the first son of a bitch I ever saw suffering with gold fever," Burke said.

Black stared at Sam and Burke.

"You best watch your step real close if he makes you ride out of here with him," Black said to Sam.

"I'm not riding anywhere with him unless he takes you both," Sam said. "We're still partners, remember?"

Black gave him a sheepish look. "To tell the truth, I don't know what I would do if I had a chance to ride away from this furnace and split the gold two ways. Gold has a way of dissolving a partnership damn fast."

"Not with me, it doesn't," Sam said firmly.

Burke craned his neck and looked off toward three soldiers who carried food toward them. One carried the same large bean pot they'd seen at breakfast. Another carried a tray full of steaming bear meat.

"Look what's coming here," Burke said. "It's our handful of beans and bear."

But when the soldiers drew closer, Sam and the other two saw tin plates stacked on the tray.

"I have gotten plates for you," Roberto

said quietly to the three. The soldiers stopped and one started handing out plates.

"We are much obliged, Private Roberto," Sam said, "very much obliged."

CHAPTER 10

When the meal was finished, the shadows of night had fallen long from the hilltops and stretched out across the desert floor. Sam, Clyde Burke and Stanley Black watched the roaring fire still burning high into the looming darkness. Black smoke and sparks flew up away across the purple starlit sky.

"They couldn't have sent a better invitation if they tried," Burke said under his breath.

Black shook his head, took off his hat and rubbed his eyes before he set his hat back atop his head.

"I'd say we're pretty much dead here," he commented.

Sam glanced at the Apache, the fire glittering in their dark eyes. He couldn't help noticing, even through their blank stoic expressions, that there appeared to be renewed energy about them. As he looked at them, the young warrior he had given water came very near nodding, as if telling him he was right in what he saw.

"We might be dead," Sam said, turning away from the warrior back to Black, "but I can't see going down without a fight."

"Well, me neither," said Burke in a mock tone of sarcasm. "Especially when we've got so much to fight with." He spread his tied hands all around, indicating their helpless and unarmed condition. "I say we need to attack —"

"Come on, Clyde," Sam said, cutting him off. "You know what I mean."

Burke scratched his head and gave him a curious look.

"I do?" he said.

"Yes, you do," Sam said. "I'm saying we're going to be ready when the Apache hit. We're not going to sit here and let ourselves get mowed down like wheat."

"Hell no," Black said, leaning in closer. "When they hit, these soldiers are going to be too busy to worry about us. We need to have a plan and be ready to skin out of here."

"That's what I mean," Sam said. "Luckily we're all three on the same rope." He shook the rope running through their rawhide-tied wrists. "But if we're ready when it comes, we can all three run together, knock out this nearest guard, take his rifle and knife, cut ourselves loose and run for the horses."

"What could be easier than that?" said Burke in the same sarcastic tone.

"I'm not saying it's easy," Sam replied.

"I know, *I know,*" Burke said dismissingly. "I'm with you on all of it. What I can't understand is, as much Indian fighting as these boys have done, how come they don't see what they're doing here?"

"Arrogance and stupidity," Black put in. "The captain might think he's too damn good to get ambushed. He's got more men here than the 'pache are accustomed to taking on. Maybe the captain figures they'll be afraid to try anything."

"I don't know," Sam said. "Whatever he thinks, he can die thinking it. Starting right now we keep watch on the desert." He nodded down toward the wide, rolling sand below. "First sign of anything, we're gone." He gestured toward the Apache warriors who sat watching the three of them talk. "Keep an eye on these warriors too," he said. "I don't know how, but something tells me they know what's getting ready to happen here."

"Damn 'pache," Burke growled. He spat on the ground in the Indians' direction. The blank dark eyes only stared right back at him.

"What about the sergeant?" Black said. "He wants that gold something fierce. He'll make you take him to it if we ain't careful."

"I'm not taking him to it," Sam said with determination. "You can count on that."

"No offense, Jones," Black said. "But you say that now. What about if he gets you off and goes to work on you with a knife? Are you sure you'd die before you'd give it up, if it meant him cutting off all your toes, your thumbs and fingers —"

"Jesus, Stanley," Burke said in rebuke. "What goes on inside your mind?"

"I'm just saying, is all," Black said. He turned back to Sam and asked, "If he done all that stuff to you, would you give up and take him there?"

"That's a hard thing to answer, Stanley," Sam said. "After all that, I probably would take him there."

Burke and Sam both stared at Black, waiting to see what he made of Sam's answer.

Finally Black nodded.

"I don't blame you," he said. "I would too. I just wanted to hear you say it."

Sam and Burke looked at each other.

"All right," Sam said. "Let's start watching, two hours apiece until morning."

In the middle of the night, Sam awoke as Burke shook his shoulder. Sitting up, Sam looked all around, seeing the guards at either end of the ropes sitting still in the darkness, making it impossible to tell if they were asleep or awake.

"How's it been, Clyde?" Sam whispered.

"Quiet as a whisper," said Burke. "Nothing's moved on the desert that didn't have red eyes and bushy tails."

"I'm hoping it stays that way," Black whispered, surprising Sam and Burke.

"Damn it, Stanley, you're supposed to be asleep," Burke whispered harshly.

"I couldn't get back to sleep after my watch," Black said. "Anyway, I'm not a big sleeper." He gathered up one of three ragged striped blankets given to them by Roberto Deluna before dark. "I'm hoping this is all for nothing," he added.

"So am I," Sam whispered, gathering his blanket tighter around him as well. "Nothing would please me more than being wrong about this." He paused, then added, "But I don't think I am."

"Neither do I," said Black. "That's the real reason I'm still awake."

"You two palaver about it until daylight," said Burke, turning away with his blanket drawn to him. "I'm gone for shut-eye." He grunted and settled onto the cold ground. "Wake me when the 'pache get here."

"I will," Sam said.

But throughout his watch, Sam saw nothing move on the desert floor, as Burke had said, that didn't have red eyes and bushy tails. After a while, Black had leaned over back onto the ground and gone to sleep, in spite of his fear of the predicted Apache attack. As Sam watched the desert floor and gazed out as far as he could see for any signs of human life, he also kept an eye on the Apache prisoners.

The warriors sat in a row, as silent and motionless as death. Their dark silhouettes had not moved or seemed to have varied since darkness had set in. Every ten minutes two walking guards moved along between them and the American gunmen like clockwork. *That's the way, keep a good eye on them,* Sam caught himself thinking as the guards passed in the moonlit darkness. He watched the distant rolling sand, the rock land and the stony ledges behind them on the hillside above the water hole. Nothing, he reported to himself after each wide close sweep.

Good. . . .

As he watched, he listened. The night around him carried the sound of quiet snoring, of crackling fire, but of little else. When the next round of the walking guards moved toward him, he glanced at the Apache. *Still there,* he told himself, seeing their black silhouettes against the purple, same as he'd seen them all night. Then he looked up at the guards as they filed past him and he watched them as they walked on.

All right. . . .

He relaxed for only a second before looking again toward the Apache. Yet this time as his gaze swept past them against the darkness, he stopped suddenly and batted his stunned eyes. They were gone! *What the . . . ?* They were gone! He jumped to his feet, dragging the rope with him. Burke and Black, feeling the hard tug on the rope, scrambled up beside him.

"What's wrong?" Burke mumbled, half-asleep. Black staggered in place and rubbed his eyes.

"They're gone," Sam said, not keeping his voice as lowered as he'd intended to.

"You down there, gringo!" a walking guard called out in stiff English, "get on the ground, or I will shoot!"

"All right, all right," Sam called back, the

148

three of them raising their hands high, hearing the sound of a rifle hammer cock in the darkness.

But before Sam and the others could drop to the ground, another guard rose to his feet at the end of the rope line.

"The devils are gone!" he shouted loudly. "Look, they are all gone!"

"Drop down," Sam said quietly to Burke and Black. As he spoke, he stooped down and pulled on the rope connecting them. "This could get *real* dangerous *real* fast."

"You bet, I'm down," said Burke as he and Black dropped quickly on either side of Sam. Soldiers came running from every direction in the campsite. Lanterns flared and turned on, glaring and flickering in the night.

Torch after torch reached into the large campfire and came out lighting the campsite.

"Jesus! Why don't they tie bull's-eyes to their backs?" Burke asked, the three of them huddled down, trying to stay out of sight, hopefully out of mind.

A guard ran down from the end of the rope line and stopped in front of them. Stooping, he jiggled their rope and looked at the tightly knotted rawhide on their wrists.

149

"The pistoleros are still here, *Capitán,*" he called out in the direction of Captain Flores' open-sided tent. "Only the devil Apache are gone."

"If the pistoleros move, shoot them!" the captain called out in reply, through the chaos that had gripped the camp.

"*Sí, Capitán,*" said the guard. He aimed his rifle down at Stanley Black and cocked the hammer. "You heard the *capitán,*" he said with a shrug.

"Hold it! We didn't *move!*" Sam shouted at him, seeing he was going to fire. Black threw his hands in front of his face as if the flesh and bone the bullet was made to destroy would somehow save him.

"You haven't moved yet, but you will," the soldier said. "So . . ." He pulled the trigger. The bullet missed Black's head, but a streak of fire skimmed along the crown of his hat, leaving a blue flame dancing and flickering behind it. Black sat stunned, his eyes wide, staring through his gaping hat brim.

Seeing his shot fail, the soldier levered a fresh round into his rifle chamber. Sam and Burke half rose, ready to grab the rifle from him. But before either of them could, Private Roberto Deluna shouted at the guard as he came running up. "No, stop! Sergeant Bolado does not want them shot!"

"But the *capitán* does," the soldier said stubbornly. "He said if they move —"

"I know what he said," Roberto shouted, snatching the rifle from his hands. "Sergeant Bolado will have you whipped and gutted if you shoot them. How does that suit you?"

"I'm only following orders," said the young soldier.

"Get out of here," said Roberto. "I will guard these men, as I have been most of the night."

"But what about my rifle?" the soldier said.

"Use my rifle. It is hooked to my saddle beside the horses. The sergeant is there assembling riders. Go now, quickly," he said. "Ride with the sergeant. Bring back the prisoners."

The young soldier turned and raced away toward the line of horses where saddles were being thrown and cinched, bridles hitched and gear readied. As the young guard disappeared into the chaos of soldiers scrambling back and forth, Sam and Burke looked up at Roberto.

"Gracias, Private Roberto," Sam said.

Roberto gave him a nod. Then his eyes cut quickly to Black, who still sat stunned by his close call with death.

"Your hat is on fire," Roberto said to him.

"Jesus!" shouted Burke, snatching Black's flaming hat from his head with his bound hands and pounding it against the ground. "You didn't have enough damn sense to know your head was on fire?"

"Go to hell, Clyde!" Black shouted in loud reply. "I thought I was dead!"

Sam ignored the two, looking up at Roberto as he saw Sergeant Bolado and a column of men mounting their horses and falling into line.

"Is that a good idea, Roberto?" he asked. "Them going off after the Apache in the middle of the night?"

"I don't know," said Roberto. "What are you saying?"

"I'm saying what if there's other Apache just waiting out there? These prisoners get half the camp chasing them, and then the others ride in and kill everybody still here. Who's going to keep that from happening?"

The soldier's expression stiffened with pride.

"I and my fellow soldiers will defend the camp," he said. "Do you not think us capable?"

"I think you're capable," Sam said, realizing there was no point in discussing the matter. "I was just curious." He and the other two would just have to be ready to make their move when the Apache hit. And he was certain they would hit most any time once the sergeant and his patrol were far enough out of camp. "Let me ask you something, Roberto," he said. "Is the sergeant carrying my Colt?"

"*Sí,* he is carrying the gun that he took from you," Roberto said. "But I think it is not your gun anymore." He gave Sam a sympathetic look. "I believe it is *his* gun now."

"I suppose you're right, Roberto," Sam said. "To the victor goes the spoils, I reckon."

"*Sí,* to the victor goes the spoils," Roberto repeated with a friendly smile.

CHAPTER 11

When Sergeant Bolado led his patrol out of the camp and onto the desert, Roberto stood guard as Sam, Burke and Black looked down watching the dark shadowy figures head out across the rolling sand.

Black still wore his sliced, and now burnt, hat, but held his sagging brim up with the tip of his finger as he watched the soldiers disappear out into the night. The smell of the burnt hat permeated the chilled night air, wafting into Sam's and Burke's faces as they stood beside Black.

"I should have torn that hat to shreds when I had it in my hands," Burke said in a sour tone. "It smells worse than a wet whore's —"

"Never you mind what it smells like," Black said, cutting him short. "It's my damn hat, and I'm wearing it. I'll hear no more on the matter." He deliberately removed his finger from under the brim and let it drop back down beneath his eyes. He stared at Burke.

Burke chuffed and shook his head. Then he took a breath for patience' sake.

"All right," he said. "I'll give you ten dollars to get rid of it."

"Have you got ten dollars?" Black asked.

Burke replied, his voice getting a little louder as he spoke, "I will have, soon as we get to where it is we're going —"

"Both of you quiet down," Sam said, watching with dread and concern as the patrol made its way deeper onto the desert floor. "Keep an eye out for anything moving toward us up here."

"If they don't get back in time, we'll be like tin ducks at a shooting gallery here," Black said, returning to his lowered voice. He straightened his burnt and battered hat. He pushed the brim back up with his finger, now that Burke had stopped chastising him.

"Don't count on them coming back," Burke said, also lowering his voice. He looked all around the campsite, its number reduced now by half. "These beaners had better hope they didn't lend any of them any money." He cackled a little into his cupped hand, muffling the sound of it.

Sam looked at him, then gazed back out into the purple starlit night.

"Stay ready," he whispered sidelong to the other two. "They'll be coming anytime."

Yet, as the night progressed and Sam kept watch, nothing stirred on the desert below or the hillsides above. Finally, as Sam rubbed his eyes and decided to take a break and leave Burke watching for a while, a hard barrage of rifle fire resounded from far out on the desert floor.

"What do you think, Roberto?" Sam asked the guard as he ran up from the end of the rope line and stopped in front of the three prisoners. "Think the Apache ambushed them?"

"No," Roberto said. "I think the sergeant has *ambushed* the escaped prisoners."

Sam fell silent, but he didn't share the young private's optimism. As he watched the desert floor, far out on the dark horizon sparks streaked back and forth, followed by another hard volley of rifle fire. After the volley a silence set in, but only for a moment. Then came single rifle shots one after the other. Then dead silence.

"Good, it is over," said Roberto. He looked relieved. He turned and smiled triumphantly at Sam. "I told you so," he said.

Sam didn't reply. He chose to wait and see what would happen next. He watched as Roberto walked back to the end of the rope line and sat down on a rock.

"What do you think, Jones?" Burke asked. "Think we've misjudged these birds? Think the sergeant is tougher and smarter than we thought?"

"I don't know," Sam said. "I'm staying ready anyway. If we're wrong, I'll celebrate."

"Me too," said Burke. "Get yourself some shut-eye. I've got this covered."

The three sat down as one; Sam and Stanley Black stretched out on the ground with their blankets over them while Burke kept watch. But the two's sleep was not long-lasting. The hour before dawn as the first silver-gold thread of sunlight mantled the eastern hill lines, Burke shook Sam and Black by their shoulders. They awakened to the sound of pounding horses' hooves galloping up the trail into camp. Sam stiffened and started to jump to his feet.

"Easy, Jones," Burke said. "It's the patrol coming back. Roberto told me the camp guards spotted them down there ten minutes ago. Said some of them are riding double."

Sam rubbed sleep from his eyes and looked all around in the purple-gray morning light.

157

"You should have woken me sooner," he said.

"And I should've been born rich instead of so damn smart," Burke said. He looked at Black and shook his head in contempt. "You're just wearing that hat to aggravate me," he said as the three rose to their feet as one. They stood watching, Roberto right beside them, as Sergeant Bolado and his men stepped down from their saddles. Two of his men had been riding double owing to the sergeant's horse going lame and having to be shot. Two other men rode double, one leading his horse behind them, the bodies of two Apache draped over its back.

While two soldiers came running to the sergeant leading three fresh horses, another soldier ran over to Roberto with an excited look on his face.

"Sergeant Bolado's patrol has killed two of the devil Apache in a deadly shoot-out!" he said. "They only return now to replace the sergeant's lame horse."

Roberto beamed at Sam and the other two.

"The devil Apache are no match for our Mexican army. Soon there will be no more Apache left in the Blood Mountain Range, perhaps not in the whole of Mexico."

Sam, Burke and Black just looked at one

another.

"The sergeant said to bring the prisoners to the horses and let them see what happens to those who try to escape."

"Go loosen the other end of the rope," Roberto told the younger soldier.

Burke gave Private Roberto a confident grin.

"Don't do all this on our account, Roberto," he said. "We've seen plenty of dead 'pache in our time —"

Private Roberto turned on him with a fiery look in his eyes.

"Keep your mouth shut unless you are spoken to," he snapped at Burke. "Do you realize the trouble I am in if I'm found consorting with prisoners? You must not cause me trouble."

"You're right, Private," Sam said, giving Burke and Black a disapproving look. "We'll keep quiet."

The three shut up and stood waiting until the other guard took the rope behind them and another guard took the rope in front.

"March," Roberto commanded, moving forward alongside them, his rifle at port arms.

Stopping at the place where the sergeant and his patrol were gathered, the three looked down at the dead Apache that had been pulled from the horse's back and pitched in the dirt. Their bodies were riddled with bullets. Their scalps were missing. Sam saw the grizzly trophies hanging from the saddle horn of the horse Sergeant Bolado rode in on.

The sergeant turned to them from a horse he'd saddled and inspected for the trail.

"Take a good look, gringos," he said. "This is what happens when you try to get away from me." Although he spoke to the three of them, he purposely singled Sam out. "The army owns this desert." He thumbed himself on his chest. "And *I am* the army," he declared. "If you value your life, you will try nothing like this on our way to Fuerte Valor. Do I make myself clear to you?" As he spoke he stepped in close to Sam, again singling him out for a response.

Sam stood almost nose-to-nose with the sergeant, not about to back off from such an aggressive gesture.

"Yes, you've made yourself clear, Sergeant," he said flatly. He wanted to ask what was going to happen if the Apache attacked the camp while Bolado and his patrol were out chasing the escaped prisoners. But he knew that asking would do no good. Anyway, he decided, maybe he'd been wrong. Maybe the Apache weren't coming after all.

"Good," the sergeant said, still standing close. He said in a lowered voice just between the two of them, "When I am finished with the devil Apache, I will have you take me to where the gold is hidden, eh?"

Sam didn't reply. He only stood staring, not backing an inch.

As shadows began giving way to the glitter of daylight on the far hill line, Sam and the other two finished a breakfast of bear meat and coffee and shook out their blankets and rolled them to carry under their arms. It had been over an hour since Sergeant Bolado had led his patrol back out onto the desert to take up the chase of the escaped prisoners. Having seen the faces of the two dead warriors the patrol had brought back to camp, Sam realized that neither of the dead bloody faces belonged to the young brave that he'd given water to over a month ago.

Good for him. . . .

Sam gazed out across the wide desert floor, Burke and Black on either side of him. All around them, soldiers were busy, dismantling camp, saddling and readying horses for the trail and loading the cart and hitching the team of mules to it. The mules brayed and honked and sullied in place. The soldiers struggled with the stubborn animals, one pushing them forward with his shoulder to their rumps while another pulled on a rope around the mules' muzzles. Soldiers loaded bloody canvas-wrapped bear meat onto the two-wheel mule-killer cart.

"So, you were wrong, Jones," Private Roberto said to Sam with a wide smile. He stood two feet back, his rifle at port arms as he spoke. "Do not feel foolish. I know there are many who discount our army. But not I. When the devil Apache vanished into the night, I knew they were not coming back to this camp. They know how loco it would be to try to —"

His words seemed to melt away inside his mouth as a rifle shot exploded. Sam saw his head kick hard to the side, then bounce back. A pleasant yet surprised look came to his face in spite of the spray of blood that jetted out the other side of his head.

"Holy Mama Amanda!" shouted Burke, the three of them dropping to the ground instantly. "They're here! The sons a' bitches have come after all!"

"But where?" Sam shouted, looking all around as bullets zipped back and forth from both the hillside above them and the boulders and rock below.

Mexican soldiers began falling where they stood, some without knowing what had hit them. Others, realizing they were being attacked, made for whatever cover they could find. As a fierce battle settled in and both sides staked out their firing positions, Sam grabbed the rifle that had fallen from Roberto Deluna's dead hand. He checked and cocked it. Beside him, Burke reached out and snatched the dead private's battle knife from its sheath and began slicing his and Black's rawhide bindings.

"Here," he said to Sam. "Get you some of this."

Sam held his bound hands around and watched the knife's sharp edge slide between them. He took a second to rub his wrists as rifle fire exploded back and forth just above their lowered heads. Burnt black smoke had already begun to loom and drift slow on the chilled morning air.

"Let's go," Sam said, realizing that they were doing exactly what they had planned to do should the attack come. They dared not stand, even in a crouch during this early fast stage of battle. Instead they crawled out across the rocky ground toward the place where the horses stood off to the side of a

163

large boulder that was providing them cover so far.

Beside the boulder they rose into a crouch and raced across ten feet of open ground and ducked in among the frightened milling horses. The rifle fire had the animals panicked, and rightfully so. One of the army horses lay dead in a dark pool of blood from a ricocheted bullet. Another hapless animal stood bleeding from a graze across its hip. Luckily, Sam found both the dun and the white barb half-spooked but in good shape, jerking nervously on their tied reins, ready to go.

"Easy, fellows," he said to the horses, standing between them, rubbing their necks, settling them as the battle raged. He noted as he stood there how improbable it had been to crawl through all that gunfire and no one get so much as a scratch. But he had no time to marvel on it now. Burke had run to the end of the horse string and came back dragging three saddles across the dirt.

"Throw these on and get the hell out of here," he said to Sam and Black.

Sam grabbed his saddle and pitched it over his dun's back and cinched it. He untied both his horses' reins from the rope line and started to back them and turn them toward a thin path leading up around the

164

boulder. But then he stopped.

"Wait," he said suddenly. He stared off, searching all along the upper hillside above the water hole.

"Wait?" Burke repeated incredulously, bullets zipping back and forth across the campsite. "Are you out of your mind, Jones?" he shouted.

"Something's wrong," Sam said.

Above the exploding rifle fire, Burke shouted, "I sure as hell won't argue with that!" as if amazed at Sam's curious behavior. He jerked around to Black. "Do you notice anything wrong here, Stanley?" he shouted. *"Anything at all?"*

Black stood crouched, staring at him wide-eyed above his sagging hat brim.

"Listen to him, Clyde," he said to Burke. "Apache don't act like this! There *is* something wrong here. I can't say what it is right now, but something —"

"Jesus, Stanley!" Burke said, cutting him off as he scrambled up into his saddle and backed his horse. "If it comes to you, write me a letter first chance you get." He swung his horse and booted it toward the path up around the boulder.

"Cover him," Sam shouted, pitching Black the rifle. He gathered the reins to the white barb and began to climb atop the dun. But

165

as he saw Burke's horse reach the path and start up it, he saw a half dozen men in soiled white peasant shirts and straw sombreros descend out of the rock behind the boulder and fall upon Burke and take him, horse and all, to the ground.

Sam saw machetes on the men's waists, but he saw none being raised or put to use. He saw Black raise the dead private's rifle to his shoulder and take aim. But he reached down and grabbed the rifle from the side just as it fired. The bullet sliced away wildly into the grainy morning sky.

From the rock behind the boulder, a man jumped out wearing a dirty poncho, ammunition bandoliers criss-crossing his chest.

"Do not shoot, Jones! Do not shoot. It is I, Marcos!"

"Marcos . . . ?" Sam stared at him as the battle raged on the far side of the boulder. *Marcos . . . ?*

"You sold me rifles for the revolution," the man shouted as if hearing his questioning thoughts. "We have come to save you, *mi amigo*! We are your *compañeros de armas*!" He spread his hands, a French rifle in one of them.

Brothers in arms . . . ? Sam translated.

But suddenly a light of recognition came on for Sam as he looked the stout scar-faced

Mexican up and down. He did not recognize the name, but he recognized the man, the voice, the striped poncho.

"Don't shoot, Stanley," Sam said to Black. "He's right, I know him." Sam booted the dun over to the place where the rebel leader and his men stood out of the gunfire in the sheltering safety of the boulder. As he arrived, the rebels had lifted Burke to his feet and stood brushing him off. Behind Sam, Black rode up with his burnt and severed hat tugged down atop his head. The Mexicans looked curiously at Black, then at Sam as the battle continued.

"Come, Jones, *mi compañero de armas.* Follow me," said the stocky, scar-faced rebel leader. He turned quickly and moved on foot up the narrow path. Seeing him leave, Black needed no further encouragement. He booted his horse forward and up the path into the rocks behind him.

"Want to tell me what the hell is going on here, Jones?" said Burke, his horse having risen onto its hooves, standing beside him shaking itself off. The rebels stood nearby gesturing for the three of them to hurry on up the path behind their leader, Marcos.

"I don't know, Clyde," said Sam, already nudging his dun forward, pulling the white barb beside him. He gestured a nod back toward the fierce fighting. "You want to wait here, I'll write you a letter first chance I get."

"You can write it," Burke said, swinging up into his saddle, falling in behind him. "But you won't like where I'll tell you to send it."

CHAPTER 12

On a stone cliff near the top of the steep hill, Sam, Stanley Black and Clyde Burke stood in the cover of a low stone ledge and looked down on the fighting below. The rest of the rebels had gone farther down the hillside to join the fighting. Marcos Renaldo, the scar-faced leader of the rebels, stood with the three gunmen, seeing his men taking over the hillside and water hole below.

"That went right well, ol' hoss," Burke said to Marcos, assuming a familiarity, as if having known him his whole life.

Marcos let it go. He held up one of the French rifles he'd purchased from Sam a month earlier.

"I have your amigo and mine to thank for it," he said, hefting the rifle admiringly. "It is he and the woman who delivered these fine arms to my men and me when we were struggling to just stay alive out here — now look at us, eh?" He gestured a hand toward the dead soldiers lying strewn on the hillside and down the trail, the sight of them obscured by the thick drift of burnt powder.

"My, my, but ain't you just the huckleberry?" Burke said with a chuckle to Sam. "You've had your thumb in lots of pies."

"He does get around," said Black through the sagging hat brim, the smell of burnt felt.

"When we saw you and your compañeros walking across the sand with your hands bound, I said to my men, 'This will not do.' We waited and looked for our chance. When we saw the sergeant and his men ride back out, we decided to strike hard."

"We are obliged, Marcos," Sam said, not wanting to get too deep into the rifles and how he had come to be the one delivering them to the rebels.

Below, two of the rebels found time in the waning battle to pull a body from the water hole and drop it on the gravel bank. On rocks nearby, the buzzards had taken time from picking at the dead bear the Montana Kid had killed, as well as the guts and scraps left over from the one the soldiers had butchered for meat. The big birds watched the carnage with particular interest, flapping their shiny wings as if applauding the arrival of such a deadly species as man.

"Ah, and now it draws to a close," Marcos said, listening to a few sporadic shots pop here and there among the wounded soldiers. "I have heard nothing as sweet as the sound of silent peace." He smiled and looked back at Sam. "Come, let us get you armed and send you on your way. The sergeant has listened to the resounding gunfire below. His patrol will be arriving back at any time. We will wait here and ambush him," he said.

Burke and Black looked back and forth between Sam and the rebel leader.

"Shouldn't we stay and help out here?" Burke put in.

"Yeah," said Black. "To show our appreciation for all you've done for us?"

"No," said Marcos. "This is all a part of my gift. You must do nothing here, only continue on your journey, and go with God."

Burke chuckled darkly.

"So far God ain't been all too keen on keeping our company, ol' hoss," he said to Marcos. "But we're obliged, him sending you when he did."

Marcos nodded and swept a hand toward the lower hillside.

"Come, then, let us lead our horses down." He looked at Black's burnt and battered hat. "Perhaps among the dead you will

171

find for yourself a better piece of headwear."

"See, Stanley?" Burke said to Black, picking right up on the rebel leader's words. "Nobody likes looking at that mess you're wearing."

"Nobody likes looking at you, Clyde!" Black said heatedly. "I'm not giving up a four-dollar hat until I've gotten my money's worth from it."

Sam nudged Marcos. The two of them turned away and led their horses ahead of the arguing gunmen and down the steep path toward the water hole.

At the path leading out to the edge of the water hole, Burke and Black caught up to them. Together the four walked into the smoke-covered campsite as the rebels lined up the soldiers who had thrown up their hands in surrender. They disarmed the frightened men and threw them to the ground, prodding them with rifle barrels until the soldiers sat trembling in fear, their hands clasped behind their heads.

As Sam and Marcos walked past the captured soldiers, they stopped and looked back when behind them Burke spoke up.

"Wait a minute. Look who this is," he said, staring down at a young soldier with blood trickling down the corner of his lips.

"Por favor, señor," the soldier begged, star-

ing up at Burke, tears running down his cheeks.

"*Por favor,* your ass," said Burke.

"It's No Talk," Black said with a surprised chuckle, gazing down at the trembling soldier.

"Imagine finding you here, No Talk," said Burke. He reached down and loosely back-handed the sobbing man across the top of his bare head.

"This man has personally wronged you?" Marcos asked Sam.

"Every time one of us tried to speak, he told us to shut up," Sam said. "But there was no real harm —"

"The son of a bitch like to have drove me loco," Burke cut in. "I was hoping I could get my hands on him." He backhanded No Talk's head again, not too hard, but hard enough to keep him frightened.

"How would you like him to pay for wronging you?" Marcos asked Burke. "Whatever you decide, so will it be."

"What about this, No Talk?" Burke said to the sobbing man. "Look who's rolling all the marbles now."

"Let's go, Clyde," Sam said, seeing Burke getting more and more worked up.

"Not yet," said Burke. "I'm going to cut No Talk's tongue out and stick it in his shirt

173

pocket for him."

The young soldier's eyes went wild with terror. The other soldiers drew away from him, as if his grim fate might be catching.

Marcos produced a knife and handed it handle first to Burke. "Here, do what you must do."

Burke took the knife with a cruel grin and looked down at the trembling bowed head.

"Huh-uh, Clyde," Sam said strongly. "Let this go. We don't have time for it."

"How long can it take?" said Burke. He grabbed the soldier by his hair and jerked his head back. Gripping the knife tightly, he readied himself to pry the man's tightly shut mouth open with the blade and do his worst. But he stopped short, the tip of the blade ready to plunge between the soldier's tightened lips, and glanced at Sam.

"Let it go," Sam said in a low firm voice. He shook his head slowly. "This is no good."

Burke waited, his hand tight on the knife handle, his other hand entwined in the soldier's hair. Finally he let out a tight breath, turned loose of the soldier's hair, actually smoothed it down with his palm.

"Well, No Talk," he said, drawing the knife blade back from the soldier's lips, "looks like this is your lucky —"

Burke's words stopped beneath the blast

of a pistol in Marcos' hand. The soldier pitched backward with a bullet hole in his forehead. A red mist blossomed in the air and melted away as the soldier hit the ground, his dead eyes staring skyward.

Sam, Burke and Black turned wide-eyed in surprise.

Marcos shrugged and lowered the smoking pistol.

"He was going to die anyway," he said. "His tongue would not matter." He turned the pistol to the next soldier sitting in the row and shot him, then the next, and the next.

Sam winced as the soldiers struggled to rise but were pushed back down by rifle butts. Glancing toward Captain Flores' felled tent, Sam saw Flores thrown to the ground by three riflemen. The captain was only half-dressed, a nightshirt hanging down over his uniform trousers. Having been awakened by the melee, he had been sleeping off a night of smoking fresh tar opium. He had staggered out waving his saber wildly, but to no purpose. Now that he was down, his saber gone, the men laughed and poked at him with their French-made rifles Sam had helped deliver to them.

"Shoot the rest of these poltroons,"

Marcos ordered his rebels, lowering his smoking pistol. "I must go say *hola* to the captain, and shoot him too. Leave no prisoners alive here," he demanded. He looked all around and smiled widely. *"Viva revolución!"*

Before an hour had passed, Sam sat atop his dun riding along the edge of the desert at the foot of the hill line. He led the white barb beside him, having found the supply pack and strapped it to the animal's back. Clyde Burke and Stanley Black rode on either side of him, the three keeping their horses at an easy gallop ahead of the day's oncoming heat. Vision across the desert floor was still clear, but with so much fighting and gunfire in the hill line, the day had started out with no secrets, Sam reminded himself, riding on. Anyone on the desert floor or surrounding hills knew there had been fighting throughout the night.

"How much farther?" Black asked above the soft plop of hooves in sand as he sidled up close on Sam's free side.

Sam looked sidelong at him, seeing his face beneath a straw sombrero given to him by one of the rebels before they'd left the water hole.

"Tomorrow," said Sam, and he turned

forward and rode on.

The three had taken on enough firearms and ammunition from the dead soldiers to get them out of any scrape, if their odds were anywhere near defendable.

Sam had found a large bandana and tied himself a head cloth. Over the head cloth, he placed a black sombrero he'd found among the captain's belongings. The sombrero's crown stood so tall that the top four inches of it folded over and flapped a little with the gallop of the dun. The initials LF were thinly embroidered in dark gold thread on the front of the tall crown.

He'd replaced his shredded shirt with a dark loose-sleeved shirt and a black embroidered vest. Under the shirt he wore a bandage on his healing wounds. Across his chest he wore a single bandolier of ammunition; on his hip he wore the captain's gun belt with an Army Colt riding in a black slim-jim holster, the holster flap cut off for quicker handling. On the dun's saddle horn hung four canteens of water. A French repeating rifle swung on a saddle ring. A knife with a brass Spanish handle stood in its sheath inside his boot well.

Black and Burke both carried French rifles, as well as battered Colts inside holsters and bandoliers of ammunition across their chests. Additionally, Black carried a short double-barreled shotgun of a kind once carried aboard Mexican traveler coaches. Black had stuffed his burnt and battered hat down into a pair of saddlebags he carried behind his horse's saddle. Burke ate from an open tin of blanched peaches as he rode, spearing the peaches on the tip of a big knife he'd acquired. A bottle of rye whiskey and a bottle of tequila stood peeping from under the edge of his saddlebags.

They only stopped for a moment at midday and looked back in the direction of the water hole, hearing the new outbursts of gunfire from the hillside. As they sat half-turned in their saddles, they saw black burnt powder rise and drift along the hillside rocks and boulders.

Burke speared another peach half and raised it to his lips. He held it there for a moment as if in contemplation.

"Mexicans love to fight, don't they?" he finally said, grinning back and forth.

"You'd think so, as much as they do it," Black replied. Sam just looked at them.

Burke stabbed another dripping peach half and held it out to Sam on the knife blade.

"Eat a peach?" he said, juice running down his beard stubble, dangling from his chin. He belched long and loud.

"Obliged, but no," Sam said, turning forward in his saddle as the new battle raged. Burke turned the knife blade to Black with the same offer. Black grabbed the slippery peach half and downed it in a gulp, then looked expectantly at Burke.

"I didn't take you to raise," Burke said.

They rode on.

A full hour had passed when the shooting behind them waned, then trickled to a stop altogether. Without slowing or looking back, they continued forward until the desert to their right became obscured by the day's wavering heat. When they realized that riders could come as close as a thousand yards or less without being seen by them, they reined their horses a sharp turn and rode onto the sloping hillsides. Once in the labyrinth of boulder and stone, scrub pine and stands of flowering ironwood, they sheltered themselves on walled paths and trails as old as the conquistadors and native peoples who'd formed them.

In the heat of the afternoon, they lay in rock shade and watered their horses from their hats and canteens.

"I could eat a snake while it's still crawling," Burke revealed, rubbing a brittle pine branch in the rocky dirt. "Peaches are

179

monkey food. They go down good, but they're too soft to fill the gullet. . . ." He let his words trail as he watched Black curiously.

Without a word of response, Black had stood and dusted the seat of his trousers and walked to the white barb. He fumbled with something in a canvas bag down among the supplies.

Burke cocked his head, even more curious.

"He comes back and throws me a snake, he's a dead man," he said to Sam in earnest.

But when Black returned from the barb, he pitched Burke and Sam each a piece of jerked goat he'd pirated from the soldiers' supplies. As he sat down, he took a bite from a chunk he'd kept for himself.

"Obliged, Stanley," Burke said.

"Obliged," Sam repeated.

As the three sat eating the dried goat meat, the horses turned nervous and whinnied under their breath. They nickered and pulled at their reins that were tied to a pair of scrub pines.

Sam stood, his rifle ready, and looked all around.

Burke stuffed the chunk of meat in his mouth and stood with his pistol up out of his holster.

Beside Burke, Black levered a round into his rifle chamber.

"Another bear, you figure?" he whispered to Sam.

"I don't know," Sam whispered in reply. "This place is good for about anything you can think of."

Burke chewed quickly, looking around, not trying to speak. The horses grew more nervous. Black's horse tried to rear, but its reins stopped it.

The ground trembled violently, as if a large hand had reached deep into its belly and shaken its guts back and forth.

"There it is," Sam said, his attention turning quickly from searching for some hill predator to keeping his balance on the tilting, wobbling ground.

"There's no letup in this godforsaken desert," Burke said, having managed to swallow the stiff goat meat almost whole.

"Soon as one thing's over, another thing starts!" Black said, spreading his feet to keep from falling.

"How does a man ever plan his day?" said Burke.

Sam stood waiting, listening, feeling the tremendous rumble underfoot draw closer, closer, then seem to dissipate and move on. Pines towering above them on the hillside swayed and shook like dogs shedding rain. Pine nuts, pine needles and dried bird nests showered down.

"Watch for rocks," Sam cautioned, hearing heavy stones thump and crash and tumble and bounce down the hillside in the tremor's wake. As soon as the steep hillside seemed to jar to a halt and settle, Sam said, "All right, get the horses, let's get out of here."

As they gathered the animals and pulled them along down the trail toward the desert floor, a boulder the size of a house rumbled down the hillside less than a hundred feet from them. But seeing it tear down the hillside raising a high spray of dust behind it didn't slow the three of them down. On the contrary, it sped them up.

They ran down the path pulling their horses by their reins until they thought the land was safe enough for them to risk being on horseback. Then they stopped and mounted and rode the rest of the way down the hill. They did not stop on the bottom slope but rather rode out onto the sand before turning their horses quarterwise to the hill and looking back.

Suddenly, as they sat their horses, staring in amazement, a large portion of the lower sloping hillside, trail and all, crumbled like a stale cake and fell straight down into the lower bowels of the earth. Remnants of rock, trees and boulders toppled over the crumbling upper edge and disappeared, leaving behind a spinning, swirling funnel of dust that was within another instant sucked down out of sight.

"Tell me if I'm mistaken," Burke said meekly when the roar of the sinking hillside diminished enough for him to be heard. "Did that hillside just fall into the ground?"

Sam and Black both sat in stunned silence. At length, Sam took a deep breath to collect himself.

"It did," he said quietly.

"All right, I'm gone," Burke said with finality. He jerked his reins to turn his horse around. But Black grabbed his horse by its bridle, stopping it.

"Wait. You can't leave," Black said.

"Try to stop me," said Burke, throwing his hand to the butt of his pistol.

"What about the gold?" Black asked, turning loose of Burke's horse. "We're almost there."

"What good is getting there if the whole Twisted Hills, the Blood Mountain Range and half the damn Mexican Desert falls out from under us?" Burke shouted.

"What do you say, Jones?" Black asked,

weakening a little on the matter himself. "Are you still going on after the gold?"

Sam just looked at the two of them, the whole hill line in front of them covered in a long wall of dust.

"For now, yes," Sam said. "After all we've gone through, I'm not stopping here. We'll be there tomorrow. If these quakes and slides get worse, we know how to stop and turn around, don't we?"

Burke calmed down; so did Black.

"You ever see anything like that?" Burke asked Sam, jerking his head toward the large missing gap in the hillside.

"I have now," Sam said calmly. He turned his dun and the white barb and rode off at an easy gallop along the sand flats.

Burke and Black sat looking at each other for a moment.

"He *has now,* he tells us," Burke said with a bemused look.

"I heard him," Black said, turning his horse, putting it forward behind Sam. "He has. So have we," he said over his shoulder.

Burke shook his head and maneuvered his horse alongside him.

"A man's got to be a damn fool . . . ," he grumbled, leaving his words trailing as he rode away.

CHAPTER 13

Looking back on the sunken hillside an hour later, they could see the dust had settled enough to reveal the rim of a black hole on the hill's lower slope. Above the black rim stood a towering cutbank of earth and stone over a hundred feet high where the trail and its boulders and rock had been.

"Sumidero . . . ," Black said in Spanish. The three of them sat dust-covered atop their sweat-streaked horses.

"A *sinkhole,*" Burke translated, shaking his head. "Now I can say I've seen everything." He looked all around, then added, "This whole damn land could fall right out from under us, far as we know." He paused and gave Sam and Black a troubled look. "You don't think it will, do you?"

"It already has," Black replied, nodding toward the missing hillside. "That much of it anyway."

Burke shook his head and managed a dark

chuckle.

"None of Madson's men is going to believe a word of this," he said.

"Why not?" said Black. "They've felt all these quakes, same as we have."

Burke didn't reply. Instead he let out a breath and studied the missing hillside that appeared to have been carved off and flung down into the earth's belly by some reckless giant.

"I don't know about you two," he said, "but I'd just as soon sleep on the flats tonight, take my chances with whoever might come prowling around."

"What's the difference?" said Black. "A *sumidero* can fall out from under us anywhere."

Burke stared at him.

"If you can't say something good, why don't you keep quiet, Stanley?" he said.

"He's right," Sam said. "You can't hide from a sinkhole. One can drop out anywhere. All these quakes and tremors have got the earth's insides stirred up and shifting around."

"At least we can shoot any son of a bitch that comes upon us. I don't know what to do with the likes of this." He gestured another nod back at the hillside.

Sam gazed at the rolling sand flats all

around them, then up the lower slopes beneath the steep hills. "We can camp down among the lower rocks tonight and go up first thing come morning and get the gold," he said.

"Yeah, if the hills are still standing when we get there," Black added grimly.

"All right, that does it," said Burke. He turned in his saddle, reached back and pulled out the bottle of rye. Sam and Black watched him uncork the bottle with a shaky hand and take a long swallow. When he lowered the bottle and let out a whiskey hiss, he passed it to Black, who sat his horse nearest to him. "You're aggravating the living hell out of me, Stanley. See if this does anything for your ugly frame of mind."

Black tipped the bottle back and took a long swig. He lowered the bottle and ran the back of his hand across his lips.

"Obliged," he said, in a whiskey-strained voice. "I've been needing that ever since I saw the hill fall into the ground." He passed the bottle on to Sam, who took it, turned up a short drink for appearance' sake and passed the bottle back to Burke.

"You've had your drink. Now put the bottle away," Sam said, taking charge. "We need to keep a clear head until this is over."

Burke gave him a look, but then he nodded, corked the bottle and put it away. The three turned their horses back along the edge of the sand flats and rode off into the long evening shadows.

Burke, Black and Sam spent the night among the cactus and smaller stone skirting the lower slopes on the hill line. On their way into the cover of rocks, they passed a forty-foot pine that had been freshly uprooted, twisted, broken and hurled down onto the slope as if it had been a twig in the hands of an angry child. They looked the tree over as they led their horses past it on a rough upward path. Thirty yards above the downed pine, they made a small fire behind a stand of rock and boiled coffee and heated more dried goat meat.

"It doesn't look like it was as bad here as it was back along the trail," Black said, sipping coffee, his newly acquired straw sombrero off his head, sitting atop his raised knee. "Maybe this will be easy pickings."

" 'Remain hopeful but expect the worst,' " Burke quoted with a raised finger for attention's sake. "That's what my uncle Paul always said." He sipped whiskey-laced coffee and chewed the stringy jerked goat.

"That makes no sense at all, Clyde," Black commented.

"I never said it made sense," Burke replied. "I just said he said it."

"Maybe he was a lunatic, your uncle Paul," Black said, the tension of the day coming out.

"Maybe if you'd been there, you could have told him that to his face," Burke said, half snapping at him. "I bet he would've been obliged to hear —"

"All right," Sam said, standing, picking up the small coffeepot from a writhing bed of flame and ember. He rubbed his boot back and forth through the fire, breaking it up, and poured the remains of the coffee onto the smoldering twigs and brush.

"Hey! I would have drunk that," Black said testily as the coffee steamed and hissed.

Sam just looked at him in the failing light.

"It's been a long day," he said. "Let's back away from here and get some sleep." He tossed a nod up the hill. "No telling what we're looking at come morning."

"Well," Burke said, standing stiffly, "I've seen enough for one day — saw a hill turn into a sinkhole. That's enough for me."

The three backed away to their horses and led the animals twenty yards higher up the slope and into another stand of rocks overlooking the darkened campsite. Throughout the moonlit night they shared watch on the lower slope and the wide, rolling desert floor. Before first light they had eaten more goat meat and drunk tepid water from their canteens. They'd watered their horses from their upturned hats the night before, and now the horses breakfasted on a handful of grain from a feed bag in their supplies. They saddled and readied the animals for the trail.

Atop their horses, they sat for a moment gazing up, negotiating the dark grainy upward stretch of rock, stone ledges, boulder and earth all held together one by the other, the whole of it standing tall, penetrating a gray-silver sky. Their eyes moved sidelong across each other; their breaths wafted thin curls of steam in the chilled air. The horses milled and scraped their hooves.

"Let's get to it," Sam said quietly, nudging his horse forward, leading the white barb beside him. The barb probed its muzzle against his sleeve and blew out a steamy breath.

Behind Sam, Burke and Black rode single file, checking the land on their way up for any signs of yesterday's earth turbulence.

"So far, so good," Black said under his breath, as if in fear of the hill itself overhearing him, somehow taking offense. In front of him, Burke only gave a short nod as he looked from side to side and felt for anything unusual beneath his horse's hooves.

After winding along a rock-strewn switchback trail for the better part of an hour, the three stopped as they came upon another long huge pine twisted diagonally across the trail. The broken root ball of the tree stood twenty feet high on its side, circling upward filled with dirt and rock. The top of the tree rested against a stony cliff abutment on the other side of the trail and served as a stop for a mammoth unearthed boulder that had rolled that far and halted. It appeared to loom perilously, as if deciding whether to stay there and reembed itself over time, or crush the large pine into splinters and roll on.

"Damn . . . ! Don't nobody breathe," Burke said. Yet he nudged his horse forward behind Sam, who turned the dun and the supply horse wide enough to circle below and beneath the root ball hanging half out over the edge of the trail.

Behind Burke, Black rode forward, the three of them smelling sweet fresh pine sap from the tree's bruised innards and the dark musty smell of overturned earth as root tentacles bobbed overhead and trickled fresh dirt onto their hat brims and their horses' manes. To their right, the hillside dropped straight down over a hundred feet of merciless stone and onto spiked treetops a-sway on a thin morning breeze.

As their mounts rounded under the tree root and ascended the other side onto the trail, Sam kept his two horses moving forward as he'd decided he would do now until they reached the crevice where he'd hidden the three sacks of gold Marcos and his rebels had paid for their French rifles.

Behind Sam, Burke pulled his horse to the side long enough to look back at the tree, the unseated boulder and the large root ball and shook his head.

"Sometimes I think being a rake and a thief is the hardest damn work in the world," he said.

Sam and Black rode on without reply.

As morning spread fiery white along the far horizon, the three stepped down from their horses on a wide level terrace that encroached into the hillside. Across the level ground, the steep hillside continued reaching skyward. A narrow game path led up around a boulder, through brush and trees, around and over rock until reaching the hill's uppermost peak.

"This is it," Sam said, looking all around.

Burke and Black looked at each other.

"Are you sure?" Burke asked quietly.

Sam just looked at him.

"Of course he's sure," said Black. Seeing Sam step forward leading the dun and the barb behind him, Black jerked his head toward him in a follow-him gesture and led his horse along behind him.

Halfway across the level terrace, Sam stopped for a moment and looked all around at large rocks he didn't recall lying there before. He looked up at the towering hillside and appraised it closely.

"This is it, but it's been shaken up," he said. "The boulder there looks different."

Black and Burke squinted at the large boulder.

"Different how?" Burke asked.

"Just different," Sam said. "But this is the place." He gestured at wagon marks and fading hoofprints on the rocky ground. Then he led the horses across the terrace and tied their reins to a stand of scrub ironwood. Burke and Black followed, looking all around, and tied their horses beside his.

Rifles in hand, the two followed Sam on the path around the boulder. But rounding the boulder, they immediately stopped. Sam stared down into the crevice he had climbed up through leading to where he'd hidden the gold. The crevice had been shallow, easily climbed. Not now. The recent quakes had widened the crevice to twice what Sam remembered it to be. The depth of it was now unfathomable in the slanted morning sunlight. Looking down the newly shaped walls of stone and clinging surface dirt, he could see the crevice had turned into a wide slice of blackness seventy feet down.

They stepped back from the edge as a small rock broke free and tumbled down. They listened, and listened, and listened. Finally they heard a clattering sound falling farther away from them.

They stood in silence for a moment, waiting expectantly. Finally Black broke the silence.

"I never heard it land," he said.

"Maybe it didn't yet," said Burke.

After another pause, Black shook his head and said, "I'm not a man to quit easily — but we ought to think about quitting this."

"Neither am I . . . ," Burke said, trailing off.

"Neither are you *what*?" Black said, he and Sam staring at Burke.

"A man who quits easy," Burke finished.

"But you quit too?" said Black.

"Yes, I do," said Burke. "Unless you know a way we can get out there and hang on to the sides and —" He stopped short, seeing Sam let out a breath, turn and walk back to the horses.

Following Sam, Burke reached out to untie his horse's reins and swing up into his saddle. "I don't know about you two, but I'm damn glad we're turning back, getting with Madson and his men and —" He stopped short again, this time seeing Sam take the coiled rope from his saddle horn.

"The hell are you fixing to do, Jones?" he said. As he asked, he saw Black taking the rope from his saddle horn as well. "Stanley, damn it?"

Black shrugged, shouldering his coiled rope.

"Tying off on these rocks, I'm thinking?" he said with uncertainty, glancing at Sam for confirmation. "Going down over the side?"

"You've got it," Sam said with deliberation. He turned with his rope on his shoulder, rifle still in hand, and started to walk back to the path around the boulder.

"Damn it, pards, you might not believe this," said Burke, reaching for his own coiled rope. "But I thought the same thing a while ago. I just didn't say it." He hurried and caught up with Black and Sam. "Hear me?" he said. "I just didn't say so."

"We heard you, Clyde," said Black.

They all three stopped a few feet back from the edge.

Sam leaned his rifle against the boulder and hung his tall-crowned sombrero on the tip of the barrel. He stripped off his bandolier and laid it beside the rifle.

"You can both toss a loop that far, can't you?" He gestured toward the width of the crevice that had now become a canyon.

"I can for damn sure," Black said.

"And then some," Burke said, eyeing the distance. "I was born throwing a lariat farther than that," he chuffed.

"Good," Sam said. "Wait here until I call for you."

He walked over to the right rim of the crevice. Black and Burke stood watching, having also leaned their rifles against the boulder that had hung their headwear in the same manner.

"Why don't he tie his rope off on something and tie it around himself?" Burke whispered to Black.

"I don't know, hush up," Black whispered back.

Sam walked out along the broken surface in a low crouch, the edge slanted inward to the crevice, loose and unsteady, slippery with small gravel and dirt.

"Jesus, he's crazy, Stanley," Burke whispered.

Black stood staring out at Sam, afraid to say anything, as if so much as a quietly spoken word might topple him over into the gaping crevice.

Looking down the deep rocky wall as he moved along, Sam stopped fifteen feet out and took the coiled rope from his shoulder.

"It's down in there," he said quietly, gesturing to a thinner crevice eighteen feet down in the larger crevice wall.

"All right, now what?" Burke called out to him in a hushed tone.

"Take the end of both your ropes across from me on the other edge and tie them off real good," Sam said calmly. "Toss them across to me."

"Huh?" said Burke, looking out along the other edge of the crevice.

Seeing Burke's fear, Black said to him, "Come on, Clyde. It's flatter over there. We're all right."

"Hell, I know we're *all right,*" Burke said. "You don't need to tell me."

On their way around to the other edge across from Sam, Burke called out, "Why didn't you go down on this side?"

"Because the gold's in the wall on *this side,*" Sam called back to him.

"Just asking," Burke said. To himself he murmured, "I should have drank that whole damn bottle before doing this."

As the two tied their ropes around rocks, Sam tied the end of his rope around an earth-stuck stone standing five feet back from the broken crevice edge. He hurled the rest of the rope out and watched it fall and uncoil down the crevice wall.

"Why doesn't he tie the other end around his waist?" Burke asked Black.

"Don't ask me. I got here when you did," Black said, watching Sam closely. After a moment, he said to Burke without turning to face him, "I get it now. He's going down that side, but he's coming up this side. We're going to hold him, help pull him up — it's wider over here. We'd have a hard time over there."

Burke looked down the crevice wall across from them to where Sam stood waiting.

"But how's he going to get from there over to here . . ." He stopped himself. "Jesus! He's not going to jump, is he?"

"I would have to say yes, he is," Black replied.

"All right, he *really is crazy,*" Burke said. He called over to Sam, "Are you going to leap this thing? It be a good fifteen, twenty feet across."

Sam called back to him, "Do you want to stand over here and pull me up, Clyde?" Beneath his feet, a trickle of dirt and gravel spilled over the edge.

Jesus . . . !

Burke fell silent; Black shook his head.

"Are you sure this is where the gold is?" Burke asked.

"Yep," Sam said without hesitation. "I wouldn't do this otherwise."

"Good thinking," Burke said. "Do us a favor. Before you jump over here, how about sending the gold up ahead of you?"

"Not a chance," Sam said. "You'll be pulling it up with me. It'll keep your attention until I'm safe over the edge."

Black chuckled to himself. He raised a loop in his lariat and spun it slowly over his head.

"Coming at you," he called out to Sam.

Burke readied his rope and shook his head.

"I never seen nothing like it," he murmured under his breath.

CHAPTER 14

With his loose rope wrapped a turn around his forearm, and the other two ropes tied around him chest high, Sam climbed down the side of the crevice, feeding his rope out a little at a time. Above him on the other side, Burke and Black handled their ropes expertly, keeping tension even on both ropes and feeding them out sparingly as they watched him descend.

Sam found good footing step after step, lowering himself smoothly, slowly, steadily. Eighteen feet down the rocky dirt wall, he stopped on a two-foot-wide stone ledge that had been to the floor of the crevice back when he'd hidden the gold there. Now, looking down, sunlight spilling deeper into the gaping chasm, he still saw no bottom, only a narrowness that sank deep into the hillside, then appeared to gradually close over two hundred feet below.

"Is that the spot?" Burke called down, getting anxious, excited.

"It's the spot," Sam said, standing sidelong at the thinner crevice in the rocky wall. He rooted his arm and shoulder into the wall and pulled four fist-sized rocks one at a time and let them fall behind him. "And here's the gold," he called up to Burke and Black.

Watching intently, the two saw him pull out a large bulging canvas sack, then a second, then a third, pitching each one down onto the ledge at his feet.

"Holy Mother Amanda!" Burke said to Black, his eyes wide. "I have to be honest, Stanley. I didn't believe it would happen."

"Well, it sure enough *has,*" Black said, equally elated at their good fortune. "What do you need us to do for you, Jones?" he called down to Sam.

"Nothing right now . . . stand by," Sam replied up the wall.

He drew his rope up and cut a length of it off with the brass-handled knife from his boot well, leaving plenty of rope length to accomplish what he needed to do.

"What's he doing?" Burke asked Black, both of them staring down as Sam tied the sacks together.

"I don't know, Clyde," Black said, getting a little bit put out with Burke. "You see everything I'm seeing."

"Don't get cross with me, Stanley," Burke warned.

Black ignored him and watched Sam down on the narrow ledge. Sam hefted the length of rope over his shoulder, two bags hanging down his chest and one down his back for balance.

"Get ready up there," he called out to the two faces peering down at him.

"Tell us what you need, Jones," Black replied.

"Take a taut hold on me," Sam said. "I'm going to back off this ledge onto your ropes and let myself fall slowlike, over the other side. Soon as I get there, start hauling me up. I'll be climbing too, to help pull me up."

"Hold up, Jones! I'm getting a bad feeling about this," Burke called down to him.

"You'd better get yourself a *good feeling* about it, Clyde," Sam called back to him. "I'm coming up with the gold, or I'm staying down here with it."

"Don't pay him any mind. We've both got you, Jones," Black called down, reassuring him.

"Tighten up, then," Sam said. "Here I come."

The two drew the ropes tight as Sam let himself step back off the ledge. They watched gravity draw him across the open

202

crevice as Sam held firm on his rope and let it out slowly.

"Why, hell, this ain't nothing," Burke said, seeing things move along nice and easy.

"Don't get cocky on me," Black said. "Be ready to pull him up when he tells us to."

"I'm not being cocky," Burke said sourly. "I could have done the same as he's doing it, now that I see how —"

No sooner had he finished his words than the familiar rumble moved along the hill line under their feet.

"Oh no," said Black. "Not now!"

Sam felt the rumble down in the crevice just as he felt the opposite wall against his back and started to turn around to it.

"Tie me off, fast," he called up to Black and Burke. The two scrambled backward, keeping their weight against the ropes. They took up the slack and wrapped the ropes quickly around the same rocks they were tied to.

"You're tied," Black called down as the ground beneath them trembled a little.

Sam felt the tremor as he turned and stood out against the wall with both feet.

"Keep the slack out," he said. "But haul me up before it gets worse."

The two pulled with all their weight, hand over hand, as Sam climbed hard to keep up with them. Another tremor rippled deep through the hill line. Sam ignored it, continuing to climb. The two gunmen pulled up on their rope for all they were worth. They wrapped the slack around the holding rocks, keeping the ropes taut.

"Uh-oh, here's the big one!" Black said, knowing the feel of the quakes by now, and what to expect. "Don't lose your footing," he shouted at Burke.

"I won't," Burke shouted in reply. "Don't lose yours!" They strained and pulled as a large distant rumble bored along the hill line like a charging locomotive.

Sam climbed hard, as if running up the side of the wall. As the underground rumble grew closer, he felt large tree roots sticking out of the dirt and stone wall. He climbed the roots as if they were some wildly shaped ladders.

Atop the edge, the rumble worsened; both gunmen swayed with their ropes, losing strength and balance. They heard their horses whinnying in fear.

"Hold tight, pull!" Black shouted loudly, the rumble roaring in their ears.

But as the earth jarred and swayed, there was nothing they could do. The earth pitched them aside. They held the ropes, yet they were powerless to pull or even hold the slack tight for a moment.

"He's gone!" Black shouted, noting the weight of their climber had gone slack between them and the crevice edge. As suddenly as the rumble had come upon them, it was gone. The hills gave their familiar shake and settled, then halted with a hard, sudden jar.

Black and Burke looked at each other even as they began to pull frantically on their ropes. But there was nothing on the other end now.

"Jones is dead," Black said in sickened tone. "We lost him."

"Our gold too," Burke said. He turned and leaned against the rock, his rope hanging loose in his hand.

"Hey . . . I'm not dead . . . over here," Sam called out just below the edge of the broken ground.

The two raced to the edge, seeing a dirty scratched-up hand reach over the edge and grasp at the dirt.

"We got you, Jones!" shouted Black, leaping to the edge, Burke right beside him.

The two grabbed Sam, one by his outstretched hand, the other by his forearm and his shoulder. With a long, hard pull they dragged him up, gold sacks and all, over onto the edge. The sacks of gold jingled like bags full of bells when he flattened onto his back on the sack he'd hung behind him.

Sam pushed the two sacks off his chest, Black and Burke helping him. He sat up, coughing and spitting dirt and bits of pine roots from his lips.

"Damn!" said Black. "We thought for sure we'd lost you. The ropes went slack. We couldn't do nothing while the quake was under us."

"I figured . . . as much," Sam said, catching his breath. "I climbed some tree roots . . . held on until it was all over."

Black pulled the sacks of gold off Sam, and he and Burke pulled him to his feet and steadied him for a moment. Burke untied one of the sacks from the other two. He loosened the top of the sack and pulled it open.

"My, my," he said as if in awe. "Look at all these pretty Mexican *monedas.*" He dug a hand down into the bag, raised a palm full of gold coins and let them trickle from his hand. The coins jingled as they fell back into the sack.

"How much do you figure is here?" Black asked. He took the sack from Burke and hefted it in his hand.

But before either Sam or Burke could

answer, a thin tremor moved under their feet.

The three looked at one another. Burke lifted two sacks of gold onto his shoulder. Black held the one Burke had opened.

"More quakes coming?" Black asked Sam.

"I don't know," Sam said. "But let's pick up and get out of here just in case." Even as he spoke, another tremor rippled along deep inside the hill line.

With their rifles, ropes and sacks of gold, the three hurried back along the path behind the boulder. But when they got to the clearing and looked toward the place where they had tied the animals, they found that the horses were gone.

"Oh no!" said Black looking all around, the sack of gold hanging from his right hand. "The quake spooked them. They've broke loose."

Sam and Burke gave each other a look.

"I don't think so, Stanley," Burke said quietly, the two other sacks of gold hanging down from his shoulder.

Sam started to raise his rifle as he looked all around. He saw their horses standing hitched to a pine on the other side of the terrace where someone had moved them to. *Just out of reach,* he told himself. *This is bad.* . . .

From behind the stand of ironwood, Sergeant Bolado stepped out, hatless and dirty, with a thin line of dark dried blood on his forehead. He held Sam's big Colt cocked and aimed in his right hand.

"Well, well, my friends the gringo pistoleros," Bolado said with a tight humorless grin. He eyed the gold. "And look what they have brought for me."

As the sergeant spoke, soldiers in dusty bloodstained uniforms appeared slowly all around the rocky terrace. They stepped from behind rock and brush and formed a half circle around Sam and the other two gunmen. Aside from Bolado, Sam counted seven soldiers, each of them bloodied, bandaged and battered from narrowly escaping Marcos and his rebel army's ambush. Each stood with a rifle in his hands, cocked, poised and ready.

"I vowed I would shoot you with your own gun," the sergeant said, wiggling Sam's bone-handled Colt in his hand. "And look, my vow has been fulfilled."

Sam looked down at himself, examining, spreading his hand a little.

"Funny, I don't *feel* shot," he said.

"Ah, that is a good one, gringo Jones," Bolado said. "You show us all what a brave, bold pistolero you are. But it serves you no purpose. Still you must all die. There is no other way." He gave a slight shrug.

On Sam's right, he heard the jingle of gold coins as Burke and Black dropped the sacks of gold to the ground. The sergeant and his men snapped their eyes toward the sound.

"Begging your pardon, these are heavy," Burke said to both Sam and Bolado.

"Yeah," Black said. "If you two are going to palaver all day . . ."

Sam raised his gaze back up to Bolado, managing to keep his right hand poised near the Army Colt standing holstered on his hip. He wondered if Bolado realized he'd just taken a position — he was ready, and if he'd learned anything about these two gunmen at his side, he knew they were ready too. He didn't have to check, or wonder. When he heard the coins hit the ground, he knew. All he had to do now was make his move. Blood would spill.

But Sergeant Bolado was confident and cool to the point of arrogance. He chuffed and grinned. He raised a finger and wagged it slowly.

"Ah, you gringos, always with the bravado, eh?" He eyed each of them in turn.

Stanley Black stood poised, ready, his expression cold, resolved.

The sergeant cut his eyes to Clyde Burke. Burke stood ready too, wearing the same expression as Black. But as the sergeant looked at him, Burke spat at the ground in his direction.

Bolado gave a short, tight laugh, his eyes taking on an excited glint.

"I have always wished to find myself in such a bold standoff as this," Bolado said seriously. "Killing devil Apache is fun, yes, it is true. But this! This is what a true fighting man wishes for in his life."

"Probably not as much fun as you've built it up to be," Sam said quietly.

All around Bolado, the soldiers held ready, but they were not as eager for action as their sergeant. Sam saw it in their eyes. Fighting the Apache and Marcos' rebels had more than sated any thirst they might have had for blood. Bolado hadn't offered them part of the gold, *huh-uh . . . ,* Sam told himself. The fighting spirit Bolado was counting on wasn't there. Sam was certain of it.

Here goes. . . .

Sam snatched the Army Colt up from the black slim-jim holster. Bolado saw his move and wasted no time making his own. Beside Sam, Black and Burke drew as one. Shots erupted back and forth between the gunmen and the soldiers.

Sam's first shot nailed Bolado a split second ahead of Bolado getting his shot off. Sam's bullet hit Bolado high in the right shoulder, knocking out the sergeant's aim. Sam felt Bolado's bullet zip past his cheek. Another bullet from a soldier's rifle hit the tall-crowned sombrero and knocked it backward off Sam's head. The sombrero hung behind his shoulders by a rawhide hat string.

Sam had to turn from the wounded sergeant and fire at the soldier before another rifle shot came flying his way. Sam's bullet hit the soldier dead center and sent him sprawling backward on the rocky ground. Now other soldiers fired at Sam, avenging one of their own, as Burke and Black fired relentlessly and more soldiers fell to the ground.

Sam swung the smoking Colt back at Bolado and fired as Bolado staggered in place, but raised the bone-handled Colt and got off another round at him. This time Sam's bullet hit Bolado squarely in his chest. Bolado went down with a mist of his lifeblood swirling in the air.

A soldier fell as Sam swung the Colt toward him, Black having nailed the man as he levered another round into his rifle. Burke hit a soldier in his hand; severed fingers flew away in a string of blood. The man fell back among the brush, dropping his rifle, squeezing his hand.

Bullets streaked through the black smoke looming above the terrace, stirring it, reshaping it. Sam saw three soldiers on the ground. He saw others trying to get back to the cover they'd appeared out of, still firing, but taking no close aim. Once inside the cover of rock and brush, Sam noted there was no gunfire coming from them. He'd been right; they'd had enough gun-fighting. They didn't want more — not like this anyway.

Turning toward Black and Burke, Sam waved them toward cover. They moved back beside the boulder but kept firing, keeping the soldiers moving down the trail away from the four horses. After a moment, Sam stopped firing and held the empty Army Colt up beside him, keeping the smoke away from his face.

"They're leaving. Let them go," he said. "Unless they start firing again." As he spoke, he took bullets from the bandolier hanging from his shoulder and reloaded the Colt as he walked toward Bolado lying groaning on the ground. Across the clearing three soldiers lay dead.

"Was it everything you'd hoped it'd be?"

he asked flatly, spinning the loaded Army Colt's cylinder, then cocking the hammer.

"You gringo son of a —" A bloody cough stopped him from finishing his words. The sound of the soldiers' horses raced away on the hill trail.

"Shhh, too late for cussing," Sam said to Sergeant Bolado, hushing him. "Let me ask you something," he said. "Did you think those two would give the gold up without a fight?" He nodded toward Black and Burke.

"*Those* two?" The sergeant looked confused. "What . . . about you?"

"Yeah, what about me . . . ?" Sam said. He brushed the question aside and let out a breath. Holstering the Army Colt, he reached down and picked up his bone-handled Colt from beside the dying sergeant's wrist. "Obliged you brought it back to me," he said, turning his Colt in his hand, inspecting it. He looked back at the sergeant and saw his dead eyes staring up at the sky. Behind him he heard Burke's voice and looked around.

"Stanley, get up. Don't be fooling around," Burke said. "Look, I brought you your horse and everything."

Black stood leaning back atop a rock, his feet spread apart on the ground, supporting him.

"I'm not fooling around, Clyde. I'm shot," he said. "I'm not making it up."

Sam stood and walked over to them, noting Black holding a forearm tight across his stomach. Burke stood holding the reins to their four horses. Seeing the question in Sam's eyes, Burke gave a bewildered shrug.

"Says he's shot, but he won't show me where," Burke said. Sam saw a worried look on his face.

"I don't have to show you, Clyde," Black said. "Take my word for it, I'm shot through, and I'm about gone here." The sacks of gold lay on the ground between his spread boots.

Sam stepped around behind him, saw the gaping exit wound in his lower back and gave Burke a look.

"Can you move your legs if you try?" Sam asked Black.

"Hell no," said Black. "Not unless I want to fall over on my face." He gave a weak grin. "Tell him what you see, Jones," he said.

Sam didn't say, he just stared at Burke and shook his head.

Seeing the look on both their faces, Black reached inside his shirt, took out a pair of wire-rim spectacles and began wiping dust off them. He looked down at the sacks of gold on the ground between his boots.

"We would've had ourselves a hell of a

time with all that," he said with regret. He slid the spectacles onto his face, batted his eyes and stared back and forth. "I meant to try these out months ago."

"Want some water?" Burke asked. "A swig of rye?"

"Nope, I don't want nothing," Black said. "Go on and get out of here. I was standing on my feet the last time you saw me," he said. He looked from Burke to Sam and gave a grin. "I had gold lying at my feet, didn't I . . . ?" His voice trailed away.

Sam only nodded.

"You sure as hell did," Burke said quietly. The two stood in silence as Black's eyes closed slowly. He started to topple sidelong off the rock, but the two caught him and eased him to the ground. They stood a moment longer. Burke reached out and pulled the brim of the straw sombrero down over Black's face.

"As far as no-good sons a' bitches go, you couldn't find one better than Stanley," he said. "If he said he sided with you, he meant it."

"I know," Sam said. "I saw that in him." He stepped away and sat on a rock for a moment, letting Burke clear his mind over Black.

Deep in the hillside another tremor passed underfoot.

CHAPTER 15

A half hour had passed when Sam and Burke rode down along the trail toward the lower slope beneath the rocky hillside. Two of the sacks of gold lay across the dun's rump, tied down to Sam's saddlebags.

The other sack lay atop Burke's saddlebags, flattened as much as possible and tied down in the same manner. Burke led Black's dark-legged chestnut bay beside him on a short lead rope.

"Two men and four horses carrying three sacks of gold Mexican *monedas* — *el oro acuña,*" he added, appearing amazed at their good fortune. "Jesus, Jones . . ." He gave a short laugh. "Who the hell would have ever thought it?" He half turned in his saddle and slapped a hand on the lumpy sack of coins.

Sam only nodded, riding on.

"I'm going to buy me a first-class whorehouse saloon and close it to the general public," Burke said. "I'm getting a bird from one of them islands and teaching it to cuss like a damn fool — teach it to drive nails with its pecker." He cackled like a madman. "They do that, you know?"

"You mean its beak," Sam corrected him.

"Maybe, I don't know." Burke shrugged. "The point is, I've got plans, big plans."

Sam nodded again, searching along the edges of cliffs and gullies.

They rode in silence for a ways, the land beneath them having remained settled for a while.

"Had it been anybody but Stanley, I might have buried him," he said out of the blue.

"Oh?" Sam said, watching the trail ahead of them closely.

"Yeah, digging a grave, saying words over it, all that," he said. "It would have embarrassed the Stanley Black I knew."

"I understand," Sam said. "We wrapped him up good, covered him with rocks. That's better than Bolado got."

"Yeah, the son of a bitch," Burke growled under his breath. They rode on until Burke said, "I wasn't going to cut out No Talk's tongue either," he said. "Just so you know."

"I hear you," Sam said. "I'm glad you didn't, even though he wound up dead all the same."

"Yeah, even though . . . ," Burke said, pondering the matter. "Not that I'm squeamish about that sort of thing."

Sam had given everything some thought ever since the incident with No Talk and Marcos.

"You've got some serious money there, Clyde," he said. "Ever think of getting out of this business altogether?"

"Fact is, I have thought of it," Burke said. "Stanley and me even talked about buying us a plug spread somewhere and hanging up our guns. We were going to see if you were interested too —"

"Hold it," Sam said suddenly, stopping his dun and the white barb midtrail.

On either side of the trail, one of Bolado's soldiers stood up with a rifle pointed down at them from a distance of thirty yards. The other two soldiers who had fled from the gun battle appeared out of nowhere and stood on the trail in front of them. They also held rifles aimed and pointed at Burke and Sam.

"You know why we are here, gringos," said a tall, serious-looking man with a wide black mustache. "Throw down the gold. It is over for you."

"Oh," said Burke. "So you went off and got your nerve up, and decided, who needs

219

the sergeant? You can take this gold —"

"Shut up," the Mexican shouted. He was nervous, ready to fire, Sam could tell.

"Take it easy," Sam said. "*Facil,* eh?" He held his hands chest high. His rifle lay snapped to the saddle ring. His big Colt could handle these two, but the two higher up in the rocks were a different story. "Look," he said, half turning slowly in his saddle. "You can have it."

"Like hell they can," said Burke. "Let them go find their own gold somewhere."

"Let them take it, Clyde," Sam whispered sidelong. "We'll get it back."

But Burke would have none of it.

"No, no, no," he said, staring coldly at the two Mexicans in the middle of the trail. "Either pull them triggers or stick your rifles right up —"

A rifle shot exploded somewhere far up the rocky hillside. Sam, Burke and the two Mexicans in the trail turned their heads quickly in the direction of the shot. As the shot echoed off along the hills, they saw the soldier on their right pitch forward limply, half of his head flying away in a spray of blood, brains and bone matter.

"Holy Missouri!" Burke shouted, he and Sam turning at the same time, back to the two soldiers in front of them. As they turned, another rifle shot exploded high up. The soldier on the other side of the trail fell dead before he realized he'd better take cover.

Sam and Burke fired; both soldiers fell dead in the trail, but not before one got off a wild shot that whizzed past Burke's head and caused him to stare wide-eyed and fire again.

Sam looked at him as the two leaped from their saddles and jerked the horses over to the cover of rock beside the trail.

"Are you all right?" Sam asked.

"Yeah, I'm all right," said Burke. "But what if that had hit me?" He looked at the gold sacks. "I'm going to be more careful —"

"Don't shoot, down there," a voice up high in the rocks said, cutting him off. "It's me, Jarvis Finland — the Montana Kid."

"Jesus, the Montana Kid?" Burke said. He turned and called out up the hillside, "Show yourself, then, before we cut you to chunks up there."

"Ha, from there?" said the voice. "If you could do that, I wouldn't have had to shoot these two for you."

"We were fixing to deal them dirt," Burke said defensively. "Did you hear me say show yourself?"

221

Montana stepped into sight high up in the rocks and spread his hands.

"See? It's me, sure enough," he said. He started stepping down among the rocks. "You are the hardest bastards I ever seen to catch up with. I've been on you since the ruins. All I find is what you've left lying for the birds, much of it unfit to handle."

"You know us, Montana," Burke called out. "We don't stick long once the party's over." He turned to Sam as Montana worked his way down the hillside. "Watch him show up acting like he's got a claim on this gold."

Sam gave him a curious look.

"He was in for a part of it, Clyde," he said. "He just kept two riflemen from getting down our shirts."

"So you're saying cut him back in?" Burke said as if in disbelief.

"That's what I'm saying," Sam replied.

Burke sucked his teeth and shook his head.

"I don't get it," he said. "But I guess I'll go along, good-natured soul that I am. . . ."

Sam raised a finger for the sake of seriousness.

"Listen to me," he said in a grave tone. "Don't say it, then shoot him unexpected."

"Ah, hell, I won't," said Burke, brushing

the matter away with a toss of his hand. "I said I'd go along with it . . . so I will. I just don't understand what makes you think this way."

At the bottom of the trail that led down onto the desert floor, Sam, Clyde Burke and Jarvis Finland sat in the shade of a boulder sipping water from their canteens. Overhead the afternoon sun bore down on the scorched desert hill country like an enemy of old with scores to settle. On a stovepipe cactus a buzzard sat in the heat watching the three, appearing hopeful that one or more of these earth-grounded bipeds might pitch forward dead on the spot.

"I'll tell you, had there been a way to stay and fight, I'd've stayed and kept fighting," said Montana. "I took a bullet graze" — he raised his hat, stuck a finger through a bullet hole in the crown and wiggled it — "got knocked senseless, rolled backward off a rock and landed at my horse's hooves. I took landing there as a sign to *get,* so I *got.*"

As Montana placed his hat back down on his head, Burke reached over and raised it again. He looked at the recent bullet scar along Montana's scalp. Seeming satisfied, he nodded to himself and lowered the hat back into place.

Montana stopped talking and stared at him. Sam watched and listened.

"Where I come from, what you just did comes awful close to calling a man a liar," said Montana.

"I *know how* to call a man a liar," Burke said. "If I thought you was lying, I wouldn't have checked your head."

"Then why did you?" Montana said flatly.

Burke gave a stiff but cordial enough grin.

"Just call it my Missourian nature," he said. "You needed to stop and take a breath anyway."

A silent pause set in while Montana examined the implication of Burke's words.

"Anyhow . . . ," he said finally. "I got on your trail as soon as I could. Thought it would be hard trailing you at first, but then I started following gunfire and buzzards." He gestured toward a buzzard perched on the cactus. "I picked this one up at the *federale* campsite. Gives me the willies, but he's stuck right with me." He shook his head.

Burke listened with a sullen begrudging expression.

"I thought sure the soldiers would hang you," said Montana. "But the rebels showed up and there you went. Couple of times I thought about firing a few shots in the air, see what I drew in. I even wondered how I could get close without you shooting me."

"You found us the best way," Sam said, nodding up the trail where the four soldiers lay dead. "And we are obliged. Right, Clyde?" he added, reminding Burke that Montana was still in on the gold.

"Yeah, obliged," Burke said halfheartedly.

"Think nothing of it," said Montana. "That's what pards do for each other." He gave a thin smile and looked back and forth between the two of them. "So . . . how much do you figure we're splitting up there?" He gestured toward the sacks of gold tied down atop Sam's and Burke's horses.

Sam gave Burke a warning look. He turned to answer Montana, but Burke cut in.

"A bunch," Burke said begrudgingly. He sat staring at Montana, a smoldering look in his eyes.

Montana gazed admiringly at the sacks of gold.

"It sure looks like *a bunch,*" he said. "How much do you figure? Enough to buy myself a —"

"All right, that's enough! Damn it to hell!" Burke shouted, springing to his feet. Montana shot up too. Burke clenched his fist around the butt of his Colt standing holstered on his hip. The Montana Kid followed suit.

Sam rose to his feet slowly, his hand close to the butt of his bone-handled Colt, not on it.

"Easy, now, both of you," he said coolly. "We've all three come through a lot to get here. Now that we've got what we came for, let's not go splattering each other all over the place."

"Damn it, Jones!" Burke said. "It ain't right, him getting a share. He never got captured, bound up like a hog for slaughter!"

"He did the same as any man would do, Clyde," said Sam. "Except for being captured, he's taken every step we've taken. He shot two Mexican soldiers that had the drop on both of us."

"Damn right, I did," Montana threw in. Both gunmen were ready to draw and fire. "Had I known getting a bullet graze threw me out of the game, I would have turned back that night —"

Burke cut him off.

"How do we know the *federales* grazed your head? For all we know you might've —"

"Stop, Clyde," Sam demanded. He backed

226

away a step and laid his hand on his gun butt. "If I hadn't taken us to the gold, we wouldn't be arguing over it right now."

The two turned their eyes to Sam, seeing him entering their dangerous standoff.

"Wait a minute, Jones," said Burke, his voice already losing some of its heat and venom. "Nobody's arguing that you've got the bigger stake in this. Right, Montana?"

"Yeah, right," Montana agreed. He watched warily as Sam spread his feet a little. "All I did was ask how much we've got here. I didn't call down all this thunder."

Sam didn't appear to hear them. As they stared at him, he slowly raised his Colt from its holster, lowered it down his side and cocked it.

"One man takes all," he said. "Ready when you are." He looked back and forth between the two, his eyes cold, his Colt poised and ready in his hand.

"Whoa," said Burke. "You're already drawn and cocked. You took the drop on us."

"It seemed like a smart thing to do," Sam said flatly. "Want me to count to three?"

"Hell, this is crazy. I want no part of it," Montana said. He dropped his hand slowly from his gun butt. "You two settle it." He backed away a step. "I'm out."

Sam turned his cold gaze back to Burke. "One," he said flatly.

"Don't start counting until you holster that shooting iron, Jones," he said. "It ain't fair! And I don't want to kill you anyway."

"Two," said Sam, the same cold, resolved look on his face.

"Damn it! Stop counting, I'm not going to do this," Burke said. "I don't want to fight you, Jones." His hands came up chest high. He backed away beside Montana. "As much as we've been through, we ought to be sided *with* one another, not *against.*"

That had been his point a moment earlier, Sam reminded himself, but it had taken all this to go full circle and come back to it. He relaxed a little, keeping the Colt in his hand. Burke and Montana watched closely for his next move.

"Here's how it's going to be," Sam said coolly. "The three of us are taking an even share of gold, no ifs or buts about it. For safety's sake, we're sticking together until we reach Madson and his men. After that, everybody's free to go their own way." He looked back and forth. "Everybody got that?"

The two nodded. Their hands were away from their guns now. Their thumbs hung hooked over their gun belts.

228

Sam lowered his Colt back into his holster and nodded toward the horses.

"Let's ride," he said. "The sooner we reach Bell Madson, the better. I don't need to tell you that he'd better never learn about this gold coming from Segert's gun deal, or your next gunfight will be with him."

Burke and Montana both eased down, seeing Sam's Colt standing uncocked back in the holster.

"What good's having gold that you can't show around a little?" Burke said.

"You can show it around," Sam said. "Just don't tell him where it come from."

Burke grinned.

"Tell him we robbed a Mexican bank south of Durango." He added proudly, "It was the first Mexican bank I ever robbed — Germans ran it at the time. It's still there, though — gets robbed so often I'm surprised they lock their doors."

"That's our story, then," Sam said.

The three dusted their trouser seats, picked up their canteens, capped them and walked to their horses. Atop the cactus, the big buzzard rose with a powerful batting of wings, swooped up and circled wide overhead. When they'd swung up onto their saddles, Montana gazed up at the soaring scavenger.

"He sticks much longer, I suppose I ought to name him," he said.

Burke chuffed.

"Don't name him after me," he said, the three of them backing their horses, turning them down toward the desert floor.

■ ■ ■ ■ ■

PART 3

■ ■ ■ ■ ■

CHAPTER 16

Shadow River Valley, Mexican badlands

Three weeks had passed when Clyde Burke, Jarvis Finland — the Montana Kid — and the Ranger, impersonating a gunman simply known as Jones, sat their horses abreast on a trail atop a wide limestone ridge cliff. They looked down on a small Mexican town where only moments earlier three gunshots had split the midmorning quietness. A man sat bleeding in the middle of the street below, his hand limp on the ground beside him, yet still holding a gun. Guitar and accordion music spilled from the open doors of a cantina.

"It's a mite early for killing or celebrating either one, wouldn't you say?" the Montana Kid commented.

"Depends on *who* you're killing and *why* you're celebrating," Burke replied matter-of-factly. "If I was down there, I'd likely be celebrating something myself. Music

233

cordial-lizes me something fierce when I'm drunk." He jiggled a bottle of tequila he held resting atop his saddle horn. He'd opened the bottle at the crack of dawn. He and Montana had been nipping steadily at the fiery liquid since then.

Sam looked at the two of them.

"You mean it *affable-ize*s you," Montana said.

"Either one," said Burke. "Maybe both." He paused, then said, "I know what we can celebrate. We can drink to us hiding our cuts of the gold without being seen — or without any of us killing each other." He grinned and held the bottle of tequila over to Montana, who took it and threw back a swallow. The Kid held the bottle toward Sam, but Sam turned it down.

Burke shook his head as Montana passed the half-full bottle back to him.

"It worries me how little you drink, Jones," he said. "I fear it's a sign of oncoming ill health."

Sam didn't reply. He looked down where, along the edge of the street below, four gunmen stood watching as if to see how long the man would sit bleeding in the dirt before he fell over dead. He looked up from the town below and at a wooden sign standing beside them on the edge of the trail.

The sign read in English WELCOME TO LITTLE HELL. In the dirt a faded discarded sign — this one splintered and bullet-riddled — read BIENVENIDO AL ENSOMBREZA EL RÍO.

Welcome to Shadow River, Sam interpreted to himself.

Noting the sign, Burke and Montana cocked their heads sideways to read it.

"Ha," Burke said. "Looks like Madson and his men have been here long enough to bring about some change."

"That doesn't surprise you, does it?" Montana asked as the three turned their horses back onto the trail.

"Nope," said Burke. "I figured he wouldn't waste any time taking this town over once he got settled in."

"I expect if he buys himself enough politicos and *federales,* he can do whatever he wants," said Montana. He grinned. "I'm eager to hear his position on free whores and whiskey."

"I wouldn't get my hopes up for anything being free," Burke said. "Anything he gives free today, he'll take back tomorrow, with interest."

The three followed the winding trail down onto the streets of Little Hell — formerly Shadow River. Entering the town, they rode

235

across a fifty-foot-long iron and wooden bridge spanning a swift river that spilled down from inside the steep hills behind them.

When they'd crossed the bridge and their horses started to step off it onto the dirt street, two riflemen appeared from inside a wooden shack and stood in front of them, stopping them. Two more gunmen appeared behind the riflemen and stood with a hand resting on the butt of their holstered pistols.

"Welcome to Little Hell. That'll be a dollar a head for each horse crossing," said one of the men standing behind the riflemen.

"A *dollar*!" said Burke, instantly outraged. "To cross one damn river?"

"You heard me right," said the same gunman. Sam and Montana sat watching.

"Jesus!" said Burke. "The river must be full of gold."

The gunman stared at Burke coolly with a smirk on his pockmarked face.

"If it was, we'd be squeezing it instead of you," he said. His words drew a muffled chuff from the other three men.

Burke fumed. He stared at Sam, then at Montana, gauging their support. Neither gave him any encouragement. He fished grudgingly in his vest pocket as he spoke.

"You need a sign up, telling folks beforehand," he grumbled.

"Say, now, that's a good idea," the gunman said to the other men who surrounded him. "Why didn't one of you think of that?"

"I did," said one with a jaw crammed full of tobacco. "I just forgot to write it down." Flecks of brown spittle flew from his lips as he spoke. He turned his head sideways and let a stream of spit go to the ground.

Burke eyed the tobacco chewer closely. Sam and Montana paid their toll fees.

"Atzen Allison . . . ?" Burke said, pondering the tobacco chewer. But as the man raised his face a little more and looked at him, Burke nodded. "Hell yes, it is you," he said. He flipped a Mexican silver coin to the gunman with the smirk and the pockmarked face. He faced the tobacco chewer and said, "I heard you got hung for burning out a sheeper in Tejas."

"No Texan ever hung a man for burning sheepers out," said Atzen Allison. He spat again. Recognizing Burke, he said, "Anyways, it was an accident, Clyde. I was trying to cook one of his sheep. The fire got out of hand."

"Clyde, huh?" said the man with the pockmarked face.

"Yep, Clyde Burke," said Burke. "I was riding for Madson and Raymond Segert when you was still learning to squat without soiling your shirttail."

The man with the pockmarked face bristled. He clenched his gun butt. So did Burke, Sam and Montana. The two riflemen clenched their Winchesters. Allison saw the trouble coming and headed it off with a dark chuckle.

"Hell, Jaxton here still has a little trouble not soiling his shirttail," he said jokingly. "Don't you, Junior?"

"Hell no, I don't. I never did," said Jaxton Brooks, the pockmarked gunman. But he cooled down, following Allison's unspoken advice.

"Who're your pals?" Allison asked Burke, eyeing both Sam and the Montana Kid.

"This here is Jones," said Burke, giving a jerk of his head toward Sam, "and this is Jarvis Finland — the Montana Kid. Montana has been with us awhile. You just haven't been here long enough to meet him."

"I've heard of him," said Allison. He looked at Sam. "Heard of this one too," he said. "Rumor is he killed Raymond Segert."

"That's no rumor," Sam put in, wanting to be completely honest about the matter. He had nothing to hide. "It's a plain fact; I killed him." He stared at Allison.

Allison grinned.

"Don't be so bashful about it," he said jokingly. "Once everybody knew he was dead, turns out nobody much liked him anyway." He turned his head sideways and spat. "Right, Junior?" he said to Brooks.

"I never cared much for him," Brooks admitted grudgingly.

"Then I expect I should feel welcome here," Sam said.

"I expect so," said Brooks, still wearing a severe expression.

Sam touched his boots to the dun's sides and put both horses forward at a walk. Burke and Montana rode flanking him on either side across the dirt street toward the cantina. Atop the cantina a young Mexican dove stood on a wooden platform beside a tall well-dressed American. She held a parasol over his head while he smoked a black cigar and stared at the three of them.

"There's Bell Madson," Burke said without looking directly up at the man.

They rode on and then recognized the man they'd seen earlier lying wounded in the dirt. Now he lay flat, his eyes staring up blankly at the burning Mexican sun. The gunmen who had been watching were now back inside the cantina. An old man stood tying the end of a rope around the dead man's foot, the other end tied to a donkey's pack frame, ready to pull the body away.

Stopping out in front of a recently white-washed adobe building, Sam and the other two stepped down from the saddles and hitched their horses to an iron rail. A red-and-green sign on the front of the building read LITTLE HELL CANTINA. Below it hung a smaller sign that read the same words in Spanish: INFIERNO PEQUEÑO CANTINA.

Burke grinned as he stepped onto the boardwalk and walked through the front door.

"Welcome to Little Hell," Burke said under his breath to Sam and Montana. "I feel at home already." As they walked to the bar, he added, "Let's just get some whiskey and relax a spell. I give Madson about five minutes before he sends down for us."

On a newly built platform atop the roof of the Little Hell Cantina, Bell Madson sat behind a wide desk in a tall Spanish *padrón* armchair. Providing shade for the platform, an overhead canvas flapped lazily on a hot wind. Three of Madson's gunmen sat in folding chairs off to one side. A Chinese-Mexican gunman, Jon Ho, stood to Madson's right. A distinguished-looking Mexican in a white linen business suit sat across Madson's desk with a petite glass of wine in his thick hand. The Mexican looked around nervously and attended his sweat-beaded forehead often with a clean white handkerchief.

"What I must make you understand, Señor Madson, is that we are overdue to carry out our plan," he said in well-spoken English. "It is imperative that we strike right away."

Bell Madson relaxed back in his chair and sipped from a glass of bourbon.

"*Overdue* depends on whose calendar you look at," he said. "If I rush in and rob Banco Nacional shorthanded, it won't matter if we're overdue or not. Are your men in Mexico City sure all the big money is there, ready and waiting?"

"They are," said the Mexican, Roberto Deonte. "But they cannot wait much longer. It will look suspicious. These are government officials — they grow nervous."

"They won't be waiting much longer," said Madson. "I just saw some of my men ride in. We'll be in Agua Fría next week. Tell any of your government pals if they don't want to get shot, don't be in the Banco Nacional with money sticking out of

241

their pockets. Does that ease your troubled mind?"

"Ah, Señor Madson, you cannot realize how much it does," he said, sitting back in relief. He blotted his forehead and started to sip his wine. But Madson gave a nod to Jon Ho. The Chinese-Mexican gunman stepped around the desk and expertly removed the glass of wine from Deonte's hand, stood it on the corner of the desk and stared down at him expectantly.

Deonte wilted quickly under the dark flat gaze. He stood up, catching his straw hat before it fell from his knee.

"Yes, then, we are through here, I take it?" he said.

"We're through," said Madson. "Jon Ho is going to escort you down the back stairs to your coach. Will your *federale* escort be able to get you to Agua Fría without the devil Apache eating your brains?"

Deonte's eyes widened.

"*Sí,* I must hope so," he said. He stopped his hand from making the sign of the cross.

"Good, then I won't need to send any of my men tagging alongside you," Madson said. He nodded toward the new wooden stairs leading down the back of the cantina. "Jon Ho, show him out," he said to the Chinese-Mexican gunman.

As soon as Jon Ho and Roberto Deonte disappeared down the rear stairs of the building, Madson turned and spoke to Manning Wilbert, one of the gunmen who sat waiting to do his bidding.

"Manning, go fetch Burke and Finland up here," he said.

"What about that drifter with them?" Manning asked.

"Yeah, bring him too. We need more gunmen — but don't tell them I said that," he added, catching himself. He took the last drink of bourbon and set the empty glass on his desk.

"You got it, boss," said Wilbert, already turning, hurrying down through a newly built stairway to the cantina below.

As Wilbert left, a gunman named Fritz Downes stood up from his folding chair, stepped over to the desk and filled Madson's empty bourbon glass.

"Just so you know, boss," he said quietly, "the third man is the one who killed Raymond Segert."

"I know that," Madson said, eyeing him sharply. "But it's good to see that you're awake." He picked up his fresh glass of bourbon and swirled it in his hand.

The third seated gunman, Clarence

Rhodes, took a deep breath and let it out slowly.

"Boss, I'll ride with whoever you say to ride with," he said. "But I thought highly of Segert. When the time comes, it will make me happy to kill this Jones fellow for you."

"I'll keep that in mind, Rhodes," said Madson. "Since my main reason for being here is to make you happy."

"Boss," Rhodes said quickly, "I didn't mean to —"

"Shut up, Rhodes," said Madson. "I don't care if you kill him. But nobody kills nobody until we get the bank robbed. Understand?" He glared at the belittled gunman.

"Got it, boss," Rhodes said.

The three of them looked over as the sound of boots came up the stairs and onto the roof. They watched Manning Wilbert lead Sam, Burke and Montana over to Madson's desk.

"Clyde Burke and the Montana Kid," said Madson, leaning back in his chair. "I was beginning to think you two were dead. Where've you been?" he asked pointedly.

"Oh, doing a little robbing," said Burke. "Enough to hold us over till we heard from you."

"You can't hear from me if you're not here," Madson said.

244

"That's true," Burke said. "But we're here now, ready to back any play you make." He gestured a nod toward Sam. "This is Jones. He's a damn good man if you need another one."

"Oh . . . ?" Madson stared at Sam appraisingly. "I'm full up with gunmen right now — maybe some other time." He paused for a second, then said to Burke as he stared at Sam, "I know he's good with a gun. He shot and killed my partner. Crazy Ray was as good as they come, gunwise."

"That's right, I killed Raymond Segert," Sam said. "I'd kill any man who had me beaten and dragged on the end of a rope." He stood returning Madson's hard stare. Madson was the first to look away.

After appearing to consider matters, Madson said, "I might need another gunman after all. Jones, why don't you go down and have yourself a drink on me?"

"I didn't come for a free drink, I come for a job," Sam replied firmly.

Madson let out a breath.

"See . . . that was just me being polite, Jones," he said. "What I meant was, haul your ass out of here so we can confab about you behind your back."

Sam looked at Burke.

"Go get you a drink," Burke said quietly.

"We'll be on down shortly."

Sam gave Madson a respectful nod, excusing himself, and turned and walked away.

"He's good, boss," Burke said, as soon as Sam left the roof platform. "We robbed a bank over in Durango —" He chuffed and shook his head. "I can't begin to tell you what all we went through coming back." He looked at Montana.

"It's true, boss," said Montana. "Jones saved our hides a couple of times."

"A brave pistolero, huh?" said Madson.

"And then some," said Burke. "I believe the man would goose a bull rattlesnake if one got in his way."

Madson rolled his cigar in his mouth and glanced at Clarence Rhodes.

"Rhodes has a mad-on over Jones killing Segert. Says he thought highly of Crazy Raymond." Madson added, "Says for two cents he'd shoot Jones down like a dog."

"You thought highly of *Crazy Ray*?" said Burke, he and Montana turning to face Rhodes. "All this time I figured that like everybody else, you couldn't wait to see somebody kill the no-good son of a bitch. Guess I was wrong." He gave a thin, sharp grin. "I'll up your two cents, Rhodes, and throw in an extra dollar to see you take Jones on man-to-man."

Rhodes didn't reply. He just stared sourly at Burke.

"So, you're standing good for Jones?" Madson said.

"That's right, boss," said Burke.

"So am I," said Montana.

Madson drank his bourbon.

"All right," he said finally. "Tell him he's in. We're getting ready to make a big strike next week. If he shows me something, I'll have more work for him after that." He raised a thick finger for emphasis. "But if he messes up . . ." He let his warning trail.

"He won't mess up, boss," said Burke. "We'll be ready to ride when you are."

"Good, see that you are," said Madson. He looked at Montana and nodded toward the door. "Now you go get a drink, let me and Burke talk some. Rhodes, you and Wilbert go with him."

When the three had turned and left, Madson looked at Burke and motioned him to the chair where Deonte had sat.

Burke sat down.

Madson shoved a glass and the bourbon bottle across the top of his desk to him. "Tell me everything you know about your pal Jones," he said.

CHAPTER 17

Clyde Burke raised a glass of bourbon, took a long swig and let out a satisfying hiss. He held the glass in his hand and swished the remaining liquid around as he glanced at the half-full bottle standing atop the desk. Seeing the look in his eyes, Madson reached over and pulled the bottle to his side of the desk. Burke gave a dark chuckle.

"Crazy Raymond had Jones beaten and dragged around the Twisted Hills," he said. "But I suppose you knew all about that."

Madson tossed a hand, relaxed in his tall Spanish armchair.

"Yeah, I knew, more or less," he said with a shrug. "Segert had a mad-on over Jones coming into Agua Fría, taming all the rowdies at the Fair Deal Cantina. Jones came looking for work with us, but he ended up a bouncer for the Fair Deal. He was a little overambitious for my taste, Segert's too." His gaze leveled expectantly.

"That's where the bad blood started between him and Segert," said Burke, trying to stay away from anything about the gun deal Segert had set up with Marcos' rebels. He wasn't sure Madson knew about the rifles, or the gold involved. "Segert had everybody down on Jones. Was down on him myself. But after riding with him awhile, I have to say, he's a man who fears nothing. We had Apache on our tail, *federales* capturing us for no reason at all. Through it all, Jones stayed tough, helped Montana and me get through it. I'd trust him with anything I've got. He won't run out if things get hot."

"I wanted to hear the kind of outlaw he is, Clyde," said Madson. He gave a slight laugh. "I wasn't looking to send him to Texas and run him for office."

"I know," said Burke. "But you asked me, so I told you. I trust him as much as any man you've got swinging a saddle — so does Montana."

"But you haven't mentioned a word about where he's from or who he's ridden with," said Madson.

Burke drank his bourbon and reflected on the matter.

"No, I sure enough haven't," he said. "Jones never says anything about who he rode with. Hasn't said where home is either." He eyed Madson. "But aren't you always saying you want men who know how to keep their mouths shut?"

Madson let out a breath.

"You got me there," he said. Seeing Burke's glass go empty in an upturned gulp, he slid the bottle back across the desk to him.

"Obliged," said Burke, filling his glass and setting the bottle down. He stared at Madson as he took another sip. "If you wanted to hear dirt on the man, I expect you asked the wrong two. Montana and I both vouched for him. What more do you want? I've never vouched for anybody before, have I?"

Madson considered it for a moment.

"No," he said finally, "you haven't. Neither has Montana. Jones killed Raymond Segert, but that worked out well for me. Raymond needed killing. I caught wind of him having his hand in the pot on all kinds of deals." His eyes leveled tight onto Burke's. "I even heard he had a gunrunning business with the peddler woman in Agua Fría."

"You're joking?" said Burke, looking unaware of any such thing going on.

"Yeah, I always joke a lot about somebody beating me out of money," he said with sarcasm.

250

"I know you wasn't joking. I was just surprised hearing it, is all," Burke said. "I knew he was crooked as a snake. But I never figured him and the peddler woman for gunrunning."

"Well, figure it," said Madson. "So, as far as killing Segert goes, I suppose I should thank Jones for it. But still, there're things about the man that bother me."

"I've said as much as I can say for him, boss." Burke gave another shrug, took another sip of bourbon. "What more can I say?"

"Nothing, I suppose," said Madson. "But there is something you can do for me."

"Name it," Burke said. Downing his bourbon, he set the glass on the desk. He had done a good job getting through all this without mentioning the rifles, the gold or the fracas they'd had with the *federales* because of it.

Madson drummed his thick fingers on the top of his desk. Then he stopped and sighed as if having come to a hard decision.

"Here it is, Clyde," he said. "Jones has tried too hard for too long to ride with us. Soon as we're finished with this job, I want you and Montana to kill him." He paused for a second to study Burke's eyes. "I don't trust the son of a bitch, and that's all there

251

is to it."

Burke sat in silence for a moment as a hot breeze licked at the canvas overhead.

"Jesus, boss," he said quietly. "Jones is my pal, Montana's too."

"So?" said Madson. "Haven't you ever killed a *pal*? It's no different than killing a stranger, except they're more surprised, more apt to beg you not to." He gave a cruel grin.

Burke just stared at him.

"If I say no to doing it? Where does that put things between us?" he asked.

"It puts us where we are now," said Madson. He tapped a thick finger on the side of his head. "Except I'm going to always remember asking you and Montana to do something for me and you turned me down."

"And what about Jones?" Burke asked.

"He'll still die, you can count on it," said Madson casually. "Rhodes wants to kill him. Him and Wilbert will do it." He paused, then added, "They'll do it slower and make it more painful. But Jones has a seat at my table. He's dead no matter who kills him. I figured him being a *pal,* you and Montana might make it easier on him."

"Damn, I need to do some serious thinking," Burke said. "If I do it, and I'm not saying I will, I don't know if I'd tell Montana until afterward. He might not stand still for it."

"He'll stand still for it, or I'll kill him too," said Madson. "But you decide whether or not to bring him in on it."

"I never thought I'd be considering killing Jones," Burke said. He shook his head in regret.

"Take your time, Clyde," Madson said softly. "I don't want to push you into anything." As he spoke, he reached out and slid the bottle of bourbon back across the desk to Burke. "Have another drink before you give me your answer."

Sam and the Montana Kid made a camp on the outskirts of Shadow River at the swift water's edge. While they waited for Burke to join them, they spent the afternoon graining, watering and grooming their trail-weary horses. Afterward they bathed, washed their trail clothes and groomed themselves. As their clothes dried on a rack made of cottonwood limbs standing near the fire, they sat with blankets around their waists, cleaning their firearms.

When they'd finished cleaning their guns, they put their clean clothes on damp. They ate warmed jerked goat meat and beans they'd cooked in a small pot atop the open flames. They sat in the broken shade of a weathered *acedera* tree as the sun stood low on the red western sky. When a lone coyote appeared slinking on the desert skyline against the falling sunlight, Montana looked at the remaining beans turning cold in the pot. He rubbed his palms on his knees.

"A few more minutes if he's not shown, those beans are gone," he said.

Sam didn't reply. He sipped coffee from a tin cup and imagined what Burke and Madson might talk about so long.

A few minutes later, Burke's horse clopped along the hard-surfaced trail at a walk, from the direction of town. Sam and Montana saw Burke slumped low and swaying in his saddle. When the horse walked on without stopping or turning off the trail toward the camp, Montana trotted out and led the animal in by its bridle.

"Drunk?" Sam asked quietly, standing as Montana brought horse and rider to a halt across the campfire from him.

"Smells like it," said Montana. "Else he's died and refused to fall."

Sam stepped around the campfire and helped Montana lower Burke from his saddle.

"Get the back end of the house raised,"

254

Burke shouted, thick-tongued and mindless, the two holding him up between them.

"Yep, he's drunk himself slack-jawed blind," said Montana.

The two sat Burke down a safe distance from the fire lest he toppled face-forward into it. Montana stood over him, a hand on Burke's limp shoulder, while Sam pulled the saddle from atop the tired horse, brought it over and dropped it on the ground behind the drunken gunman's back. Two bottles clanked together in Burke's saddlebags.

Montana turned loose of Burke's shoulder and gave him the slightest nudge. Burke collapsed backward, his mouth agape toward the grainy purple sky. His hat pitched backward off his head.

"He's not going to want those beans," Montana said. He reached a finger down under Burke's chin and lifted his mouth shut.

Sam dropped Burke's hat over his face. While he unrolled the blanket from behind Burke's saddle, Montana ate the cold beans out of the pot from the flat side of his boot knife.

"I've seen him drunk enough he couldn't scratch one ear with both hands — but never like this," he said, chewing the cold beans.

Sam flipped the dusty blanket out and up with both hands and let it settle down over the passed-out gunman. He slipped Burke's gun from his holster and shoved it behind his saddle under the edge of his saddlebags to keep it from getting rolled in the dirt.

"Well," said Montana, "I've got his horse." He set the empty pot down and rubbed his knife blade back and forth across the sandy ground. "I'd hate to be wearing his head come morning." He turned and led Burke's horse over to the water's edge to let it drink its fill.

Sam cleaned up around the low, glowing fire, scraped the bean pot clean and washed it out with a few drops of canteen water. He slung the pot dry and put it away.

When Montana led Burke's watered horse away from the river's edge to grain it and wipe it down beside the other horses, Sam started to rub out the glowing embers of the campfire with his boot. But before he did, he turned as Burke mumbled in his sleep.

"Jones? *Jones . . . ?*" Burke said, mouthing the name from within his drunken stupor. His hat had fallen from over his face.

Sam turned and stepped over to him. But

he saw that Burke was still knocked out, only rattling some senseless whiskey litany. Sam picked up his hat, started to place it back over his face.

"I don't like sneaking, boss . . . ," Burke mumbled under his whiskey-sodden breath. "Don't like it. . . ." He shook his head.

Sam stopped and listened. He watched Burke wrestle with something dark and troubling, even in his drunken mind.

"All right. *All right* . . . ," he argued. "Didn't I say I would, damn it?"

Instead of laying the sweat-stained hat back over Burke's face, Sam dropped it on the ground beside him. Seeing Montana walk back from the horses, Sam walked over to the glowing firebed. But Burke fell silent.

"What's he mumbling about?" Montana asked. "I heard him all the way over there."

"Nothing," Sam said, "just whiskey-drunk. Let's get some shut-eye." He reached his boot out and dragged the embers back and forth until they died and the camp darkened beneath a wide starlit sky.

Late into the night, Montana sat up, awakened by Burke's snoring and the replying yelping howl of a curious coyote. Looking all around blurry-eyed, he saw the silhouette of Sam against the sky, keeping watch on a clustered group of red eyes moving back and forth, blinking in the direction of the darkened camp.

"Coyotes?" Montana whispered, easing over close to Sam in a crouch, his rifle poised in his hands.

"Yeah, most likely," Sam whispered back to him.

A long rattling snore rose from Burke's bedroll, followed by mumbling, drunken mindless jabber.

"Is this drunken fool bringing wildlife in on us?" Montana asked, gazing at Burke's outline lying stretched out in the dirt.

"They hear him," Sam said. "But his snoring isn't bringing them in. They're drawn more by scent than sound."

"If they draw from scent, they must think somebody broke a keg of whiskey and left it," Montana whispered.

"The thing is," Sam said, "if coyotes are hearing him, so will anybody else happening by." Standing up in a crouch beside Montana, he moved toward the snoring, mumbling Burke, Montana right beside him. They stopped over Burke. Sam raised the passed-out gunman's hat two feet and dropped it back down over his face.

Burke puffed a breath in and out and groaned. The drunken snoring fell silent.

"That won't stop him for long," said Montana. No sooner had he said it than Burke let out a long gurgling snore.

"Think if we knocked him out with a rifle butt?" Montana said, only half joking.

"Go on back to sleep," Sam whispered in reply, ignoring Montana's suggestion. "I'll sit here for a spell and keep him quiet."

"I'll sit and help," Montana offered.

"Go on to sleep," Sam said. "I'm all right here. Anyway, it'll be coming up daylight in a couple more hours."

"Obliged, I'll owe you one," said Montana. He moved back over to his blanket, wrapped it over himself and went back to sleep.

A few minutes later when Burke began to snore again, Sam gave him a sharp nudge, quieting him. In another moment a familiar rumble moved along under the desert floor. Sam waited in anticipation, but the tremor seemed to have dissipated and stopped.

"Good enough . . . ," he whispered to himself. In front of him, the red eyes had appeared to freeze for a moment in the wake of the tremor. Yet, as he sat in silence, he soon watched the red eyes play in and out of sight along the desert floor. He knew the younger coyotes among the pack were curious about the shadowy sight of him, about his scent, the scent of man and horse, and all the accompanying scents that man brought along with him.

Using the coyotes as a warning system, he watched them as he relaxed, resting without sleep. But after a while, when he saw the pack suddenly break up and disappear, he stretched out on the ground, rifle in hand, and stared and listened out into the silent desert night.

He waited and waited, relying strictly on the coyotes' behavior. Had they simply decided it was time to go on, they would have drifted away slower, one and two at a time. But they weren't walking away, they were fleeing, he told himself. Nothing made creatures of the wild flee like the coming of man.

And there they were.

He saw the silhouettes of horses and riders emerge against the sky, cross the crest of low sand and submerge once more back down into the lower puddle of blackness. He counted eight, six of them riding single file, two riding abreast, thirty yards out. Indians, white men? Mexicans . . . ? He had no idea. They had risen and fallen steadily, none of them clearly enough to be identified by horse, hat or clothing.

He lay flat and still, gauging by the speed of their passing how far they were. He continued listening closely, his finger on the trigger of his cocked rifle, hoping that Burke, Montana and their horses stayed as quiet as stone until whoever was out there had long gone on their way.

As motionless as a dead man, he held his lone vigil across the roll and the sweep of the sandy terrain, of stone and upreaching cactus. He remained in place even as a dim wreath of light swathed the land and mantled the eastern hill line gray-gold on the far edge of vision.

Behind him, Montana rose just before dawn and ventured forward, rifle in hand.

"Jones?" he said quietly. "Are you all right there?" He remained as crouched as he'd been earlier.

The silence broken, Sam looked back over his shoulder and let the hammer down on his Winchester.

"I'm all right," Sam replied quietly. "We nearly had some company. The coyotes warned me." He pushed himself to his feet and dusted the front of himself. "Stay back twenty feet and keep me covered," he added. "Let's go out and see what they're riding."

"I've got you," Montana said. "I'll wake this drunken sot up too, if I can."

As Sam walked out across the sand,

Montana stepped over and shook Burke by his shoulder.

"I'm awake," Burke said after Montana's third hand shake. "Jesus, who hit me?"

"Nobody hit you," said Montana. "Wake up. Somebody rode by. Jones is gone out to see who's out there. We need to lag back and keep him covered."

"Aw, man, Montana," Burke groaned, sitting up, holding his throbbing, hammering head with one hand while he fished for the bottle in his saddlebags with his other.

"Get it done, Clyde," Montana said. "He might walk himself right into a gun battle."

"I'm coming," said Burke. He stared at the half bottle of bourbon with a confused look on his face. Finally he shook his head and took a long swig, the conversation with Madson coming back to him. "I made a bad mistake," he said.

"Come on, tell me later," said Montana. "Jones needs backing."

Burke staggered to his feet, jerked his Colt from its place under the edge of the saddlebags and hurried staggering along behind Montana.

They walked forward warily until they saw Sam wave them toward him. When they reached him, he had stooped down over the tracks of unshod horses.

"Apache," he said quietly. "The tremors must've sent them down here. Ordinarily they stay up where it's easier to leave no hoofprints."

Burke looked back toward the camp, seeing the horses in the grainy rising light of the desert.

"Jesus, I was knocked-out drunk," he said. " 'Paches riding this close?"

"Don't worry, Clyde," Sam said. "I had you covered."

Burke gave the two of them a hangdog look.

"Obliged, again, to you, Jones," he said.

Sam saw a dark expression pass across Burke's drunken, bloodshot eyes. *What is it? Remorse, shame?* He wasn't sure, Sam told himself. But he was sure it had to do with meeting with Bell Madson. He watched Burke look away, avoiding both his and Montana's eyes as the hungover gunman pushed his hair back from his face.

"Let's get some coffee and goat meat in our bellies," said Sam, pushing the matter aside, rather than tipping Burke that he saw what was at work here. "We've got a long ride to Agua Fría."

"I'm wondering," said Burke, "do we need to be robbing something this soon? We've all three got gold laid up. Why are we doing this? We could be off celebrating."

"I've never heard you talk this way before a robbery, Clyde," said Montana. "Did you fall off your saddle and hit your head?"

"Naw, damn it, Montana," Burke said, catching himself, looking away again. "I was just wondering, is all." He shrugged.

"Well, don't wonder on an empty belly," said Montana. "It's the worst thing a man can do."

CHAPTER 18

At daylight the three drank coffee boiled over a low smokeless fire and ate more goat meat, this time with hardtack from the supplies. Sam and Montana kept a watchful eye on the rolling desert floor in the direction of the unshod horses. Burke sat near the fire, blanket-wrapped but still shivering, his arms hugging around his drawn knees. He drank his coffee laced heavily with rye whiskey to still the drumbeat in his head and the feel of snakes and squirrels fighting in his belly.

"How'd your palavering go with Madson?" Montana asked.

Burke shook his bowed head and cut his bloodshot eyes to Montana and Sam.

"I wish you hadn't asked," he said in a shaky voice. He sipped the strong hot liquid and lowered his head again.

Sam and Montana looked at each other.

"Yeah, but I did ask," Montana pressed.

"So, how did it go? I see there was no short-age of beverage on hand." With a thin smile, he continued tormenting the suffering gun-man. "Did he get you drunk and take advantage? Because if he did . . ."

"What — ? Hell no," said Burke, jumpy and shaking. "I mean, yeah, sure we drank us some of his fine bourbon. He told me all about the robbery, our jobs and all." He paused, then let out a breath and said to Sam, "Look, Jones, you're not going to like it — neither did I. But Madson's got you relaying fresh horses for us."

The three fell silent. Sam sipped his cof-fee, deciding how to best respond to Burke's words. Finally Montana ventured a com-ment.

"Did he say why he's doing that?" he asked as if outraged. "Did you tell him what a good man Jones is?"

"Hell, of course I told him about Jones," Burke said. "He said just because you and I know Jones is a good hand doesn't mean that he does." Burke shrugged. "I couldn't very well tell him about Jones without spill-ing what we were up to out there, now, could I?" he posed, getting irritated and red-faced.

Montana considered it, realizing Burke was right.

"Damn it, this stinks like rotten fish!" he said. "If Jones is staking our horses, then so am I." He finished his coffee and slung the grounds from his tin cup.

Burke swung his bowed aching head back and forth slowly, his rye-laced coffee steaming in his hand.

"Jones, Montana's right. This is a stinking deal for you. I wouldn't blame you if you rolled up and rode off. Maybe we'd meet you down the trail and stick back together someplace." He turned his bloodshot eyes to Sam, but only managed to look him in the face for a second. He looked away.

Sam sipped his coffee and took a deep breath.

"What is the big job?" he asked.

"He never said," Burke replied. "But if it's in Agua Fría, there's nothing worth robbing there except Banco Nacional."

"Banco Nacional de Méjico," Montana said. He gave a short grin. "I knew somebody would rob it someday. I never thought I'd be a part of it."

Sam, watching and listening, realized that robbing the bank would draw *federales* on the outlaws' trail immediately. He needed a way to keep himself in the game without appearing too humiliated by being the relay man for fresh horses.

"In that case, my job providing horses is a whole bigger thing than it sounded like at first," he said.

The two snapped their eyes to him.

"You mean you're all right with doing it?" Montana asked, sounding surprised.

Burke looked almost disappointed.

"Don't do it, Jones," he said. "Leave this one alone. Meet us later on, like I just said. I'll even share a piece of my cut with you."

Montana looked stunned at hearing Burke offer a part of his share of the robbery.

"Man! You really did fall on your head last night," he said.

"I'm just trying to do what I figure is right for all of us," he said. He looked at Sam. "You're not going to take the lowest rung on the ladder and work for chicken feed. Ain't I right?"

"Huh-uh, you're wrong, Clyde. I'll do it — but just this once," Sam said, turning down Burke's offer for part of his cut. He gave a shrug. "We've got to look at it from Madson's point, a big job, he's never ridden with me. Who says he's supposed to trust me right from the get-go?"

"But we both vouched for you," Montana said.

"Obliged," Sam said, "but maybe you shouldn't have." He stood and slung the

268

grounds from his empty cup.

"That's a hell of a thing to say," Montana replied. "We faced bears, soldiers, Apache, earthquakes and landslides —"

"And Bell Madson knows none of that," Sam said, cutting Montana short. "Let's not start all over on this," he said. He looked at Burke. He had to ask himself why Burke would offer a part of his cut for him to ride away now and meet up after the robbery. He didn't like the only answer he could come up with. "Madson wants a horseman, I'm his man," Sam added. "How many horses and where does he want them?"

"There's a man named Ace Turpin runs a horse spread near Fuego Pequeño — we'll go there with you, then split up," Burke said. He drew a small pouch of gold coins from inside his shirt and pitched it to Sam. "He'll have seven horses strung and waiting," he added, his hangover seeming to be under better control. "Take them just off the trail below Mesa Rocoso, twenty miles from Agua Fría. There's a cave there at the base of the mesa. Be waiting for us, ready to switch horses."

Having caught the pouch of coins, Sam hefted it on his palm. They felt light, different; they made a dull sound.

"Anything else?" he asked. As he inquired,

he opened the drawstring on the pouch.

"One thing," said Burke, "because of the size of this job, you need to kill Turpin. Madson wants nobody alive who might have his name on their tongue."

Sam shook the contents of the pouch out onto his palm and saw it wasn't gold at all, only iron screw washers.

"I told him you'd have no qualms doing that," Burke said.

Sam just looked at him, scooping the washers back into the pouch.

"Madson said the only men he's known of you killing is outlaws, Raymond Segert and his own men," Burke continued. "Said killing Turpin would say something for you, gain his trust, so to speak."

"Save your breath, Clyde. I understand," Sam said quietly. "I'll do it." He drew the string on the pouch and put it away inside his shirt.

"You *will*?" Burke looked surprised.

The three stood and dusted the seats of their trousers. Burke finished the whiskey-laced coffee in a gulp while Sam and Montana put out the fire with their boots.

"What'd I say?" said Sam. He started toward the horses. "How far to Fuego Pequeño?"

"Three days on the sand flats," said Montana. "More on the hill trails."

"Let's pull up and get riding, then," Sam said. "I've got relay horses to gather."

Fuego Pequeño (Little Fire)
Three days later
At seventy-five feet, Sam, Burke and the Montana Kid spread out abreast facing the adobe and weathered plank shack standing at the end of a sandy narrow path. The trail wound through a sand lot strewn with pale clump grass, prickly pear, cholla and nopal cactus, all of it presided over by a small herd of lank and wandering Mexican cattle. Beside the shack stood a corral; inside stood a string of horses tied to the gatepost. At the gate stood a man holding a shotgun, a black beard hanging on to his chest. He straightened at the sight of the three riders.

"We'll ride on in with you, Jones," Burke offered.

"Why?" Sam fired back sharply. "Do I look like a newcomer at this?"

"No," said Burke. "I was just offering. Looks like Ace Turpin is sporting a shotgun." Instead of nudging his horse forward as he'd planned, he drew up and sat staring straight ahead.

"Means nothing to me," Sam said, keeping his voice hard. "You can wait here and still see all you want to see." He put his dun forward at a walk. Montana moved his horse over beside Burke, leading the white barb supply horse beside him. The two sat watching.

"How many times you say Jones'll shoot him?" Montana said, staring straight ahead, squinting against the sun's glare.

Burke considered it.

"Three times at least," he said. "I figure he won't take a chance with that shotgun staring at him."

"Huh-uh, one shot is all, I figure," said Montana. He raised his voice for Sam to hear. "I've come to know Jones as a fragile sort. He'd not waste three bullets when one will do the job, shotgun or no."

Sam looked back over his shoulder and rode on. He wasn't going to kill this Ace Turpin. He'd already decided that much, he reminded himself. His plan was to lure Turpin out of sight, knock him in the head, fire a shot in the ground and get the horses out of there before the man regained consciousness.

Simple enough, he told himself. Yet he began seeing a snag in his plan as soon as he got within twenty feet of the man and recognized the moon face hidden beneath the long black beard. He didn't recognize him by the name of Ace Turpin. He knew the man as Henry Tabbs, a man he had escorted to Yuma Prison a year ago. As soon as the bearded face looked familiar to him, he ducked the brim of his sombrero enough to keep his face partly hidden.

"Are you Madson's horse man?" the bearded man asked. He held the shotgun in a way that it could be easily raised and fired at a split second's notice.

"I am," Sam said. Keeping his sombrero brim low, he swung down from the saddle and walked forward. This didn't change anything, he told himself. He only had to keep his face shielded a little in the black shade of his sombrero and go on with his plan. "I see you've got the horses ready and waiting," he added, walking along the corral fence, checking the animals as he went.

"I don't fool around," the man said with a straight harsh grin that showed Sam a familiar gap left by a missing front tooth.

Yep, Henry Tabb. . . . Sam walked back, stepped inside the corral gate and continued looking the horses over. They were fine, strong animals, no question about it. He raised a hoof on a silver-gray, checked it, set it down — lifted the lip on a big roan, checked the wear on its teeth, then rubbed its muzzle and went on.

"What's your name, mister?" Henry Tabbs asked, following along beside him.

"No offense," Sam said quietly. "I don't use one on a deal like this." He reached inside his shirt, pulled out the pouch of phony coins and held it up for the man to see. "Here's all you'll need to know. I'm the man who brought you this gold."

Henry Tabbs, aka Ace Turpin, grinned again.

"At least we're speaking the same language, amigo," he said. He started to reach for the coin pouch, but Sam expertly moved it away from him and kept it close to his chest as he stepped away, inspecting the horses some more.

The bearded man stood watch, giving Sam a curious look as if pondering something familiar about him. The sound of his voice? He wasn't sure.

"Have I seen you before?" he asked.

"Not that I can recall," Sam said. He turned back to the man, needing to get this done before Tabbs' memory caught up to him. Gesturing a nod toward the rear of the shack, he said, "Let's get in some shade while you count this." He held the pouch back up for the man to see.

"Sounds good to me," said Tabbs. He turned around to walk, but only took a step before he stopped and froze. "Damn it, I know you!" he said, already turning back to Sam, the shotgun coming up into play. Sam heard it cock. "You're that damn Ranger from Nogales!"

This changed everything. Sam's Colt was up and cocked. It caught Tabbs as he turned. Sam's bullet nailed the man dead center in his forehead and sent him spilling backward onto the dirt. A bloody mist settled on him. The string of horses stirred, wanting to bolt, but only for a second. Sam stepped over to them, his Colt smoking in his hand. He rubbed the first horse's muzzle, patted down its withers. He settled the skittish animal and, with it, the rest of the string.

This wasn't what he'd wanted at all, he thought, looking over at Henry Tabbs. But this was how the hand had played itself out. He couldn't let the man turn and kill him. *No, sir. . . .*

Seeing Sam shoot the bearded man, Burke and Montana rode forward quickly and slid their horses to a halt outside the corral. They stretched up in their stirrups and looked over the corral fence at the body lying dead in the dirt. Sam walked out of the corral, replacing his spent cartridge and slipping the bone-handled Colt into its holster.

"You were right, Jones," Burke said. "You're no newcomer. We both saw you kill him faster than a cat can scratch its behind."

"Is that what you'll tell Madson?" Sam said stiffly. He stepped up atop the dun and turned it to the corral gate.

Montana and Burke — neither one answered. They watched as Sam stepped the dun inside the corral, untied the string and led the horses out. He stopped in front of the two gunmen.

Montana stepped his horse and the barb forward.

"You'll be needing these supplies more than we will," he said. He handed Sam the barb's lead rope. Sam held it with the other lead rope.

"Obliged," said Sam. He sat gazing coolly at Burke, seeing the same troubled look in his eyes he'd seen ever since Burke had returned mindless and drunk from Shadow River. Burke was sober three days now — still the look was there, Sam noted. "Anything we need to talk about before we split up?" he asked Burke.

Burke returned his gaze, keeping himself steady, not revealing a thing.

"No. We've done all the talking we need

to," he said with a note of resolve in his voice. "We'll be seeing you at Mesa Rocoso."

"Then Rocky Mesa it is," Sam said, translating the name. He touched the brim of his sombrero toward Burke, then toward the Montana Kid.

As he nudged his dun forward, leading the barb and the seven-horse relay string, Montana called out, "Jones," getting his attention.

Sam looked around.

"I won a five-dollar piece on you," Montana said.

"Yeah, how's that?" Sam said.

"I bet Clyde here you'd kill Ace Turpin with one shot." He chuckled. "Ain't that a hoot?"

"Yeah," Sam said, pushing forward, "that's a hoot sure enough."

CHAPTER 19

Mesa Rocoso
Mexican Desert badlands

Leading seven fresh horses and the white-speckled barb, Sam approached the wide mesa on a narrow meandering trail that bore no sign of recent hoof prints. In their place, looking down, he saw a laden bed of coyote tracks trafficking back and forth and straying out into the rock across the mesa's rocky sloping base. When he spotted a black hole on a high wall above him, he rode upward toward it with his rifle lying ready across his lap.

In moments he led the horses onto a flat clearing that appeared to have been leveled and laid out just for this purpose — to shelter and hide him and the horse string, and to offer a long wide view of the desert floor below. As he surveyed the mesa and the terrain surrounding it, he searched any path or trail leading up off the desert floor, knowing that horses drew Apache as a magnet draws iron shavings.

This will do, he told himself, gazing off in the direction of Agua Fría. Sometime tomorrow Madson and his men would arrive hell-bent along the main trail below. He would see their dust for miles. He would hear their gunshots if any *federales* had gotten close enough on their trail when they'd ridden away carrying sacks of Mexican gold.

But all of that remained to be seen, he told himself, nudging the dun forward toward the black cave entrance, leading the horse string and the supply barb behind him. What he did not want to do was get himself caught or killed by *federales* in his attempt at supplying fresh horses to a gang of bank robbers. Working undercover or not, that would be a hard situation for Ranger Captain Morgan Yates back in Nogales to explain to the U.S. consulate in Matamoros.

He had taken his participation in this as far as he could. Stepping any further would be crossing some serious legal lines. There was no question he wanted Madson dead. Just as badly, he wanted Jon Ho dead, and this gang of thieves and gunmen broken up. But it had to be done coolly and it had to be done right, he reminded himself, stopping the horse out in front of the cave entrance and looking back on the lower trail behind him, seeing the hoofprints of his horses leading down the slope toward the desert floor.

So get started, he said to himself.

Swinging down from his saddle, he led the horses to a standing spur of rock, tied one end of the string there, spread the horses out and tied the other end around a waist-high rock near the cave entrance. He took a small lantern from the supplies atop the barb and carried it with him inside the cave.

Once inside the narrow black opening, he stopped long enough to light the lantern with a sulfur match and hold it up, revealing a wide floor in a clearing a few feet in front of him. Somewhere in there among the cavern's rocky perimeter, the warning rattle of a snake rose and fell as the lantern light probed into its domain.

"Easy, big boy, I'm not here to eat you," Sam whispered to the snake.

Rifle in hand, he walked forward in time to see the snake slide silently out of sight farther back into the rocky interior. In the loose fine dust on the cavern floor, he saw more coyote prints everywhere. Across the floor, he saw half of a human skeleton still

280

partly clothed in thin crumbling rags. A few feet away, he saw a loose leg bone. A few feet farther on, a battered miner's boot lay on its side. Sam saw a lizard dart into it. He stood for a moment longer, then turned and walked back out into the afternoon light.

He took his battered telescope from the supplies atop the barb and walked to a rock that stood as high as his chest. He stretched the telescope out and rested on his elbows, scanning the desert floor as far out as the afternoon sunlight would allow. *Nothing,* he told himself. He scanned closer, clearly seeing the hoofprints his horses had left along the edge of the sand flats to the unwinding mesa trail. He looked left and right for any sign of rising trail dust, but he saw none. Letting out a breath, he laid the telescope down atop the rock for later, then turned and walked back to the horses.

From atop the supply horse, he took down some kindling he'd gathered on his way to Rocky Mesa. He laid out the kindling for a firebed and gathered dried scrub branches and piled them atop it. Searching all around the sloping terrain, he found a downed, weathered pine and dragged its brittle carcass back and broke it up as much as he could and banked it atop the brush and kindling.

He walked back to the rock and picked up the telescope and looked out again. The depth of vision had grown clearer with the lowering of the afternoon sun, yet the lower edges of the distant hill line still wavered and hid in the dissipating veil of heat. He scanned in every direction, the same as he had earlier.

Still nothing. He closed the telescope and carried it under his arm. He looked at the horses, then at the fire waiting to be lit, then at the long afternoon shadows stretching out from Rocky Mesa onto the desert floor.

"Time for some coffee," he said aloud to himself, "maybe a little goat meat."

Turning to the waiting fire site, he lit the kindling deep under the brush and downfall pine and let the fire feed and grow. He put a small pot of coffee on to boil and stood a stick of impaled goat meat to sizzle in the flames. While he waited for his evening meal, he walked to the horses, took a few meager supplies from atop the barb and filled his saddlebags behind the dun's saddle.

Early darkness began turning purple as the coffee boiled and the jerked goat meat sizzled on the stick. After he'd finished his food and coffee, he lit a small lantern he'd taken from his supplies and carried it inside the cave. He set the glowing candle to one rocky side of the clearing and walked back out.

Out front he looked at the black cave entrance, seeing the glow of light begging to be investigated. Then he walked to the fire and piled on thick layers of loose brush he'd gathered. He watched the dried tinder flare and crackle and send sparks spiraling and racing skyward on the growing darkness. Beneath his feet came the familiar rumbling deep in the earth. He steadied himself in place, took a breath and looked out onto the darkening desert floor below.

When the deep rumble jarred to a halt, he settled the horses and rubbed the barb's muzzle as if saying good-bye to a friend. Then, rifle in hand, he took the dun's reins and led the horse up onto a path across a narrow stone shelf and let the deep crevices and steep-cut walls of Rocky Mesa swallow them up.

Agua Fría, Mexican badland hills
The Banco Nacional de Méjico, a sprawling whitewashed adobe, stone and timber building, stood at the end of Agua Fría's main tiled street. At that point, the street divided into two lesser-width streets and went around the powerful bank. On a six-foot-

high stone terrace out in front of the bank, two large field cannons sat staring out at the town as if in warning. A long stone ramp ran twenty feet wide from street level up the terrace, to the bank's elaborately colored tile porch. Along the front of the wide porch stood thirty feet of iron hitch rail.

"She is a fat pretty thing," Montana said to Dan Crelo and Clyde Burke, standing beside Crelo outside a large open-front cantina two blocks from the bank. Burke leaned deep against a streetlamp pole, quiet and sullen, his thumbs hooked behind his gun belt.

"Yeah," said Dan Crelo. "She's fat and pretty. . . ." He checked his watch quickly, snapped it shut and stuck it down into his vest pocket. "If fat and pretty is most generally your style, that is. But it ain't mine." He made sure the gold watch fob hung just right below his vest pocket.

The Montana Kid looked at him curiously.

"I'm just saying," Crelo said. He looked back and forth uneasily beneath the brim of a straw skimmer hat. "I myself prefer a slim neat little place with piles of cash — no cannons staring up my backside on my way out of town. But that's just me."

Burke mumbled something dark and

284

inaudible under his breath, and looked back down the street at the bank. He and Montana wore the same dusty trail clothes they'd been wearing since leaving Sam at Fuego Pequeño.

Dan Crelo wore a clean white linen suit and a black ribbon-style bow tie beneath a soiled white canvas riding duster. He wore black tooled Mexican riding boots that stood up to his knees, his trouser legs tucked inside the wells. He carried a folded Mexican newspaper up under his arm, for show, being barely able to read English, let alone Spanish.

"Maybe I need to skin away from the two of yas, get on down the square," he said to Burke and Montana. He clutched a lapel of his suit coat behind his duster. "It don't make a lot of sense — an important-looking rooster like me, consorting with . . . Well, can I say *men like yourselves*?" He smiled. A gold-capped tooth glinted in the morning sunlight.

"Go bite a dog turd, Crelo," said Burke without looking around at the well-dressed gunman. "Last man I saw dressed like you tried to stick a hand in my blanket."

Crelo stiffened and bristled.

"Why, you — !" he snarled, his teeth clenched, his hand instinctively jerking back the left side on his duster.

"Whoa! Easy, now!" said Montana. He half stepped in between the two, Crelo ready to draw a big nickel-plated Smith & Wesson from a cross-draw holster. "Jesus, Dan," he said to Crelo. "We're all set to —" He cut himself short and looked all around the busy street. His voice dropped quiet. "You know, take care of some business here?"

"Yeah, I know that," said Crelo, cooling quickly. "But I don't tolerate blackguarding from no *son of a bitch.*" He paused, then said to Burke, "Hear me, Clyde? Hear what I called you?"

Without turning to face him, Burke continued to lean and watch the street as he waved Crelo away with a hand.

"You still here?" he said gruffly to Crelo over his shoulder.

Crelo flared again, tried to take a step forward; Montana stopped him with a stiff hand on his chest.

"Come on, Dan! Let it go," he said. "You know something, you're right. You shouldn't be standing here talking to the likes of us. You should be moving around some. Where's your saddlebags anyway?"

Crelo took a breath and settled again. He started to turn away, but first he directed a warning to Burke.

"When this is over, Clyde, you and me are going to —"

"Yeah, yeah, I know," Burke said, cutting him off, still leaning, still not looking around at him, "you're one *malos hombre.* We see that. Now, cut on out of here. You're standing where I'm fixing to spit."

"Holy Joseph!" the Montana Kid said to Burke as Dan Crelo turned in a black huff and stomped off along the tiled sidewalk. "Are you crazy, talking to Dan Crelo like *that,* at a time like *this*?"

"You asking my opinion? No, I'm not crazy," Burke said, still leaning, not looking at Montana. "You heard the poltroon — cutting us down, talking ill of how we're dressed —"

"Damn it, Clyde," said Montana. "He's got the jitters, like he gets every time before robbing something." He paused, then said, "Wait a minute. Are you still drunk from last night?"

Burke stared straight ahead at the horseback, donkey-cart, wagon and buggy traffic on the street.

"I've *been drunk* near forty of my forty-eight years, so *drunk's* no mark against me," he said. He shook his head slowly and let out a breath, still not facing Montana. "I've got lots on my mind, Kid," he said with remorse. "I mean, *lots* on my mind. . . ."

Montana looked all around. He sniffed the air toward Burke and almost reeled.

"Yep, you're drunk," he said with certainty. Then he said quietly to Burke, "I don't know what's on your mind, Clyde, but I do know that talking about your troubles never helped nobody, especially when you're getting ready to —" He looked all around again.

"I know that," Burke said. He straightened up from the pole and hiked his gun belt and turned to Montana. "Anyway, I just stood there and made up my mind." He took a deep breath and let it out slow and gave a weak grin. "There're some things you've got to draw up your belly and *do*. This is a hard life we're in. If I can't stand toe-to-toe with it, I best get out."

"That's the spirit . . . and just in time," said Montana. He gestured a nod toward the far side of the street where Bell Madson, Jon Ho and Madson's top four gunmen led their horses out of an alley and split up onto either side of the street, the four of them drifting along toward the Banco Nacional.

"Damn, how many men are we cutting up this gold with?" Burke asked quietly.

"There're *six* right there, counting Madson and Jon Ho."

"Yeah . . . ," said Montana, contemplating the matter. "There's Crelo and another one already inside, and there's us two. That makes ten." The two looked up the street toward the bank at two more of Madson's gunmen standing along the stone sidewalk. "Jenkins and Adams, that's a dozen," he summed up. "Jones only brought seven relay horses."

"I've seen Madson do this before," Burke said. "He's going to split off with Jon Ho and four men and take a different direction. He's got more relay horses waiting somewhere."

"Damn it," said Montana. "I don't like all these changes and surprises at the last minute. He acts like he doesn't even trust his own men."

"So? Would you?" Burke said.

Montana considered it.

"Naw, I reckon not," he said. "Bell Madson has never seen the inside of a jail. He must be doing right."

Burke's mood darkened again, as he thought about what Madson was requiring of him.

"He's an evil, rotten, low-dog son of a bitch," he snarled under his breath, his hand on his gun butt as he stared across the street at Madson and the gunmen. "I could cut his throat and bleed him upside down like a hog," he added.

Montana looked at him and gave a dark chuckle.

"There's nothing like keeping a good attitude toward the boss," he said.

Burke continued to stare off at Bell Madson, Jon Ho and the other gunmen.

"I'm dead serious, Montana," he said. "I could shoot him so full of holes he couldn't cast a shadow — take what's left and hand-feed it to stray dogs."

Montana chuffed and shook his head. He hiked up his gun belt and felt the broad bandana around his neck, making sure it was in place for him to jerk it up over his face when the time came.

"All right," he said. "Keeping all that in mind, what say we get on out there and help him rob this bank?"

"Yeah, let's go," said Burke, keeping his eyes riveted tight on Madson's back.

CHAPTER 20

Inside the Banco Nacional, armed *federale* soldiers stood on either side of the wide-open doorway, their rifles rigidly at port arms. Across the tiled floor an ornate wooden counter ran the width of the building. Atop the counter a row of ornate iron bars of a Spanish design caged the young men busily at work behind the counter. Against the wall behind the counter stood a large German-made safe with its thick door ajar. Another armed soldier stood beside the safe door as if at attention.

Three of Madson's gunmen who'd been posted along the street had already entered the bank as Madson, Jon Ho and the other four gunmen approached the front door. One of the first three stood only a few feet from one of the door guards. He held what appeared to be a small bag of coins as he checked a list of figures in his hand. A thick hickory walking cane lay hooked over his forearm.

At a short floor counter near the other guard, Dan Crelo stood with a pair of new and stylish saddlebags draped over his shoulder. He'd taken the saddlebags from his horse after stomping away from Burke and the Montana Kid. He wrote on a piece of paper with a pen he kept dipping in an inkwell. In each saddlebag compartment, he carried a two-pound adobe brick.

Out front, Clyde Burke and the Montana Kid had taken position among the robbers' horses lined along the iron hitch rail. The two drew their Winchesters from their saddle boots.

As Bell Madson brought his five accomplices through the bank's open front doors, he stopped and looked around. Jon Ho walked on past him and the others to the long barred counter. Madson's top gunmen, Atzen Allison, Jaxton Brooks, Manning Wilbert and Clarence Rhodes, spread out casually but remained abreast of their leader.

With a slight nod Madson set the robbery in motion.

At Madson's signal, Dan Crelo hefted the brick-loaded saddlebags from his shoulder. Drawing the bags back, he took three fast sidelong steps toward the unsuspecting soldier nearest him. With merciless force,

Crelo swung the saddlebags in a long circle and flattened the hapless soldier to the floor. The other door guard saw the soldier hit the floor and instinctively tried to run to him. But before he could take a step, the gunman, Joe Sheff, standing near him, moved in quick and jammed the tip of a hickory cane into his stomach.

When the soldier jackknifed at the waist with a grunt, Joe Sheff swung a long-barreled Colt from behind his suit coat and brought it down hard on the back of the soldier's head. The young soldier crumpled, his rifle clacking loudly as it hit the tile floor. Sheff looked around and jerked a bandana up over the bridge of his nose. He saw other gunmen doing the same.

Just as the two door guards hit the floor, Jon Ho hurried forward and pulled up his bandana. He raised a Colt from under his duster and leveled it through the ornate iron bars lining the counter. The soldier beside the safe had seen the commotion with the door guards. He tried to raise his rifle and run forward to the barred counter. But one shot from Jon Ho's Colt nailed him in his forehead. The bullet hurled him backward and sent him sliding down the wall, leaving a long smear of blood behind him.

Hearing the shot from out front, Burke

uncradled his rifle from his arm and swung it up and stepped sidelong in between the horses at the hitch rail.

"Here we go, Kid," he said to Montana. The two hurriedly jerked dusty bandanas over their noses.

The Montana Kid moved right along with him. The two quickly gathered the reins to all the horses. To save time, Burke held all the horses, ready to accommodate the gunmen when they ran out of the bank. As townsfolk turned and gazed, and began venturing toward the sound of the gunshot, the other two gunmen on the street, Dale Jenkins and Porter Adams, took position at the far end of the hitch rail and gave them a look.

"Ready them up, boys," Burke called out to them. He gestured down the street toward two soldiers trotting in the direction of the bank, their pistols out of the flapped black military holsters. One of them had run out of a brothel where he'd spent the night, his shirttails billowed loosely around him. The one in front of him held his officer's cap on as he ran.

"I can take the first one from here," Montana said, leveling his rifle at the soldiers. Farther back along the street more men in uniforms began appearing from doorways and on balconies, all of them staring toward the bank.

"Take him, then, Kid," Burke said, all business now, his drunkenness suddenly gone. "I've got the one behind him. It'll slow the rest of them down some." He gathered the horses' reins in his left hand, supporting his rifle barrel atop the wad of leather.

Montana steadied his leveled Winchester. He took close aim on the running soldier, drew a normal breath, held it and squeezed the trigger. The rifle bucked against his shoulder. Silver-gray smoke rose around the tip of the barrel following the loud blue-orange explosion. The running soldier turned limp and awkward and melted down onto the street.

Burke's rifle resounded as the next running soldier veered over to see about his fallen comrade. The rifle bullet sliced through his chest from the side. The soldier buckled down and clutched at his ribs like a man stricken by an angry hornet. He twisted and swayed painfully in place before collapsing over onto his back, his arms outstretched. The horses, spooked by the rifle shot, tugged at their reins in Burke's hand.

"Got him," Burke said, relevering a round into his rifle chamber and settling the nervous horses.

Yet even as the two soldiers lay dead or dying, other soldiers were gathering up, running along the street toward them, rifles and pistols in hand. One officer carried a long saber raised high over his head.

"We ought to both shoot him," Montana said, already taking aim on the shouting running man.

But Burke looked over at Jenkins and Adams, who stood watching the soldiers advance, running along the street. They had not yet covered their faces.

"Hey!" Burke called out. "Feel like shooting somebody today?" he asked in a bemused tone.

"Go to hell, Clyde," Jenkins shouted in reply, the two giving him a hard look. They turned quickly and began firing at the oncoming soldiers.

Burke jerked his head around toward the bank doors at the sound of two more pistol shots. A woman screamed; a man shouted loudly. Then a third gunshot resounded. Burke saw gray gun smoke begin to waft out through the open door.

"Come on, Madson, damn it to hell," he said under his breath. "Get the gold and let's cut! These cayuses are ready to leave without us."

Return fire began slicing through the air from the soldiers, some of them still running, some close enough to drop down on one knee and fight back.

"*Whoooieee!* We've got us a *whing-dinger* going now!" Montana shouted, firing four rapid shots in a row.

As bullets tore past the horses, Burke pulled the scared animals around the edge of the hitch rail.

"Fall back, take cover with us, Kid," he shouted at Montana. He pulled the bunched horses up the stone steps onto the big porch and ducked behind a large stone column. Bullets pounded against the wide columns and whistled past on either side. Burke gave a dark laugh, seeing Montana duck for cover behind the next column fifteen feet away. "What did you say to make them so damn mad, Kid?" he called out.

Montana began unsnapping bullets from a bandolier across his chest and reloading his Winchester.

"Looks like Jones might have got the best job here, setting up relay horses," he shouted above advancing gunfire. Two columns away, Dale Jenkins had dragged Porter Adams out of the gunfire. He stooped beside him and examined a blood-gushing hole in the wounded gunman's chest. Burke looked over and saw Jenkins look up from Adams and shake his head.

"Damn it, Madson, come on," Burke said beneath the heavy gunfire.

As if in answer to him, Burke and Montana heard Bell Madson's voice from the open doors.

"Get the horses inside here. We'll cover you," Madson shouted through his bandana mask.

"I don't mind if we do," Burke said aloud to himself.

"I'll come over there, Clyde, and take half the horses," Montana called out.

"Huh-uh," said Burke. He saw Montana getting ready to bolt over and join him. But he stopped him with a raised hand. "Stay over there! Fall in behind me, keep these horses covered!" he shouted over the gunfire and the sound of bullets breaking chunks of stone off the columns and kicking up sprays of adobe dirt from the front of the building.

"Get ready!" Madson shouted from inside the bank. He turned toward Jenkins. "Drag Adams in here. We need both your guns!"

"You heard him, Porter," Jenkins said to Adams. "Are you able to run if I get you on your feet?" He stuffed a wadded-up bandana onto the bleeding wound and pressed Adams' hand on it.

"Get me up . . . I'll go," Adams managed to say in a wheezing wet voice.

"That's what I thought," said Jenkins, lifting the wounded man to his feet and leaning him back against the column, awaiting Madson's signal.

Burke stood holding the horses, hugged against the column, looking over at Montana, who stood watching the front door, waiting to hear from Madson. The *federale* gunfire seemed invincible. Yet in a split second the battle turned. A heavy barrage of rifle and pistol fire erupted from the windows, upper-level balcony and roofline of the bank. The only opening that had no fire flashing from inside it was the wide-open front doors. Suddenly Madson appeared there and waved them in before disappearing from sight.

"In we go!" Burke shouted at the horses, running for the doors, pulling the frightened animals along with him. As he ran, Montana fell in behind him, moving along backward, firing his Winchester shot after shot at the soldiers hunkering down behind whatever cover they had found.

Burke kept the horses together long enough to get inside the bank. Once through the open doors, Madson and Jon Ho grabbed some of the horses from him and pulled them out of the raging gunfire. Montana charged inside a moment behind Burke and ran across the tile floor, leaping over the backs of terrified townsfolk lying facedown. From the windows the robbers kept up a steady barrage of return fire. Allison and Brooks began swinging tandem bags of gold across the horses' backs.

"What now, Bell?" Burke shouted at Madson from five feet away as bullets pinged off the iron work and bars along the wooden counter. Chinks of wood and splinters flew.

"We're heading out the back door," Madson shouted in reply. "I had two men in the livery barn scattering their horses before we came in."

Jenkins and Adams hobbled through the front door and collapsed, both of them wounded now. Three men ran over and dragged them off to the side. Seeing the shape they were in, Madson looked Burke and Montana up and down.

"Get ready to make a run for it."

The two watched Madson run over to Adams and Jenkins, who stood supporting themselves against the floor counter where blood and ink spilled down from the counter's marble edge.

"We're done for, Bell," said Dale Jenkins

in a pained voice. "Me and Porter both."

"I see you are," Madson said. "We've got to leave you behind here."

"I . . . can ride," Adams rasped, leaning on the floor counter that was now covered and dripping with his blood.

But Jenkins shook his head. He gestured down at his bloody belly, where two bullet holes had punched through his shirt.

"We didn't make it. Arm us up, and get out of here," he said to Madson. "We'll hold 'em down for you."

"That's the way," Madson said proudly. He started to pat Jenkins on his shoulder, but he saw the gesture might knock him off his feet. "Allison, Wilbert, get over here," he shouted. Running from their position at the edge of the front doors, the two gunmen came to a halt at the floor counter.

"Yeah, boss?" said Wilbert to Madson, looking Jenkins and Adams up and down, seeing all the blood spilling from them both.

"Get them bound up as much as you can, and help them load up. Then get ready to haul up out of here," Madson ordered.

"You got it, boss," said Wilbert. He and Allison helped the two mortally wounded gunmen away from the counter to one of the smoke-filled front windows.

Madson ran back to where the last of the

bags of gold were being tied down atop the nervous horses.

"We've got to get out of here quick before they figure us for the back door," he shouted. He gestured toward some customers lying trembling on the floor. "Grab a few of them, just in case."

Montana stepped over among the townsfolk on the tile and began pulling two of them to their feet.

"You heard the man," he said. "Who wants to take a little ride with us?"

While Montana shoved two men and a woman to the horses, Dan Crelo ran in a crouch beside Burke.

"Don't think I forgot you, Clyde," Crelo said acidly. "We get away from here, you'll answer to me."

Burke gave him a bemused look.

"Did you go bite a dog turd like I said?" he replied, his Colt hanging readily in his hand. He gave Crelo a goading stare.

But Crelo was having none of it right then.

"Ornery son of a bitch," Crelo growled at Burke as he grabbed his horse by its reins and pulled it away toward the rear of the large bank building. Two bags of gold hung down behind the horse's saddle.

"Get on your horses when you see they're ready," Madson said above the hard-

302

pounding gunfire. Next to him, Jax Brooks and Clarence Rhodes hurriedly hefted bags of gold up onto the horses and tied them down behind the saddles.

Grabbing the reins to his horse, Montana looked around at Burke.

"See you outside?" he asked.

"Yeah, you bet, Kid," said Burke, with a short, tight grin, "else you'll see me in hell." He grabbed his horse by its reins as Rhodes finished tying down the gold.

A gunman appeared at the top of a long set of stairs and shouted down to Madson.

"Boss, make 'em get going," he said. "Soldiers are moving around back, taking positions!"

"You heard him, men," Madson said. "Grab a saddle and get out of here. Wait for us at the top of the trail a half mile out. Keep us covered if they're on our backs!"

Burke and Montana rode their horses through the bank, gunfire slicing through the air all around them. They met Dan Crelo, who had led his horse to the back door and stood looking out warily.

"Yeehiiii!" shouted the Montana Kid, racing past the cautious gunman.

"Get on your horse and get your knees in the wind, you cowardly cur!" shouted Burke, his horse almost knocking Crelo

down as he raced past him, out the back
door.

"You arrogant son of a bitch!" shouted
Crelo, leaping up into his saddle. "I'll kill
you if it's the last thing I ever do!" He
booted his horse out the door and raced
along right behind them.

CHAPTER 21

The rear of the building was still scarcely manned as Burke, Montana and Crelo pounded along a narrow alleyway toward the top of the hill trail down to the desert floor. At a rushing stream, they slid their horses to a halt, turned the excited animals and looked back at the sound of rifle fire starting up at the rear of the building. Through the gunfire they saw Manning Wilbert coming toward them at a full run, his face masked, duster tails flapping out around him.

"One question," said Crelo, his Colt up in his hand, cocked and ready beside him. "If Madson gets chopped down, do we get to keep all this gold?"

"Good point," said Burke. "We'll be sure and ask him next time, tell him you brought it up." Their nervous horses spun in place beneath them.

"I'm joshing, damn it, Clyde!" Crelo said.

"You look like you're joshing," Burke replied as Wilbert came pounding across the last few yards to the stream bank. He gestured at the well-dressed gunman. "You got blood on your vest," he said.

"Don't worry about my vest," said Crelo. "We're still going to settle up, you and me," he warned.

"I'd like that, Dan," Burke said mockingly. But then his eyes darted to a large pine only ten yards away, seeing a soldier jump behind it. "Watch the tree, Kid!" he said.

The three turned in their saddles and pelted blistering gunfire at the large pine as Wilbert slid his horse to a halt and turned it back facing the alleyway.

"Bejesus!" he shouted at the others. "You like to scare the hell out of me."

From behind the pine a young soldier raced away, rifle in hand, and dived into a thick stand of brush as Montana sent a shot over his head.

The four spread out and kept their horses moving all around the edge of the stream as Madson and the rest of his men raced in one and two at a time.

The next two arriving were Jon Ho and Bell Madson. They stopped and turned, jerking bandanas down from over their noses.

"Jenkins and Adams are holding them back," Madson said.

"Damn shame, them two," said Wilbert.

"Yeah, I know," said Madson.

"What about all them soldiers?" Crelo asked. "Will they be dogging our trail?"

"They will as soon as they can," Madson said, seeing two more gunmen on horseback racing toward them along the alleyway. He gave a dark chuckle. "Last I looked, they were chasing their horses all over the street."

More soldiers on foot began forming out around them in a half circle as the two gunmen rode in. Gunfire still resounded heavily from the direction of the bank building. Madson turned in his saddle and fired into the brush where soldiers were slipping in and taking position.

"Keep them pinned down, men," he said. As he fired, he said through the cloud of smoke looming over them, "What the hell is keeping Allison and Brooks?"

"They're right behind us, boss," said Crelo, his voice sounding excited.

"Here they come," Wilbert said. Even as he spoke, rifle fire resounded from the sparse trees and thick brush surrounding them.

Madson and his gunmen returned fire as the last two men came pounding along the alleyway.

"It's about damn time," said Madson, firing steadily from within the cloud of gun smoke. "Get across this stream and meet us down at the desert floor."

"Let's go," Burke said to Montana, turning his horse to the swift, shallow stream. He looked at Crelo. "You best come with us, Dan," he said. "They catch you alone, they'll hurt your feelings something awful."

"Son of a bitch!" Crelo snarled under his breath.

"Stop jawing, get going — !" said Madson, rifle fire growing heavier from the brush. His words stopped as a rumble rippled down deep in the bowels of the earth. "Whoa," he said, his horse swaying a little beneath him. "We don't need none of that right now." He steadied the animal until the rumble fell away and the quaking earth made its hard-slamming halt. Rifle fire ceased, but only for a moment.

The men turned and rode away across the shallow stream as gunshots started up again.

At the bottom of the trail, they stopped and gathered up around Madson and Jon Ho.

"All right, we'll keep moving like they're on our trail whether they are yet or not," Madson said, taking an uncapped canteen that Jon Ho held out to him. He took a long swig of tepid water and passed the canteen back to Jon Ho. "Now we ride straight to our relay horses and keep moving, like Sherman over Georgia." He grinned, yanked off his hat, waved it and slapped it back on his horse's rump.

"We've done it!" shouted Wilbert, slapping a hand back on the bags of gold hanging behind his saddle.

At gray dawn, Sam had moved out of the high-cut walls of Rocky Mesa and ventured back to his campfire, which lay empty and darkened. Down from his saddle, he looked around, noting that even the lantern light from inside the cave was gone. The firebed on the ground that he had left blazing, visible for the desert floor, was now black and lifeless, and had been throughout most of the night.

The horses — supply horse, lead rope and all — were gone, as if they had all vanished up into the sky. On the ground at his feet, Sam saw unshod horses' hooves running in every direction.

Pretty smooth . . . , he told himself, looking all around.

He had expected the horses to be gone — he'd even planned on it.

But he found it surprising that listening from his position in the rocks above the camp, except for the yipping and howling of coyotes, he heard not a sound from either man or beast throughout the night.

He felt almost like telling the Apache "obliged." Stealing the relay horse had gotten him off the spot. Nobody could be blamed for losing horses to desert Apache. He'd managed to get rid of the animals and free himself from any complicity in Bell Madson's bank robbery. Now he needed to reconnect with Madson long enough to kill him and Jon Ho and break up the gang. Then back to Nogales, he reminded himself, stepping back into his saddle, turning the dun onto a partially hidden trail leading down from the southern side of Rocky Mesa.

When he reached the bottom of the mesa, he found the prints of the Apache, their unshod horses leading the relay string. They had come down from the rocks owing to the deep tremors. With this much valuable horseflesh in their possession, they weren't going to take a chance on watching them all fall into the ground or slide down the side of the hills in a huge spill of tumbling rock.

Sam followed the prints until he crossed a short stretch of flatlands. Seeing the prints run on along the edge of the desert floor, he turned the dun onto an uphill trail and rode along two hundred feet up along a long hill line until he spotted the Apache resting the horses around a water hole on the lower slope of hillside. Needing the water for the dun and himself, he sat in the cover of rock and rested the dun and watched and waited for the Indians to leave.

At length he saw the braves gather the string of horses and move out along a short trail back down onto the desert floor. As they turned left and rode along the edge of the sand, in the distance ahead of them, visible to him from his position on the long hillside, he caught sight of a large roil of trail dust moving along toward them from the opposite direction.

Uh-oh. . . .

Realizing that the odds of the dust belonging to anyone other than Madson and his gang were slim, he mounted the dun and moved along the trail slowly, keeping watch, seeing how this was going to work out before venturing down any closer. Beneath him the dun jerked its head in the direction of the water. But Sam rubbed its withers, settling it.

"Don't worry. I'm taking you down there,"

he said. "First, let's sit here — see what this is."

At the front of the riders, Bell Madson and Jon Ho rode abreast, each with two bags of gold tied behind his saddle. Beneath them the horses were winded and weakening, having spent half the day traveling at a hard pace in the scorching desert heat. But Madson had it all planned out in his mind before they'd started. All they had to do was make it to Rocky Mesa.

There were horses there for them. Jones had them there, rested, watered and waiting. And according to Burke and the Montana Kid, these were good-looking horses, he reminded himself. Whatever ground any pursuing *federales* might have gained on them earlier, they would lose once he and his men got to Rocky Mesa. What did the *federales* have waiting for them out here?

Nothing, that's what, he told himself.

He whipped his tired horse forward. Fresh horses out here meant the difference between life and death. He grinned, looking back over his shoulder. His men would soon have them, the *federales* wouldn't and that was that. Riding beside him, Jon Ho, the half-Mexican, half-Chinese gunman, sidled close, reached over and nudged his shoulder.

"What the hell, Jon Ho?" Madson said above the sound of their pounding hooves, looking around at him.

Jon Ho pointed at rising dust around an upcoming turn in the trail.

As the two drew their horses to a halt, the men bunching up and stopping behind them, Madson stared straight ahead at the turn around a twenty-foot-high edge of rock. A puzzled look came to his face.

"Who travels these flats in the heat of the day?" he asked quietly.

Jon Ho sat in silence beside him, staring straight ahead at the rise of dust, judging the riders to be less than a mile away.

"No white man," he said as if in warning.

"No 'pache neither," said Clyde Burke, nudging his horse up on Madson's other side. Montana reined his horse up beside Burke. The other men sat watching, listening, starting to hear the rumble of hooves beyond the edge of rock.

"Jon Ho," said Madson, "maybe you best go take us a little look-see." He raised his rifle from across his lap and sat holding it propped up, its butt on his thigh.

Jon Ho only gave a short nod and booted his horse forward. As the Mexican-Chinese rode forward and out of sight around the edge of rock, Burke raised his Winchester from across his lap and checked it and held it ready. Montana did the same beside him. So did the men behind them, the sound of the hooves growing stronger.

"I don't like the sound of all this," Madson said, his tone growing wary.

"Neither do I," Burke said, staring straight ahead. "Whoever's coming knows about us, same as we know about them."

"Want us to spread out, boss?" Dan Crelo asked, sitting his horse a few feet behind them.

"Yeah . . . no . . . I mean, wait a minute," Madson said as if mesmerized by the sound of hooves. "Let's hear what Jon Ho says —"

No sooner had Madson spoken than the sound of the hooves grew louder, pounding faster. Jon Ho came racing back around the turn in the trail only a second ahead of over a dozen thundering, war-whooping Apache warriors and the string of horses.

"Holy Moses!" said Montana, recognizing the white barb by the supply pack hanging half off its back. "The savages have got our relay horses!"

"Damn it," said Burke. "It's got to where you can't do nothing for these devil sons a' bitches!"

"What are you waiting for? Give them hell, men!" Bell Madson shouted. He saw no time to do anything but charge forward into a roiling dust cloud filled with thundering hooves, yelping warriors, firing rifles and swinging war clubs.

"Jesus," said Montana, booting his horse forward. "We're all dead."

Burke let out a rebel yell and charged forward, prompting Montana, Madson and the others to fall in around him. The riders fired rifles and pistols repeatedly while pounding forward at a full run. Burke fired his Winchester until the barrel was hot and smoking, neither of his hands on the horse's reins. When the rifle was empty, he held it by its hot barrel like a club and drew his Colt with his other hand. He charged into the Apache firing the Colt and swinging the rifle butt at anything that got in front of him.

Five feet to Burke's left, the Montana Kid fired two Colts. Preferring the Colts for close fighting, he'd shoved his rifle down into its saddle boot for later. He rode with his horse's reins wrapped around one of his hands beneath the butt of his gun. Charging Indians flew backward from atop their horses as the distance between the two forces shortened.

Beside Montana, a wildly fired bullet nailed Clarence Rhodes center forehead. His blood and brain matter splattered on Montana's face and chest. But Montana only tried wiping his face sidelong on his shoulder and plowed ahead into the Apache front riders as bullets and arrows whistled past him.

The relay horses were no longer strung together by rope. The unwitting combatants charged forward into the melee, eyes wide, bulged with terror, their whinnying turned to screams for mercy. On the outer edge of the charge, the barb loped along like some ridiculous element of a *comedia carnaval* caught up in someone else's nightmare. Its supply pack had gone askew, yet it clung to its side. Tins of food and wrapped packages of jerked meat worked loose from the supplies and rose one and two items at a time and flew back and bounced along the sand in the horse's wake.

"Don't stop! Ride through them!" Madson shouted above the din of screaming horses and raging gunfire. In another relentless instant, the two forces clashed head-on. Bullet, arrow and club in force, both sides appeared to rise and spill back each onto itself like powerful waves at sea.

At close quarters the battle raged, both

sides flying down from their horses' backs like wild creatures born in tree boughs and hurled to earth for man's decimation. Burke and the Montana Kid fought back-to-back like ancient gladiators given a promise of freedom.

Both gunmen and Apache alike shot and stabbed and choked, poked and bludgeoned. Blood flew, bones snapped. Scalps ripped away; limbs plopped to the ground. Horses reared and trampled, kicked and bit with bared teeth like wild dogs and whinnied long and loud, protesting at having been brought in on this against their natural will.

After seconds — seconds that weighed in as hours — the gunmen felt the turn of the fight to their favor. Outnumbered but better armed, they fought with an outlaw's fortune at stake in the bags of gold behind their saddles.

The Apache, fighting with bitter vengeance for land and lives lost, and for home and hearth — meager though it be — felt the wrath and force of ruthless desperate men driven by gold and fearless in their defense of it.

Clyde Burke grabbed a warrior out of the air by his throat as the man sailed in at him. Yelling wide-eyed, the Indian swung a bloody pistol, barely missing Burke's head. His yell turned to a gag as Burke jammed a smoking-hot gun barrel deep into his throat and pulled the trigger. Burke flung the broken Indian aside and wiped the blood and bone matter off on his blood-slathered shirtsleeve.

Behind Burke, facing the opposite direction, Montana fired a blocky German pistol he'd snatched up from a dead warrior, and began firing it as he swung a broken stockless French rifle in his other hand. Manning Wilbert ran at Montana, screaming, blinded by blood, his scalp gone and a bloody boot knife slashing back and forth in his hand. His left forearm was missing, sliced off cleanly by the blade of a broken *federale* sword a warrior swung fiercely.

Without hesitation, Montana shot him in the forehead and turned away in time to shoot a charging Indian as a bullet from the Indian's pistol grazed his forehead and caused him to stagger in place.

"We're *all dead*!" he shouted again, the words having become almost a mantra he'd adopted early on.

"All you do is *whine*, Kid!" Burke shouted behind him.

They fought on.

CHAPTER 22

All the while the sound of the battle raged below, Sam had followed the upper trails, one to another, keeping watch on the rising dust and gun smoke. By the time the gunfire and whinnying of horses had started to diminish, he sat his horse on a cliff that offered a partial view of the fighting. Scanning down with his battered telescope, he saw man and horse locked in a death waltz obscured in a swirl of fine sand, burnt sulfur, potassium and charcoal.

All the elements of hell . . . , Sam told himself.

As he looked down to his left, he saw the barb break away from a circling field of riderless horses, a couple with empty leather saddles and the loaded canvas bags bouncing heavily at their flanks. Others wore only wooden saddle frames, padded by blankets and skins. He saw several relay horses circling with the frightened herd. The barb ran back in the direction of the distant water hole as if that might be the last peaceful place of recent memory.

In a moment, as the fighting waned some more and a couple more horses broke away from the frightened circle and galloped away along the desert edge, Sam lowered the lens and stared down into the drifting dust with his naked eye. He had estimated over a dozen Apache by the volume of hoofprints he'd studied. Now as the gunfire fell away, he began to see the warriors fleeing sporadic shots, having had enough, if not to sate their blood vengeance, at least to have held it in check for the time being.

Watching the circling horses, he saw the herd thin down as more Apache grabbed their animals from within it and raced away. As the Indians fled, he noted the two horses carrying the bags behind their saddles had been cut out of the herd. In another moment, he saw Madson's men galloping after the fleeing Apache. But they appeared to lose interest after a hundred yards and slowed and circled and fired rifle shots that appeared to be more of a warning now as the last rifle and pistol shots fell silent below.

Sam raised his telescope again and studied the gunmen as they rode into sight from around tall rock edges and cliffs jutting out of the hillside beneath him. He saw Burke and Montana. The two rode along blood-covered yet appearing otherwise unharmed. In front of them, he saw Madson and Jon Ho and thought to himself what a perfect time it would be, to be there and kill the two of them and put an end to Madson's lawless reign. But he reminded himself to be patient.

The time was coming. . . .

He backed the dun, turned it off the cliff onto the trail and rode down for the next half hour until he left the hills and rode onto the sand at the edge of the desert floor.

He rode to the battle site, the dust and burnt powder still settling around him. Two of Madson's gunmen lay dead on the ground. One of the dead he recognized as Clarence Rhodes; the other was Manning Wilbert, who'd been there the day he met Madson atop the cantina roof in Shadow River. Manning's scalp was missing, as was his left forearm and a large portion of his skull both front and rear.

Hearing a muffled groan, Sam turned from the two dead gunmen with his Colt coming up cocked and pointed toward the sound.

Ten feet away, the warrior he'd given water to over a month ago lay staring at him, blood staining his clenched teeth and running down from the corner of his lips. Sam saw a look of recognition stir in the young warrior's dark eyes. He lay propped against another dead Indian, clutching his chest with both hands inside an open *federale* tunic. Sam looked all around, then stepped over to him and looked down.

The warrior took one bloody hand from under the tunic and reached it up to Sam. He murmured something in Apache, something barely audible. Sam crouched a little.

"Hablo español?" he asked the dying warrior.

The dark eyes only bored into his. The bloody hand remained upreached. Sam leaned closer. He started to try what few words he knew in Apache. But before he could say a thing, the bloody hand sprang to life suddenly, grabbed his shirt and jerked him down closer. Sam reacted quickly, seeing the warrior's other hand come out of a bloody tunic and holding a double-edge knife. In spite of his sharp reflexes, Sam felt the knife reach up and slice along his ribs before he pulled away and kicked the knife from the warrior's hand.

He felt the burn of the steel as the warrior fell back to the rocky ground and stared up at him. The knife lay a few feet away. Sam planted a boot on the Indian's bloody chest and examined the stab wound he'd just taken from him. He'd been cut deep, but luckily he'd missed the stabbing point of the blade. He saw blood flowing freely down his side. He looked back at the Indian's face and recognized something akin to satisfaction in the dark, weakening eyes.

Being a double edge, the knife had sliced twofold, diagonally along the inside of Sam's forearm and straight along his side at rib level.

What a time to get cut. . . .

Sam squeezed his sliced arm against his bleeding ribs for the moment and leveled the cocked Colt at the young warrior's head.

"If that's all you've got, you can go now," he said in a lowered tone.

The warrior stared at him with almost a faint smile on his face.

Sam started to pull the trigger, but he caught himself and stopped. He gazed out across the desert floor in the direction of Agua Fría and saw dust starting to rise against the afternoon sky.

"You've cut me good," he said. With his big Mexican boot clamped down on the man's chest, he uncocked his Colt and let it hang in his hand. With his bleeding arm, he reached out long enough to pick up the double-edge knife and stand up with it in hand.

The Indian stared at him, unafraid, a questioning look on his dying face.

"Huh-uh," said Sam. "You'll have to die on your own." He threw the knife away and took his foot off the man's bloody chest. Backing away, he reached up under his sombrero and pulled down the black cloth he wore over his head. He wadded it and placed it along the wound on his ribs, then pressed his forearm in against it. He took the bandana from around his neck and did the same thing, feeling a need for more than the one bandage to stay the flow of blood.

"I didn't see that one coming," he said quietly. He looked at the drawn face again and saw dead glazed-over eyes staring past him at the distant hills. Sam let out a breath and backed away toward the dun. "I wish you'd died ten minutes sooner," he said without malice, squeezing his forearm against his bleeding side.

He stepped atop the dun and rode back up onto the hill trails, this time staying lower, needing to make better time. He needed to get to the water, put himself ahead of Madson and his men. He kept his forearm pressed tight to his side and let the dun pick its path and its pace back toward the water hole.

Bell Madson looked down at the fresh tracks coming down toward him, both shod and unshod, as he led the riders along the edge of the sand flats. In the long shadows of evening, they'd turned upward onto the slope leading to the water hole. They had lost two men in the sudden skirmish, but they had killed over half the Apache. Montana had suffered a bullet graze along the side of his head. He'd wrapped a bandana around it.

Burke was nicked and cut all over; he bore a perfect bite imprint on the side of his neck. He and Montana led six of the relay horses they'd recaptured. The white-speckled barb's supply had been straightened on its back.

Jaxton Brooks had lost a hand just above his wrist. He wobbled in his saddle from the loss of blood he'd suffered before Atzen Allison had covered and bound the stump of his arm with a shirt he'd taken from Brooks' saddlebags.

"I — I hope we killed . . . that sword-swinging son of a bitch . . . who did this," he said in a rasping voice, Allison leading his horse along by its reins.

"Oh yeah," Allison reassured him. "If he

ain't dead, he owes me the three bullets I put in his belly."

"Obliged," Brooks replied weakly, swaying in his saddle. "We . . . got all our . . . horses, then?"

"Pretty much," said Allison. "Why don't you shut now and rest?"

Brooks held up the bloody shirt-covered stump.

"Funny," he said dreamily. "I can't tell it's gone . . . feels like it's here . . . I just can't see it."

"Yeah, *real* funny," Allison said, giving him a look. "Shut up and rest, damn it."

"I'll have to learn . . . to shoot all over again —"

"All right, that's it," Allison said. "Here, you're on your own." He pitched the maimed gunman the reins to his horses. He booted his horse forward away from Brooks. "He won't shut up," he said with a shrug to anyone watching.

As the weary riders rode up through the tall rock lining the outer perimeter of the water hole, Madson reined up fast. His hand slapped in reflex around his holstered gun butt. He sat startled for a second at the sight of Sam sitting on the ground by the water's edge. When he relaxed, he turned from startled to surprised. As the gunmen

326

moved up around him on either side, he let out a tight breath, staring at Sam.

"All right, Jones, here's the deal," Madson said. "You've got five seconds to give me one good reason why I shouldn't blow your head off where you're sitting." As he spoke, he started to pull the gun from its holster, but seeing Sam raise the Winchester from across his lap already cocked and ready, Madson left his Colt holstered.

"I don't need five seconds," Sam said calmly. He jiggled the Winchester a little. "Here's my *one good reason.*"

He almost hoped the gang leader would go for his Colt. He could end it right here — Madson first, then Jon Ho, while they both sat side by side. He might not get a better chance than this, he told himself. But he thought about his sliced arm and wounded side. Would it slow him down, cause him to lose a precious half second levering a fresh round up for Jon Ho while Madson fell backward from his saddle?

Too risky. . . . He wanted them both dead. He didn't want to give up his life to only kill one of them, have the other one ride away and leave him facedown in the dirt.

"Bell, look, he's bleeding," Burke said on the other side of Madson. "What do you suppose happened?" he asked Madson to bring his attention away from killing.

Madson, needing a reason to back away from a fight without looking bad to his men, let his hand drift away from his Colt.

"Yeah, Jones, what happened?" Madson asked Sam.

"What do you think happened?" Sam said in a voice balancing on a thin edge of anger. "I got hit in the night by Apache. They took all the horses. You had me waiting at Rocky Mesa. . . . Turns out that's one of their favorite sites."

Madson cocked his head a little to one side.

"You ever heard that, Jon Ho?" he asked the Mexican-Chinese gunman.

Jon Ho didn't reply; he only shook his head, staring hard at Sam.

Madson looked back and forth and all around the hillside above the water hole.

"All right, what are you doing here?" he asked Sam.

"I followed them here," Sam said. "I stuck to the high trails, being only one of me. I knew I couldn't take the horses back. I figured you'd be coming, I'd get ahead of them and warn you before they come riding up on you." He paused and let his Winchester lie back across his lap. "I heard the gun battle. I knew I wouldn't get there in time. I sat down here. I been here ever since."

Madson sat mulling his story over in his mind. Sam half turned and dipped his bloody bandana into the water, wrung it and pressed it back to his forearm.

"An Apache do that to you?" Madson asked, his voice calmer.

Sam just looked at him.

"Yeah, I suppose so," Madson answered himself. He gestured at Jon Ho. "Go check out his wounds."

Jon Ho started to step down.

"You send him over, you'll come scrape him up," Sam said with iron in his voice. His hand went back to his Winchester.

Undaunted, Jon Ho started to step down anyway. But Madson reached a hand over onto Jon Ho's forearm, stopping him.

"Montana, you go check him," Madson said.

Montana stepped down, walked over cautiously and stopped a few feet from Sam.

"You see what I got to do, Jones," he said with his hands spread in a show of peace.

"Yeah, I see," Sam said. He turned a little toward Montana and raised his forearm from against his side.

"Jesus . . . ," Montana whispered. "He's sliced bad, boss," he called back to Madson.

"I see it from here," Madson said.

As Montana stepped in closer to Sam he said, "Is there anything I can do for you?"

"Obliged," Sam said, "you can help me up from here." He raised the rifle barrel up to Montana, who took it and pulled, helping Sam onto his feet.

"You able to make it on up to Shadow River?" Madson asked Sam, sounding concerned. "We're going to switch these spent horses out. We'll be traveling fast," he cautioned. As he spoke, he gestured the men down from their tired horses.

"I'll keep up," Sam replied. His dun stood drinking from the water hole. As the men hurriedly stripped saddles and bridles from the sweaty exhausted horses, the animals staggered over to the water's edge and drank.

Madson looked troubled. "I just realized, Jones, we've got no fresh horse for you."

Sam just looked at him.

"But don't worry," Madson said. "Dress your wounds and stay back with Jon Ho and Burke. They're bringing up these cayuses soon as they've rested some." He gestured toward the worn-out horses. Then he looked at Jon Ho, then at Burke.

"What do you say, Clyde?" he asked. "Can the two of you take care of Jones?"

Sam caught something in Madson's words. He looked at Burke and saw something there too, something he didn't like seeing.

"Yeah, we'll take care of him," Burke said, looking away from Sam as if unable to face him.

"I can stay back, boss," Montana said. "I might even sew him up and get him to stop bleeding."

"You're a doctor now?" Madson snapped at Montana.

"I'm just saying," Montana replied, looking a little surprised by Madson's sudden flare-up at him.

"You don't have to *just say*," said Madson. "Jon Ho and Burke are staying behind. All you've got to do is swap out your horse and get the hell out of here with us. We've got *federales* ready to stake our heads on a pole, they catch up to us."

Sam stood watching, his forearm pressing the cool damp bandage to his side. Madson stepped over closer.

"I mighta been wrong not trusting you, Jones," he said. "You get to Shadow River, you're getting something more than just a fee for handling the relay horses." He paused and nodded. "Next job we go out on, you're riding up front, taking a full cut

331

for yourself. How does that sound?"

"That's what I come down here for, boss," Sam said, as if relieved to hear it. He let himself relax, looking comfortable with everything Madson had just told him — when in fact, he didn't believe a word of it.

CHAPTER 23

With some medical supplies Montana had left with him, Sam washed the wound on his forearm and, after a deep breath, set about sewing the gash shut. Burke stood watching him while the tired horses drank and rested. Jon Ho sat on a tall rock off to the side and gazed back at the dust rising back below the hill line. As Sam drew on the needle and thread and tightened the last stitch in his forearm, he looked over at Jon Ho, then up at Burke.

"Is your pal always so talkative, Clyde?" he said.

Talkative . . . ?

Appearing to have a lot on his mind, Burke took a second to understand Sam's gibe. Finally getting it, he gave a short, troubled grin.

"He's never much of a talker anyway," he said. "I don't think he likes me much."

"Yeah?" said Sam. "He seems real fond of me."

"Pay him no mind. He's Bell Madson's lapdog, Jones," Burke said. "Whatever Madson tells him to do, he jumps to it."

"What about you, Clyde?" Sam asked, just wanting to see what Burke's response would be.

"What about me?" said Burke.

Sam stared at him until Burke had to admit he'd understood the question.

"I'm nobody's lapdog," Burke said. "Haven't you seen that by now?"

"Yeah, I've seen that," Sam said. He tied off the stitch, bit the thread and broke it and laid the wet bandana along his forearm over the stitches. "So, you're always your own man?" he asked. He worked his hand and elbow easily, testing the use of it.

"You know I am, Jones," said Burke.

Sam studied his forearm, knowing it had taken the brunt of the knife thrust. After washing and looking at his side wound, he saw no need in stitching it.

"So, Madson tells you to do something, you don't blame him, you do it because you want to?" he said coolly.

Burke gave a shrug.

"That's right, I do what suits me," he said. His gaze settled on Sam. "Why? What are you getting at, Jones?"

Sam just stared at him.

"Just curious," Sam said.

He reached over and picked up his Winchester lying beside him and held the barrel up to Burke. "Give me a hand up, Clyde," he said. The two saw Jon Ho climb down from atop the rock and walk toward them. Sam took note of Ho adjusting his gun belt. With a sidelong glance, Sam also noted the horses had drunk their fill and begun pulling back from the water's edge. They stood milling, poking their wet muzzles here and there for graze.

Burke pulled him up by the rifle barrel.

"I will say this, though," Burke put in. "Soon as I get my cut, there's no son of a bitch ever going to tell me to do something I don't want to do."

Sam caught a bitterness in his tone. But before he could pursue the matter, Jon Ho stopped a few feet back from them.

"Soldiers," Ho said. He pointed off toward the distant rise of dust.

The two looked at him. Sam noted that Burke was still holding his Winchester after pulling him to his feet with it.

"Go now," Ho said. He stared at Burke expectantly. "Go now," he said more insistently.

Sam got the picture. But he waited.

Let it play itself out, he told himself.

"What's your damn hurry, Jon Ho?" Burke said tightly, taking a step farther back from Sam. "Don't tell me what to do, you damn Chinese-Mexican . . . !" He let his words trail as if an ending wasn't readily available.

"Go now!" said Ho, poised toward Burke.

Sam waited, watched.

Burke half turned between the two of them. He looked at Jon Ho, then at Sam.

"Damn it to hell, I've got all that gold waiting!" he said, as if arguing with himself. Then he swung toward Sam with the rifle and spoke hurriedly.

"He's going to kill you, Jones!" he blurted out suddenly. "I'm here to help him. Get out of here, Jones!" As he spoke, he swung Sam's cocked Winchester toward Jon Ho. But Ho was ready for him. The fiery-eyed gunman raised his Colt sleek and fast from his holster, fanned two rounds into Burke's midsection as he spun toward Sam. Burke jerked back a step when each bullet hit him.

Sam was ready for Jon Ho. His Colt came up cocked and leveled. His single shot nailed Jon Ho and sent him sprawling backward, his gun flying from his hand. Sam cocked his Colt again while smoke curled up from its barrel.

For the peddler woman, he said to himself.

He stepped over quickly to Burke, stooped down and propped him up with his good forearm. But even as he lifted him to keep him from choking on his blood, he could see the gunman was going fast.

Burke gripped Sam's shirt with a bloody hand and gave a tight grin across bloody teeth.

"Damn you . . . Jones," he said in a broken, dying voice. "A man can't . . . do right, after doing wrong . . . all his life."

"You just did, Clyde," Sam said quietly.

"Yeah," said Burke. "Look at me . . . it got me killed." He coughed; blood surged. Then he settled and said in a ragged whisper, "Aw, what the hell . . . ? Adios, pard."

"Adios, Clyde," Sam said, closing Burke's eyes with his palm. He picked up his Winchester, stood up, let out a tight breath and looked all around. Then he gazed back down at the dead outlaw and said in a lowered tone, "Don't worry. I won't leave you here."

Shadow River, Mexican Desert badland
Daylight rose in a thin golden line, mantling the upper hill peaks like long gentle arms coming to embrace the desert and its kin-

337

dred inhabitants. Yet even the dullest of these inhabitants knew that by midmorning, this gentle sunlight would turn fiery; the white-hot sky would rage against them like a lover scorned.

Sam kept the string of horses at a gallop along the last mile of trail leading up into Shadow River. Beside him the white-speckled barb loped along on a shorter lead rope. Behind the barb, the bodies of Clyde Burke and Jon Ho lay tied down over their saddles. Following the two bodies, the rest of the string galloped along in the cool but waning morning air.

At the sight of two riders coming down the trail from Shadow River, Sam slowed the dun to a walk and finally stopped ten feet back from Joe Sheff and Dan Crelo. He allowed the two gunmen to half circle him and see the bodies of Burke and Jon Ho. As they circled, he eyed the set of saddlebags they each carried over their shoulders.

"We've been expecting you," said Sheff. Then he and Crelo recognized the bodies at the same time.

"Holy, John," said Crelo, seeing the two dead gunmen he'd robbed a bank with only a day earlier. "Who killed them, *federales*?" he asked, casting a wary glance along the trail behind Sam.

"No," Sam said flatly. He paused and raised his Winchester and propped the butt of it onto his thigh, "Jon Ho killed Burke. I killed Jon Ho."

The two sat in silence for a moment. Joe Sheff shook his head slowly, staring at Jon Ho.

"Madson's going to throw a fit," he said.

"You think so?" Sam said in the same flat tone.

"I do," said Sheff. "Not that I care," he added quickly, knowing why the Winchester was standing there. "But he thought the world of that sneaking, evil-eyed son of a bitch."

"Good," Sam said. "Then he can bury him." He turned his eyes to Crelo, and saw a worried look on his face. "What're you wanting to say?" he asked.

"Nothing," said Crelo.

"He heard you and Burke and the Montana Kid are pals," Sheff cut in.

Sam just looked at him.

Sheff continued. "He's fearing you'll want to take up the trouble between him and Burke —"

"No, *I'm not,* damn it, Joe!" said Crelo, cutting him off. "I don't know why you even thought you ought to open your mouth about it. Nobody asked you nothing."

Joe Sheff shrugged.

"I'm just saying," he said.

"Well, just *don't,*" Crelo snapped at him.

"I'm not taking up anybody's trouble," Sam said quietly. "But we were pals, I guess you could say." He nodded at the bulging saddlebags over their shoulders. "Everybody's got their cut and is leaving Shadow River?"

"What? No!" they both denied. Each clasped a hand on the saddlebags. Joe said, "These are just some — uh." He stared at Crelo for help.

"Just this and that," Crelo said. Then he stopped and composed himself and said, "All right. Yes, it's our cut. We're heading a long way from here." He kept a hand on the saddlebags and his other hand close to his holstered Remington Army. "You've got a cut coming too."

"Yep," Sam said, looking away from the saddlebags to keep anybody from getting nervous. "That's why I'm here. Is Madson there?"

The two looked relieved.

"He was an hour ago," said Crelo.

"But most everybody else has cut out, with the *federales* coming and all," said Sheff. "You might not want to stick too long there yourself. Mexicans carry on something

340

awful when you take their gold." He chuckled and jiggled the heavy saddlebags up and
down on his chest.

"Damn fool," said Crelo. He looked at
Sam somberly. "Just so you know, Jones, I
liked that son of a bitch right there." He
nodded at Burke's body. "We always threatened to kill each other, but neither of us
ever took it too serious, or we would have."
He paused, looking down at Burke's body.
"But I don't expect I have to tell you how it
is. You've seen it yourself in this kind of
work. Ain't that about right?"

"Yeah," Sam said. "That's about right."

"Sit here and jaw all you want to," said
Sheff. "I'm gone." He batted his horse
forward. "Adios, Jones," he called out over
his shoulder.

"Get ol' Clyde buried proper enough, will
you, Jones?" Crelo asked.

"You bet," Sam said. He touched the brim
of his sombrero toward him and nudged the
dun on toward Shadow River.

The white-speckled barb at his side, the
string of horses and their grisly cargo right
behind him, he rode on without stopping
until he reached the edge of the swift-
running stream and followed it to the bridge
that lay unattended by any toll collectors.

Welcome to Little Hell, Sam said to himself,

gazing across the bridge onto an empty street. He led the string of horses across the bridge and stopped again and sat for a moment gazing at the cantina where he and Montana and Burke had met with Bell Madson. He recalled the dying man who was sprawled shot and bleeding in the dirt street that day he'd first ridden into town. Gunmen from within the cantina had walked out and stood watching the man die. He wondered for a moment whose day it would be to die in the dirt. But as soon as the question came to mind, he put it away.

Ahead of him at the cantina, two dust-streaked men walked out and leaned against the weathered poles. One drew on a cigarette and let the stream of smoke go on a gust of hot wind. A faded green canvas flapped and clattered overhead, then settled into silence as Sam stepped the horses forward. Looking up atop the cantina, he saw Bell Madson, Fritz Downes and three men he didn't know looking down at him. They stood blackening in and out of silhouette against the white burning sun.

CHAPTER 24

Standing atop the roof beside Bell Madson, Fritz Downes loosened the Colt in his holster and looked down at the two bodies tied across their saddles. Recognizing both dead men by their clothes and horses, he whistled low under his breath.

"Is that who I think it is leading them?" he said sidelong to Madson.

Madson still wore his trail clothes under his long riding duster. He took a thick cigar from his mouth and stared down long and hard at Sam as he spoke to Downes. On Madson's other side stood Tanner Hyatt, Boze Stillwell and Eric Waite, three men he'd hired and arranged to meet him after the bank robbery.

"If you think it's Jones, it *is*," he replied to Downes. He held the cigar drooping between his thick fingers. "But why's this son of a bitch still alive, Burke and Jon Ho lying over their saddles?" With his right hand he eased the lapel of his duster back and laid his hand on his holstered Colt.

"I don't know," said Downes, as if Madson really expected an answer from him. "Apache, maybe?"

"Keep talking stupid, Downes, and I'll send you away," Madson said menacingly. To the man standing nearest him on his other side, he said, "Tanner, is everybody gone that ought to be gone?"

"Yeah, Mr. Madson, they've all hightailed, like you told them to do," said Hyatt, a steely-eyed Texas gunman.

"Horses are ready?" Madson asked sidelong. "The gold's all packed?"

Hyatt looked around the two men beside him. Stillwell, a tall, gangly Missourian, gave him a nod.

"The horses are ready," Hyatt said to Madson. "The gold's all packed." He stood staring down intently at Sam as Sam stepped down from the dun, hitched it and the barb to the rail and hitched the string alongside them. "You want this monkey kilt and skint?" he asked.

"Yeah, I do," said Madson, gazing at Jon Ho hanging down his horse's side. He straightened and took a breath as if to clear his head. "Damn right I do."

Hyatt looked at the other two gunmen and

nodded his head. Then he turned back to Madson.

"Mr. Madson, why don't you and Fritz here head out? The three of us will take care of this fool."

Madson snapped his eyes to Hyatt.

"First day here, you're going to start telling me how to run things?" he said in a heated tone.

Hyatt just stared at him.

Madson flung his cigar aside.

"The three of you fan out along this platform," he commanded, gesturing a hand along the narrow platform walkway leading to where his outdoor office sat beneath a canvas overhang. "Fritz, there's a shotgun broke down in a desk drawer. Get over here and put it together!"

Hyatt, Stillwell and Waite looked at one another, amazed at all this preparation for one lone gunman. Yet, even as they mused at one another, Hyatt shrugged and jerked his head toward the walkway stretched along behind him.

"You heard Mr. Madson," he said.

The three of them spread out along the walkway.

Madson raised his Colt from his holster, checked it and held it down his side, ready to cock and swing up into action.

345

"We need to kill him fast," he said. "We've got *federales* riding down our shirts anytime."

"We've got this, boss," said Hyatt. He wanted to tell Madson to settle down, but he knew better than to say it.

Madson was getting nervous, starting to sweat.

"How's that shotgun coming along, *damn it to hell*!" he called out to Fritz Downes, who stood at the desk trying to assemble the two parts of a short-barreled hammer gun together.

"Boss, she's sprung or something!" Downes shouted back to him, unable to connect the two simple parts.

"Sprung?" shouted Madson, getting enraged. "A damn shotgun doesn't get sprung, you *babbling idiot*!"

Stepping around the hitch rail, Sam came face-to-face with the two men lounging out in front of the cantina. One straightened from against the pole as Sam stopped and stared at him from four feet away. The other man backed a step and stood with his feet spread shoulder-width apart. From inside the darkened cantina, the sound of boots hurried out the rear door. Sam heard the door slam shut behind the fleeing boots.

"You men working for Bell Madson?" he asked the group flatly, his hand wrapped around the butt of his holstered Colt.

The man with the cigarette took his time. The smell of burning marijuana wafted on the hot desert air. He let out a stream of smoke, tilted his head at an odd angle and held one eye closed, his cigarette pinched between his thumb and finger.

"Might be we do . . . ," he answered in a long drawling voice. "Then again, might be we don't. It all depends who's —"

You *don't have time for this,* Sam advised himself.

The barrel of his Colt swung up, cracked the man hard up under his chin and sent him backward behind a spray of broken teeth. Before the other man could make a move, Sam grabbed him by his shirt, jerked him forward and buried his knee in the man's groin. The man jackknifed at the waist, his hat flew off, his knees clasped together and his hands clutched his privates. Sam pulled the bowed man forward quickly, at a short run. He guided his bare head into the iron hitch rail with a loud *gong* and let him fall.

Sam reached down, pulled the man's gun from its holster and unloaded it into the street. Stepping over to the other man, he stooped beside him, pulled up his gun, unloaded it and pitched it aside. As he stepped inside the cantina doors, he saw a Mexican bartender raise his hands in a hurry, looking scared, appearing to have witnessed what just happened out front.

"Welcome back to Little Hell, *señor!*" he said quickly, recognizing Sam from his prior visit. He shrugged. "Or Shadow River, whichever you like best. It is all the same to me."

Sam tossed a questioning gesture toward a new set of steps reaching up through the roof.

The bartender nodded and whispered, *"Sí,"* lifting his eyes toward the roof. Sam walked to the bar with his left hand held out. The bartender reached under the bar slowly, lifted a shotgun and laid it over into Sam's hand, butt first.

Sam broke the shotgun open, checked it, snapped it shut and turned and walked to the steps. Looking up, he saw Fritz Downes at the top of the steps fumbling with the two pieces of Madson's hammer gun. His eyes widened, seeing Sam with the bartender's shotgun pointed up, cocked and braced against his hip.

Atop the roof, Madson and his three new gunmen stiffened at the sound of the explosion from downstairs. They saw Downes fly up backward in a spray of blood, bone and soft tissue. Their hands wrapped around their gun butts. They started to move forward toward the stairs. But Madson held them in place with a raised hand.

The three stood looking at Madson for a signal. He motioned them over to his desk and hurried around it himself and took his chair.

Sam stepped up into sight, one barrel of the shotgun curling smoke, the other barrel cocked, ready to fire. Blood from his wounded forearm had seeped through his stitches and his shirt and now made a thin line along his duster sleeve. He held his Colt up in his right hand, cocked and ready.

"Well, well," said Madson from behind his desk, the three gunmen spread apart on either side of him, facing Sam. "Fritz thought he heard someone on the stairs." He gave a tight grin. "Looks like he was right." He stuck his cigar in his mouth.

"You just saw me ride in," Sam said.

"Well, yes, that's true, I did," Madson admitted. "I wanted to make us all comfortable, you know . . . in case there's anything you might want to talk about."

"There's nothing to talk about, Madson," Sam said. "I came here to kill you. It's that simple."

"Nothing's ever *that* simple," Madson said, leaning back a little in his chair. "You had to have a reason to want to kill Jon Ho and me."

"How's this?" Sam said. "You had Burke and Ho set up to kill me. Turned out Burke wouldn't do it. So Jon Ho killed him." He gave a shrug. "I killed Jon Ho — now I'm going to kill you."

Tanner Hyatt cut in, saying, "You make it sound easy. Am I missing something? Don't you see us standing here?" He gestured at the other two gunmen.

Sam ignored him; Madson gave the gunman a disapproving stare.

"There's more to it than that," Madson said to Sam. "I knew you were trouble when I first heard of you back in Agua Fría. Heard you wanted to join us, but something told me you're nothing but a one-eyed Jack. Nobody was seeing your other side." He stood up, a big Colt cocked in his thick right hand. "I don't aim to die without knowing what for," he said. "So spit it out. What is your game, *Jones* — or whoever the hell you are?"

Sam saw the Colt ready to rise toward him; the three gunmen saw it too. "I've got a right to know — !" Madson shouted.

But Sam's first bullet hit him dead center before his words were finished. Madson staggered backward and fell over his chair. His Colt fired wildly through the canvas flapping overhead.

Sam spun and fired at Tanner Hyatt as Hyatt's gun bucked in his hand and sent a bullet whistling past his head. Hyatt flew backward. Sam turned toward the other two gunmen, but held his fire, seeing their hands raised chest high in a show of peace.

"Easy there, Mr. Jones," said Stillwell in a calm, soothing voice. "Let's see if we can't work this thing out between us like gentlemen." When Madson went flying backward over his chair, Stillwell's and Waite's minds had drawn immediately to the horses readied for the trail and loaded with gold, hitched to a pole, waiting out back.

Sam eased down a little but kept his Colt cocked, ready. He looked from Stillwell to Waite.

"Is he speaking for you too?" he asked the gunman with a battered derby cocked at a rakish angle.

"Oh yes, indeed he does," said Waite. "The fact is, we were leaving when that unfortunate thing happened on the stairs." He gestured toward Downes' mangled body lying on the other side of the roof. "Suits us to just leave, walk away from here and never look back."

"Show me how slow you can pick those shooters up with two fingers," Sam demanded.

"You've got it all, mister," said Waite. They both eased their guns from their holsters with their thumb and finger and let them fall.

"What happened to the Montana Kid?" Sam asked.

"The Kid?" said Stillwell. He gave a slight smile. "He lit out of here happy as a twinpeckered billy goat."

Sam took a breath and considered it.

Good, he told himself.

"Move out," he said to the two gunmen, gesturing them toward the steps with his gun barrel. "I see you waiting for me down there anywhere, I'll kill you both. That's fair warning."

"Yes, it is," Stillwell agreed. "But you won't see us down there. I'll swear it on a Bible, or whatever." He looked all around as if searching for something to swear on. Then he and Waite gave each other a look on their way to the rear stairs, both of them thinking of the gold waiting out back for them.

Sam turned as soon as the two were out

of sight. He walked down the stairs, keeping an eye out for any stray gunmen still hanging around Shadow River. Stepping out front, he saw the two men just now coming to and looking all around for their bullets scattered on the ground.

"Huh-uh, don't load them until I'm gone," he said.

"You broke my damn teeth," said a thick voice — the man who'd been smoking. "I like to have bit my damn tongue off."

Sam made no reply. Instead he turned and looked at them, and at the Mexican bartender standing in the doorway.

"I left your shotgun upstairs," he said.

The Mexican nodded.

Sam turned to the two recovering men, one holding a hand cupped under his bleeding mouth.

"You two know how to use shovels?" he asked.

They looked around on the ground.

"What shovels?" said the one still holding his groin.

Sam let out a patient breath.

"*Any* shovels," he said. As he spoke, he fished two gold coins from his vest pocket.

"*Hell yes,* we do," the man replied. "We're not stupid." He thought about it. "You're wanting your pals buried?" His hand came out expectedly. He rubbed his thumb and finger together in the universal symbol for greed.

"Just that one," Sam said, ignoring the gesture. He motioned toward Burke. "He was my *pard,*" he said quietly. He reached past the two men and gave the Mexican the coins. "Pay them when they're finished, not one minute before," he said.

The Mexican bartender closed his fist around the coins and nodded his agreement.

Sam turned and walked around the hitch rail to the horses and took the bodies down and laid them under the overhead canopy out of the bright white sunlight. He stood looking down at Burke's cold dead face for a moment. His job here was finished, he reminded himself. He would meet up with Montana somewhere along the trail; he was certain of it. The three of them had gold hidden out there. He was sure the Montana Kid would take it sooner or later, do whatever outlaws do with gold.

Clyde Burke and the Montana Kid . . . He allowed himself a thin smile, thinking about them. Then he stopped himself and turned away. It was time to lead these horses out somewhere off the desert and unstring them. It was time for him to step out of this outlaw's world and back over to the other side — to his side, the side of the law. He untied the string of horses, then unhitched the dun and the white-speckled barb. As he swung up into his saddle, he forced himself not to look back down at Clyde Burke.

Take them where? he asked himself, regarding the horses. He backed the dun and barb from the rail and nudged the string along with them. He didn't know. . . . Maybe some grassy high meadow over where the hill country softened enough for horses to graze themselves full and run themselves strong and free. A place where everything wasn't out to eat everything else? He chuffed drily. Where would that be? He didn't know that either. The best thing was just turn them loose, give them a slap and watch them run.

The ground shuddered underfoot. He swayed slightly in his saddle, but then he caught himself and let the tremor pass without so much as slowing down for it. The dun nickered and blew out a breath but stayed steady and straight.

That's just how it is here. You never know what to expect, he told himself. *So expect anything. . . .*

In seconds the desert hill country shivered and settled with a familiar hard thump. Sam nudged the dun forward and rode away, the white barb beside him, the string of horses close behind.

The employees of Thorndike Press hope you have enjoyed this Large Print book. All our Thorndike, Wheeler, and Kennebec Large Print titles are designed for easy reading, and all our books are made to last. Other Thorndike Press Large Print books are available at your library, through selected bookstores, or directly from us.

For information about titles, please call:
  (800) 223-1244

or visit our Web site at:
  http://gale.cengage.com/thorndike

To share your comments, please write:
  Publisher
  Thorndike Press
  10 Water St., Suite 310
  Waterville, ME 04901